COLD HEART

THE YORKSHIRE MURDER THRILLERS #BOOK 3

JANE HEAFIELD

BLOODHOUND
— BOOKS —

www.bloodhoundbooks.com

Print ISBN 978-1-5040-7027-0

ALSO BY JANE HEAFIELD

THE YORKSHIRE MURDER THRILLERS

Dead Cold (Book 1)

Cold Blood (Book 2)

———

Don't Believe Her

———

Her Dark Past

CHAPTER ONE

'This one,' the man in the back of the car said. He was in his twenties but looked older and worn out. His name was Rob Norman. 'I know I said that last time. But this time I'm sure.'

'Also stated last time,' the front passenger said. He was in his forties; tall, handsome. His name was Liam Bennet.

Twice previously when the driver had stopped, the man in the back seat had taken a long look at the area before shaking his head. This time the pair up front expected the same. Still, the car drew to a stop on the country lane.

'This is it for sure,' the man in the back said. 'I remember the gate. Definitely.'

'You said definitely last time,' the driver said. He was overweight and closing on fifty. His name was Darren Wright.

'Well, definitely definitely this time.'

Bennet stared at the farm gate. Rusty old metal with horizontal bars and wire mesh cladding on the bottom half to prevent small animals getting through. Just like the last, and the ones before, and probably all the ones to come. A whole day and a morning they'd been at this, travelling what seemed like every country lane in Barnsley to find the right location. A whole weekend wasted so far.

Wright sighed. 'How can he be sure when he's not even certain which village, which town? I mean, how can you not know?'

Wright had lost his patience ages ago and Bennet wasn't far behind. But he would keep it internal. 'You heard the man,' Liam said. 'Definitely definitely this time. Let's go.'

Grumpily, Wright parked on the grass verge and out they got into the hot morning sun. The gate was hampered by the rough soil and Bennet had to use both hands to move it. He got it open just far enough to get his muscled but lean frame through.

Norman was shorter and slimmer so easily made the passage, but both men had to wait for Wright to heave metal and get his plus-size frame from one side to the other. The stifling heat in the car had already moistened the big man's skin; his exertions with the gate virtually soaked him. His frustration went up a gear.

The field was fully ploughed except for a patch of grass alongside trees that ran dead straight away from them. The trio started walking under the branches, where a tractor couldn't reach. Speaking of tractors: one was deep in the field, silent until they got twenty metres away, at which point the rumble of its engine carried over to them. A moment later, it started heading their way. No doubt the landowner wanted to know their business on his property.

Bennet pointed at the approaching vehicle. 'Go tell him the score,' he told Wright.

'What if this guy runs? He's half our age. You okay with it if he gets back to the road and jumps in front of a truck?'

'Hardly my fault. Guilty conscience. And the taxpayer will save a wad of cash.'

'I won't run,' Norman said.

'See, Wright, he won't run anyway. So go tell the farmer to mind his own business.'

Unhappy with this task, the big man started lumbering across the field. Bennet and Norman continued along the treeline, shaded from the hot morning sun. Then Norman suddenly stopped. Bennet had been walking some six feet behind and he kept that distance as they both looked into the trees. The wood separated two fields and was only ten metres thick. Years back, the trees had lined both sides of a stream, but only a sunken furrow crawling with undergrowth remained of the waterway.

Norman's finger pointed and Bennet saw a clear path of flattened undergrowth. A trail laid by something heavy.

Bennet stepped forward and gave him a soft shove, enough to let him know he should get moving. Both men stepped into the woodland and down the slight slope, onto the old stream bed. The shade was a blessing.

The path through the undergrowth had led here and now ran off ahead, along the crevasse. Bennet's hopes rose as, some twenty metres ahead, he saw what looked like the top half of a stone circle.

Bennet grabbed Norman's elbow and almost dragged him.

Closer, Bennet saw that they had indeed found what he'd figured was a semicircular stone culvert angling underground. It seemed like a forgotten remnant because not only was there no stream, there wasn't a road or track for it to pass beneath. It had a rusted mesh cover that was slightly ajar. The black space beyond made him want to pick up speed, to sprint across the final distance, but Norman suddenly stopped.

'Yes, that's it. It's unlocked.'

'You never mentioned a culvert.'

'I didn't remember. But that's it. I'm not going any closer.'

'You went closer last time. Much closer.'

Bennet tightened his grip on the man's elbow and forced him onward. When they reached the culvert, Bennet squatted and made his prisoner do the same. That was when the horrendous smell hit him.

There was no lock on the mesh cover and it was open an inch. It was too gloomy within to make anything out. Bennet pulled out his phone and accessed the torch. Norman grabbed his wrist so he couldn't aim it inside.

'No, I don't want to see. We don't need to. This is the place. Just call your people in and let's go.'

Norman tried to stand, but Bennet yanked him right off his feet and onto his butt. 'Listen, you twat. You had no problem looking last time you were here, did you?'

'But she... won't look the same. You can't make me look. The police aren't allowed to do this.'

Bennet grabbed Norman's hair and forced his face towards the culvert, then shone the torch inside. 'Look, you bastard.'

Light washed over the interior of the culvert. Inside, Bennet saw a female body lying on her back on flattened weeds. Her head was about three feet from the opening and bent to one side, legs and arms also twisted haphazardly. She was naked and a week of decomposition and animal hunger had ruined her flesh.

But enough skin remained for Bennet to see a clear muddy bootprint on the back of her neck and another on her shoulder. And something else. These marks told the story: Rob Norman had sat right here and used his legs to thrust the body feet first into this makeshift tomb.

'Is this your wife, Mr Norman?'

The man began sobbing. 'Yes.'

'Say goodbye.'

Norman put his face in his hands, but his fingers were splayed and he continued to stare at his wife's corpse. 'I did. Before I brought her here. After the terrible accident.'

'I meant say goodbye to your bullshit claim that she drowned in the bath.'

Norman's head snapped round. 'What do you mean? She drowned, I told you that. What are you talking about?'

Bennet ignored him and stepped out of the crevasse. Wright had returned and Bennet stopped in front of him. Behind Wright, out in the field, were two uniformed police officers whose job was to follow, remain silent, and step forward when needed. They were needed. Bennet ordered them to secure the prisoner.

The big detective constable was looking at the culvert, and at Norman, who had digressed into wild sobbing as the two uniforms got him to his feet. 'She in there?'

Detective Chief Inspector Bennet nodded.

'Any clues about cause of death?'

Bennet nodded again.

Three weeks ago, on a late evening in July, police had attended the home of twenty-one-year-old Rob Norman and arrested him. He'd reported his wife, Matilda, missing a fortnight earlier, but Norman's violent reputation had quickly thrown suspicion on him and Bennet's murder squad had found no indication that she was alive and well. The social media addict hadn't been online. The shopaholic hadn't bought a thing. The doting daughter hadn't contacted her parents or any friends.

Upon arrest, Norman had sharply admitted she drowned in the bath and, panicked and high on cocaine, he'd hidden her body. He'd subsequently claimed no memory of loading her corpse into his car, of driving through the night, or of where he'd dumped his childhood sweetheart.

Until yesterday, when guilt had finally opened his mouth. One of Bennet's team, interviewing him in prison, had convinced Norman that his wife's family needed her body for burial; giving her up would make a judge look upon him favourably. He was young and could see release with a substantial portion of his life ahead of him. He could move out of Barnsley, start a new life somewhere. Remarry, make money, die old and happy. Sold, Norman had agreed to help find her, and here they were.

Bennet indeed wanted the body primarily for her family's peace of mind, but had no intention of instilling sympathy in a judge. Norman had said she drowned by accident; a bloodied rolling pin found in the garden claimed otherwise. He needed the body for a forensic post-mortem to establish the truth. But his own eyes had already confirmed what he'd always thought.

'Her skull's crushed,' he told Wright.

'Little bastard. I'll call it in. Let's get that fool back to prison. I reckon he only agreed to this for a couple of days away from the gangbangers.' He paused. 'Case closed, I guess. So that's you done then?'

Bennet opened his arms. 'End of an era. So say what you've long wanted to.'

'You only brought me along on this trip to ruin my Sunday off and annoy me, didn't you?'

'I don't see you as detective material. You're not a team player, and you don't like taking orders. So say your bit so I can get home.'

'Fair enough. I think you're a piece of shit and I'd love to cave your head in, and I'm glad I don't have to see your face again.'

'Good. Now that's out of your system, I'm going. Nice knowing you.'

Bennet started walking and pulled his phone to call the police station for a car to collect him. After the call, he stopped and turned his head to the blazing sun. He'd waited for this moment for a long time and had expected to feel elation. But he felt nothing.

CHAPTER TWO

When Liam Bennet arrived home, he found the house empty. He opened the back door and found his eleven-year-old boy, Joe, in the garden with Liz, playing chess on a giant board in the Sunday morning sun. He went out and they both said hi. He sat on a plastic chair to watch the game.

Except his mind turned elsewhere as he noticed the lack of sounds from his neighbour's garden. Last month Patricia had gotten herself a puppy that was always barking or panting like a marathon runner. Before the heart attack. The lack of noise was a constant reminder that his elderly neighbour, dear friend and babysitter to Joe was gone.

He returned to the kitchen and put the kettle on. On Liz's very next move, she put herself in a position to be checkmated, which gave her an excuse to chat with Liam in the kitchen while the kid reset the board. As she became more comfortable being in his house, she'd started to dress more casually. Tracksuit bottoms and a yellow T-shirt today, and no make-up. She didn't need any to look pretty.

'You're back earlier than I thought. I'm guessing it's good news. Or bad, if you know what I mean.'

He nodded. 'We found the body.'

'Any second thoughts now it's over?'

'Nope,' Liam said, but there was a pause beforehand. He still wasn't certain himself. But he had no choice, did he?

Joe's mother was dead, killed in a big-news quadruple murder nine months ago. Her death hadn't really changed much in their son's life because she'd left him when he was a baby. An alternative mother-figure had been Patricia, who loved the little guy no less than any real mother should.

As a detective heading Major Investigation Team 3 (Barnsley), one of four covering the four districts in South Yorkshire, Liam had worked long days, unpredictable hours, and was often on call. As well as planned babysitting, Patricia had often been called upon in the middle of the night to watch over him while Bennet rushed to a crime scene.

Bennet had foolishly never questioned that this set-up would endure, until Patricia was snatched away by a fatal heart attack three weeks ago. In the blink of an eye, Liam knew his career was over.

Sure, he could have found alternative childcare, but ever since he'd investigated the death of Joe's mother, he'd become aware of how little time he spent with his son. It had gnawed at him for the past six months, so the decision following Patricia's demise had been an easy one.

Any investigations that had hit his desk since could happily be handed to his replacement, but he'd refused to abandon his existing cases. They had been diligently worked to conclusion and the last had been the murder of Matilda Norman by her husband. He could have walked away the day Rob Norman was charged with murder, but he'd felt a sense of incompleteness and had vowed to remain in charge until her body was found. Now she had, and he was free.

His plan was to work from home so he could be around Joe

more. It was daunting though. Being a policeman was all he'd known. He was probably institutionalised. Hopefully, as Liz had once said, he'd soon get used to the glamour of being his own boss.

'I think the sugar is truly gone,' Liz said. He snapped back to the moment and realised he'd been constantly stirring his cup of tea while daydreaming. He took both cups to the kitchen table and they sat.

'Thanks for watching Joe.'

'Anytime. He likes having me around and he's fun to be around. And I like the chess battles.'

Liam tried not to read too much into her words. It was hard not to hear what she'd said as, *See, we can date and it won't be a problem that you've got a child.*

'What are you going to do with the rest of your day off?' he asked her, and again he couldn't help but play editor: *Are you busy later? We could go out together.*

'I'm shifting my stuff from my sister's, remember? Told you earlier?'

She had. Liz had separated from her husband a number of months ago and had been lodging with her sister's family. She wasn't happy there because Gill was pretty controlling. Now she had a new bedsit over in Woodhouse Mill in the east of Sheffield and the last of her stuff was being shifted this evening.

'I'll help. Joe will help too. When do you want to do it? Right now is good for me.'

She grinned. 'Great idea. I promised Joe one more game, though, so...'

She stopped as her phone rang. It was the theme music from the movie *Jaws*, which was pretty relevant. He knew that ringtone was attached to only one number, and if it rang everything else had to be dropped. He'd been in that position countless times himself.

'Tomorrow maybe?' he said.

'Or tonight if it's a slam dunk. See you later. Apologise to Joe for me.'

Liz answered the call as she headed for the door, fast. Liam poured away the tea he'd made for her and tried to dampen his jealousy.

CHAPTER THREE

JULY 2017

I t just wouldn't do to have busy murder detectives called to a body to discover that the deceased had died peacefully in his sleep or slipped off a ladder. In the past, homicide squads had even raced to a scene to find a sleeping drunk, a store mannequin, a graveyard resident laid out in the open for a laugh.

So, when one of South Yorkshire Police's Major Investigation Teams got a call about a body, two detective constables designated as the Review Team went out for a look. If they discovered a joke or an error, the case got passed to detectives working that area. If they found a corpse and suspicious circumstances, game on. The former was more common.

When MIT 2, covering Sheffield, got a call about a bloodstain, the two members of the Review Team were at another location, having just announced a legit kill. Those on the night shift had barely had time to dump their bags and make tea before having to shoot off. Those who'd just clocked off were heading home and thankful the call hadn't been twenty minutes earlier. Detective Inspector Liz Miller was one of the latter, but she hadn't yet reached home when her phone rang.

It was her boss, DCI Alan Bates. 'Bloodstain found at Frecheville Community Centre. Any chance you can swing by?'

'Of course. What do we know?'

'Just that. Bloodstain. Can't be ignored though. Thanks. Keep me updated.'

Only after she'd hung up did she realise what had just happened. She'd just become a one-person Review Team, a job nobody liked. And there wasn't even a body. But, like Bates had said, it couldn't be ignored. And she could go straight home if it turned out to be nothing to worry about. She loaded Frecheville Community Centre into her satnav.

Between one main side of the building and the edge of an L-shaped annex, there was an out of sight square of land the size of a standard living room. The living-room analogy fit quite well because it looked as if someone had tried to make this little nook into a home. There was a patch of grass that had been laid with a large tarpaulin. There was a portable stove and cordless kettle, various books, and a cardboard box of dried and tinned foods. Clearly it was the home of the homeless.

She saw the bloodstain up the wall. 'Looks bad to me,' a uniformed officer who'd cordoned off the nook said. 'You taking this?'

Well, that was a pretty big bloodstain. But she didn't know if it was human or even part of a crime. She called Bates. 'Unsure about this. A lot of blood, but enough to be fatal? Don't know. Something bugs me about this whole scene though. I can stay a while and co-ordinate if you want.'

'Nah. Pass it to the local detectives and if there's a dead person somewhere, we'll get it back. But, if you're eager for overtime, I could do with you down here. I've got a bloody knife but a body with no visible wounds. Looks like a strange one.'

'Okay. I've got no plans. But let me just get the ball rolling here first.'

Liz told the uniform to call in detectives from the nearest station and then she used a forensic collection kit from her car to wet-swab the dried blood. Her final task was to bag a couple of the items in the nook and dispatch an officer to the lab with them. After that, she handed the scene back to the uniforms and left. But she was still bugged by something she couldn't explain.

———

The results were back the next day. The lab had gotten a full crime-scene profile from the DNA in the blood and had uploaded it to the National DNA database. Because her name had been on the request form, the Home Office had notified Liz's station and her superintendent had called Bates, who summoned her to his office.

'Good work,' he said. He was fiddling with a paper aeroplane, which he was known for throwing around the incident room. 'The DNA is a match for a chap called James Breakspear, thirty-two. Last year he was arrested for stealing strawberries from a farm. Last known address – well, place of registration – was a day centre called The Cat and Mouse in the city centre. He's got a twin sister called Clara listed as his next of kin. Let the girls and boys know at the station dealing with it.'

She knew her disappointment was written all over her face. He said, 'You don't want to let this one go, right? That buggy feeling. I understand. But we don't even know if Breakspear is dead. I've seen your photos of that bloodstain, Liz. I've known people to stroll away from losing more.'

'And to fall stone dead from losing a lot less.'

'Like I said, if a body turns up, we'll get it back. Remember that we're talking about a homeless guy here.'

Others could have read something insensitive in that last sentence, but Liz knew what Bates meant. The usual methods for proving someone was alive or dead without a body didn't apply. The homeless weren't known for their digital footprints, such as phone, bank, and social media activity. They often had no family and their social circle usually consisted of other unregistered people.

She agreed that trying to find the owner of the blood, alive or dead, would be tough, but challenge was part of the attraction... and she was still bugged by this one. Something she couldn't identify made her certain James Breakspear had suffered an injury not easily walked away from.

Again he saw disappointment on her face. 'I know you, Liz. You want the big case, the one that will make you. You want to be able to say this was yours, you saw it from the start. Well, I don't think this will be that one. Move on to the next.'

Liz knew this opinion of her wasn't Bates's alone. Yes, she did chase the big cases, but her reason wasn't superstardom. She just wanted to do a good job. But reputations were hard to dispel and she didn't have the stamina to even try to change people's opinions. As long as they didn't get in her way, people could think whatever they wanted.

'I'm working on gut instinct here, sir. How about I get my coat, you give me two hours, and I get a missing persons report filed?'

'Why the coat and why two hours? You can do a misper downstairs in ten minutes. And we know nothing yet, Liz. The guy could be at his new home with a new family, telling the story of how he lost all that blood in a silly accident.'

'I want to go visit his sister. If he's not around and she doesn't know where he is, I'll convince her to file the misper.

Otherwise it could be months before anyone notices he's gone, if indeed he is. I just want to speed things up. I'll even use the McDonald's drive-through on the way back here.'

Bates gave a thumbs up.

Clara Breakspear lived in Fulwood, just under three miles north-west of Liz's station in Woodseats. The suburb was leafy, expensive, and the detached house she parked outside was as glorious as her own sister's. It was set back from the road behind a high privacy hedge and a block-paved driveway. In the planted lawn borders were giant water features that surely cost hundreds of pounds each. A little childish and probably in part down to jealousy, but Liz couldn't help but already dislike the woman.

As she got out, she heard merry conversation from round the back. She avoided the front door and walked alongside the building, to a wrought-iron fence blocking access to the backyard. Here she saw a long garden with a lawn, a rockery, a massive stone outbuilding. Seated on a patio in recliners were four women, all in their late twenties, dressed in classy gear and sipping wine.

They all looked as she called out and introduced herself. Before she could ask for Clara, a short, blonde, chubby woman in a dress got up and approached. She had the slight wobble of the tipsy and the face of someone loath to have her little party disturbed. She looked Liz up and down, as many did. They found it hard to believe a pretty young woman could be a high-ranking detective, assuming it was the domain of grizzled middle-aged men.

'I'm Clara. What can I do for the police? We're making no noise here.'

'It's about your twin brother. Can we speak inside, or at least somewhere private?'

'No, we'll talk right here. Why does a detective want to know about my brother? What's he done?'

'Have you heard from him recently?'

'Just tell me what he's done.'

She seemed impatient to get back to her friends, who were all watching the show. Liz cut to the chase. 'I'm afraid we found some of his blood. It was outside Frecheville Community Centre. Now there's no proof he's injured, but I'm trying to find out if he's okay.'

No change in emotion. Still that impatience. 'He'll be okay. He always is. He's been homeless for years. And I've not heard from him for years, so I can't help you. Now, if you don't mind–'

'Well, because he's homeless we don't have a way of contacting him. He was registered at a day centre six months ago but hasn't been there for a while. Do you know if he has a phone or stays at certain other places, perhaps using a false name?'

'I know nothing. He left home at sixteen. Well, he was kicked out because he was always up to petty crime. That's sixteen years ago. I know nothing. He'll be fine.'

'I hope so. Like I said, we have no proof anything bad has happened to him. Still, I think it would be helpful if you filed a missing persons–'

'You do it. If he cared about me, he would have been in contact. He'll be fine. Have you asked other homeless people about him?'

'No, we–'

Yet again she interrupted. 'There you go. Go do that and you'll probably find him. Now, I'm in the middle of a business meeting that I need to get back to.'

The obnoxious woman walked away. Liz had no choice but

to leave. Back at the station, she filed a missing persons report for James Breakspear, listed Clara Breakspear as his next of kin again, and that was that – she doubted the sister cared enough to do it. Now she could only wait and turn her mind to other things.

CHAPTER FOUR

AUGUST 2020

The call Liz took as she was leaving Bennet's house was from a detective sergeant called Larry Boeson, effectively her right-hand man. He was a former Royal Marine who'd impressed at his police interview by saying he'd heard cops were tougher than soldiers: 'So I want to give up that and try this.' He had such a constant joking tone that even the most terrible news didn't sound that bad out of his mouth.

'The Review Team just got a body in Frecheville. Mostly skeletal, still dressed. Beach body ready, I guess. Looks to have been dead a few years.'

Intriguing. Her team hadn't dealt with such a case for a while. 'Buried?'

'Nope. Dumped right out in the open. Normally I'd assume some grave robbers are trying to get a reaction.'

'But this isn't normal?'

'Donaldson recognised the body by the clothing. He told me you should think about a hessian T-shirt and a bloody wall at Frecheville Community Centre.'

The call ended as she reached her car at a jog. She got a battered notebook out of the glovebox. It was her murder book, where she'd kept her notes from all the major cases she'd worked. It was three quarters full and dog-eared. She flipped back to 2017. Nine murders that year, two unsolved, and five missing persons cases that were still unresolved. Her eyes scanned the latter until they settled upon the word *'Frecheville'*.

There it was. July 2017, back when she was a DI. A bloody smear on a wall at Frecheville Community Centre. A missing man called James Breakspear. She remembered it well because of a gut feeling that Breakspear had come to serious harm. The missing homeless man had occupied her thoughts for a few weeks and she'd asked for updates from the investigators. But no body had ever been found and she'd eventually managed to convince herself that Breakspear was fine, wherever he was. An error.

She called Donaldson, a DC on the Review Team rota this week. 'I got your message. Hessian T-shirt. Tell me you're not saying our missing man is back?'

Donaldson had been one of the local detectives handling the case. By a quirk of coincidence, Liz had interviewed him when he applied to join MIT 2 last year and they'd discussed the case; it was how Liz had learned that Breakspear had been known to wear a T-shirt cut from a hessian potato sack. Donaldson's team had acquired a photo of Breakspear in this garment taken by staff at The Cat and Mouse day centre.

'I'm sure it's him, ma'am. That's why I knew you'd be up for this one even on your day off. I remember that T-shirt, and the corpse I'm staring at right now is wearing one.'

Liz almost dropped the phone. It wasn't uncommon for missing people to turn up long dead. But she'd never heard of one resurfacing at the very same spot he'd vanished from years before.

CHAPTER FIVE

Blocking off Churchdale Road, out front of the community centre, was easy, but behind the building was open land with a lake and many pathways, which was harder. Officers were already positioned at various points to try to bar pedestrians.

Liz opened the boot of her car and retrieved her one-piece protective forensics suit, but didn't put it on yet. At the back of the boot, secured by Velcro, was a hard-shell camera case containing her £600 Nikon DSLR. She put it in her pocket.

She approached the community centre via one of the paths, walking past the lake and staring into the water to try to calm her racing mind. A uniformed officer met her. She was aware that she was visible from several houses overlooking the land, which was why she hadn't yet suited up. She showed the officer her ID as she walked past and he had to turn and match her pace.

Her ID said she was a detective inspector, so the uniform said she was the first of her team to arrive and asked who the senior investigating officer was.

'Me,' she said. The uniform had all the information he

needed, so she didn't tell him that her boss, DCI Alan Bates, was off work with a recurring knee injury and she was acting detective chief inspector. He let her into the cordon.

DS Boeson was waiting, already wearing his white protective gear. The fifty-something was tall and still had the sinewy neck and craggy face earned shedding sweat and blood as part of 40 Commando, although fifteen years with South Yorkshire Police had increased his waistline. She asked if he'd notified the coroner's office.

'Sure thing. The call about the body came in about an hour and a half ago. The caller sounded distraught and wouldn't give his name or say if he knew the victim. It was rung in from that payphone...'

He pointed behind them, at Hopedale Road about a hundred metres away, beyond the lake and past a fenced oblong of wasteland. 'We roped it off so no one touches it. I hear that you have a history with this victim?'

'Before your time.' She gave him a rundown of events three years ago and then said, 'Anyone in the community centre when the body was found?'

'Loads. It was hosting a poetry reading when the Review Team arrived. Everyone was still present when uniforms turned up to secure the area. No obvious guilty party so far and apparently no one heard or saw a thing. There's a couple of local plods inside getting everyone's details. Nineteen people. I'm trying not to worry about the headache of making all those background checks and verifying all those alibis, but I can't get past the shock of knowing there's nineteen people in the world who love poetry.'

She ignored his joke. 'Let's go look.'

Boeson led her to the nook where she'd found a bloodstain three years earlier. Out of sight of any nearby homes, Liz pulled on her protective suit and latex gloves. They entered using duckboards to step on to preserve evidence on the ground. Two other detectives were already here. The Review Team.

'Just like last time,' Donaldson said, as if reading her mind. He was a tall black man, a lifelong copper who'd hit detective constable rank just about as quickly as possible for a teenaged uniform and had decided to stay there.

Just like last time indeed, Liz noted. Back in 2017, the nook had looked pretty much the same, except for four things. One, the bloodstain. Way back, nice and thick and dripping. Today, just a faint outline because the wall hadn't been scrubbed properly by the same caretaker who'd found it.

Two, the body. Little more than a skeleton, it lay near the faded stain, right about where Breakspear – if it was he – must have been when whatever happened to spill his blood up the wall... happened. As if he'd been there the whole time and had somehow been missed. Of course, that hadn't happened. Breakspear had gone. And now he was back.

She could immediately see the grubby jeans, pulled down below the pelvis, and a T-shirt made from a hessian sack, exactly as people had described when questioned about the homeless person who had lived in this nook. Both garments were stained with old blood. His skull was smashed.

Three, the car seat. It lay next to his head, touching it. Bending over for a closer look, she could clearly see damage to the plastic frame and fragments scattered amongst the pieces of bone. Obviously, the car seat had been used to destroy the skull. But was it the murder weapon?

Donaldson pointed at the exposed pelvis. 'No ventral arc. So it's deffo a man.'

And four, the most intriguing: the personal items in the nook. Way back, the articles had had an obvious male flavour. Now Liz could see a pink deodorant, an empty tampon box, and various other products designed for women. She wasn't the first to notice.

Aware of her scrutiny, Donaldson said, 'I heard from one of the local bobbies that there's been a woman living here for months. They see her out and about. Nobody's moved her on because there's been no attempts to break into this place since. So she's like a security guard. I'll get forensics to try to get us something for an ID. We know Breakspear's got his DNA in the system, so at least we can confirm if that skeleton is him.'

Liz started taking photos of the scene, with close-ups of the personal items and especially the body and car seat. ID of the deceased was no longer her main concern. She had no doubt the body belonged to James Breakspear. Her new focus was finding the nook's new, female tenant.

CHAPTER SIX

Liz stepped out of the nook and stripped off her forensic whites. She would return here when her team arrived, but for now she wanted to walk the area and soak it in.

She headed to the road out front, where a crowd had gathered outside the cordon. Last December she'd been involved in a major murder investigation and had faced heavy media scrutiny. Back then she had welcomed the attention because she had low self-esteem and craved respect, and had foolishly believed the solving of a big case would achieve this. These days she felt she had nothing to prove and having her photo in the papers was just embarrassing and annoying. Some thrived under the spotlight and others withered.

However, facing the inevitable horde at crime scenes was something she had to endure. Every cop alive knew that some killers enjoyed seeing their handiwork create drama, and what better way to watch this than as an anonymous face in a crowd? One killer had described this habit as 'Like the premiere for my own movie'. She took a photo of the faces watching her. Some jeered or pulled poses, others shielded their faces, and a portion just stared. It was an indication of nothing. She recognised a face though.

Next, she focused on the community centre. Near the main doors was a large wall-mounted lockable poster board. She approached it and saw flyers advertising activities. Sunday morning: poetry reading. Last night: disco. She hoped the corpse had been dumped this morning and not last night. Digging into nineteen poets currently collected in one room would be a lot easier than analysing the alibis, characters and histories of thirty or forty drunken teenagers now scattered to the winds.

'What can you tell me, Elizabeth?'

The shout had come from a nerdy-looking guy of about twenty, who stood at the front of the cordon. He was the guy she'd recognised earlier, a man who'd attended at least the last five murders she'd been involved with. His name was Barry and he was never without his camera, notepad, and trademark red baseball cap. Apparently he was writing a book of Yorkshire homicides and hoped to include photographs and interviews from live crime scenes.

'I can tell you I don't like emptying the bins,' she called out. A recent budget slash had seen the evening cleaners removed and now departments had to tidy their own floor at the end of a shift. Bates had promised to give this duty to any member of his team who talked to Barry.

'Have you seen the body? I'm hearing it's someone who's been dead ages.'

She ignored him, pulled her phone to dictate notes, and returned to the nook to await the rest of her team. She also texted Liam Bennet to cancel their drink tonight. This one was going to be no slam dunk.

An on-call officer from the coroner's office had arrived while she was out front. It was a middle-aged woman Liz knew, a former police officer in the nineties. Someone not known for her enthusiasm. Liz approached her.

'Have we ID'd him yet?' the officer asked.

'No. But we have DNA from a previous injury to match him against. We'll have that answer by tomorrow morning. I'd like a post-mortem.'

'I'll have this boy stored away and I'll do a PM if you need it.'

Liz was puzzled. 'If? His head's been crushed.'

'Sure, sure. That's fresh though. This boy's been dead a long time. I bet you find he's from a local graveyard. The damage could be from when he was dug up or transported here.'

'People are usually buried in T-shirts made out of potato sacks, are they?'

'We can't be sure he wasn't redressed. Look, if this boy is from a cemetery, he might have already had a post-mortem. That's why we need his ID.'

'I can promise you now that this body belongs to a man who went missing three years ago. I know the clothing. He left a bloodstain here, and now he's back as a skeleton. Look at this man's head, look at the damaged car seat right next to it. I would very much like a full post-mortem on him.'

The officer didn't like Liz's tone, but she forced a smile. 'Okay, I'll do it. I'll do it tonight, if that makes you happy.'

'No, not you. Not a standard post-mortem. I want this sent to a Home Office pathologist for a full forensic post-mortem.'

'On a skeleton three years old? I hardly think that's necessary.'

Liz knew she was being a little demanding, but she couldn't help it. She felt as if she'd lost three years of time because she could have done so much more back when all she had of James Breakspear was a bloodstain. Her impatience was justified.

'A standard post-mortem could miss something. A lot of

homicides are missed and ruled as natural causes or accidental because somebody has decided they don't want to spend the extra money on a forensic pathologist. That was the finding of a report sent to the forensic science regulator a few years ago. I read it.'

'There's no need for histrionics, detective. My office never–'

Histrionics? Liz's blood almost boiled. 'Your office never what? In that report, the highest percentage of homicides called into doubt was by coroners. You know how the regulator got his information? Questionnaires were sent to coroners, police and Home Office pathologists. Coroners also had the lowest number of returned questionnaires. This is now a murder investigation, so you will refer this to a Home Office pathologist and if we hear back that the dead man is from a graveyard, I'll reimburse the money myself.'

'Fine,' the officer said, losing her smile. 'I'll pass it on and also pass on my opinion of your attitude to your superintendent, how about that?'

'Pathologist first,' Liz said, and left the woman's company.

Her team started to arrive shortly afterwards, just as Liz was finishing up a phone call. Little more than a hello was exchanged. Her colleagues knew their roles and their tasks. She approached Donaldson. He said, 'You okay, boss? You look like I feel. We had our orders last time, remember? So this isn't our fault.'

Easy for him to say because he had at least been part of the team that tried to find James Breakspear. Liz felt like she'd abandoned him. But the sick feeling that showed on her face wasn't because she felt she could have done more way back. 'You remember Breakspear had a sister?'

'Yeah, you mentioned talking to her. Claire, something like that. Runs a hair salon. Didn't give a toss about her brother way back. Never reported him missing. I imagine we'll all have a day in court to explain things once she finds out he'd been dead all along.'

'I think she already knows,' Liz said. 'I just made some calls, trying to find her. Her last known address was a place in Sheffield city centre, although she left over a year ago and none of the staff have a clue where she is now. But I think I know where she's been living since.'

Donaldson looked puzzled, until Liz indicated the scattering of toiletries and other products in the nook – all for a female – and said, 'That last known address was The Cat and Mouse day centre.'

CHAPTER SEVEN

L iz didn't return to her sister's house until eleven pm, some five hours after she was supposed to be back to help shift her stuff. Her sister's husband, Freddie, had hired a small van, but it wasn't in the spacious driveway. She got a bad feeling.

Justified when she went in the house. Sometimes she liked to sneak in and go upstairs to her attic room to avoid the family, especially after a long day of being around people. She didn't get the chance now. Her sister came into the hallway, puffing because she must have run to catch Liz before she had to heave her oversized frame up the stairs.

'Late,' Gill said. 'Freddie and his friend have already taken your stuff.'

'I'm sorry. Caught up at work.'

Gill rarely asked about her sister's workday, knowing Liz wasn't permitted to speak of it. 'Well it would have been nice to get a phone call.'

'But where has Freddy taken my stuff? I've got the key to the flat.'

'Because you didn't want me to see the place. And it's a bedsit, Lizzie, not a flat. Your stuff has gone to your house.'

'I hope you don't mean my ex-husband's house.'

'Current husband. You're still married.'

'Yes, okay, I'm still married and it's a bedsit, not a flat. Why did he take it there? You know I don't like to see Dan.'

'Which is just silly. He called here to talk to you just as Freddy was loading the van. So it was perfect timing. When we said you were moving out, he offered to take your stuff in and help you move it tomorrow. You should be thankful.'

Well, she wasn't. She was annoyed. She'd been separated from Dan for almost a year now, since discovering he was a cheat. After she'd moved out of the home they'd bought together, he'd moved his mistress in. This, however, hadn't stopped him constantly phoning Gill's home to try to speak to Liz, usually in the period between when his new beau dumped him and when she foolishly took him back.

She knew why he'd made the offer to shift her stuff, and it was nothing to do with being helpful. The presence of Gill's family in this house discouraged unannounced visits, a defence Liz wouldn't have at her own place. She'd planned to keep her new bedsit secret as long as possible and never give Dan the address. Obviously he wanted to help her move so he could visit. The last thing she wanted was him turning up on her doorstep the next time the new woman walked away.

It was at times like this that she wished she hadn't been so career-focused that she'd made no personal friends. She would just have to hope she could get a couple of coppers to help her shift the stuff and keep Dan at bay.

'I'll get my stuff tomorrow,' Liz told Gill.

'You mean you want to stay here again? Your room is empty. I mean, it would be best if you didn't stay, but I suppose this is late notice.'

'You know what, don't worry about it. I can afford a hotel.'

'Wouldn't it be easier to just go and stay at home? So you can move your stuff early?'

Liz wanted to rage at Gill. She'd dumped Dan months and months ago, yet her big sister still grasped the wild hope of a reconciliation. 'That would help you out, wouldn't it? Must be embarrassing to have your snobby friends know your sister has a failed marriage and no kids and a career dealing with blood and hate and evil. I do apologise.'

Gill raised her eyebrows in shock. Something else she seemed unwilling to accept was the idea that they weren't teenagers and she could no longer boss Liz around. Gill seemed unable to speak, but a finger pointed at the front door said everything.

Liz knew she'd been in a bad mood ever since the discovery at Frecheville Community Centre, but she wasn't about to apologise, even to family. Without a word, she left the house.

CHAPTER EIGHT

E arly Monday morning, Liam Bennet received his package. He opened it as giddy as his son had ever been at Christmas. He called Joe downstairs. The boy was in his bedroom, packing for a trip to his grandfather's, even though the holiday wasn't until the middle of next week.

His father showed off a business card, one of five hundred he'd purchased online. It bore an outline of a detective caricature inside a magnifying glass. Text displayed Bennet's mobile and the home landline numbers and 'Liam Bennet – Private Investigator'. Joe was impressed.

'Wow. Awesome. You should advertise online,' Joe said.

'When it's time, you can help me with that.'

It was the school summer holidays and Joe was getting bored, so he was eager to help. But his father didn't realise this until later in the afternoon, when they were both gardening. Bennet's mobile rang in the kitchen, but Joe offered to get it. He didn't just fetch it though. He answered the call as he returned to the garden.

'Bennet Investigations. How can we help?'

Liam smiled, thinking his son was kidding around. But Joe didn't hand over the mobile. 'It's a hundred and fifty pounds a day.'

Liam softly snatched the phone and put it to his ear, in time to hear a woman say, '—seven o'clock tonight? I'll text my address.'

'Hi. This is Mr Bennet. I think there's a misunderstanding. How did you get this number?'

'The Facebook advert. I assume your call-out fee will be a day's work, right?'

'Er... yes.'

'I'll text the address. Thank you. Seven to seven thirty. Goodbye.'

When Bennet hung up, Joe clapped and said, 'You got your first job. What is it? Are there terrorists to hunt?'

'What just happened? How did some strange woman know I'm already a private detective? And what Facebook advert is she talking about?'

Joe dragged his dad inside, to a computer, to show off what he'd done. Bennet was shocked when Joe loaded a business page on Facebook. Bennet Investigations.

'Good Lord.'

'Great, eh?' Joe was beaming. Bennet took the mouse and scanned the page. He'd been ready to be annoyed, to reprimand his son, and to quickly delete the boy's online creation... but the page was actually pretty good.

It included a photo of Liam standing by his car, which Joe had taken a few weeks ago. Bennet had posed next to his new BMW, little knowing Joe's ulterior motive. It listed his work history and skills and a little biography, all of which Bennet recognised as text copied from a CV he'd knocked up a few weeks ago when considering applying for work at an existing private investigation agency.

Next, Joe showed him another business page, this time on a social network for local neighbourhoods called Nextdoor. He clearly wanted praise, but Bennet was a little perturbed.

'I was planning some time off before becoming a private investigator, Joe. I'm not really ready.'

'Why wait when you got your first job?'

'I'm not licensed. There's a course you have to take to–'

'No, you don't have to. I read about it. Nothing to stop you investigating. That's all about being professional and showing off that it's all official for clients. But you just got a call. And why bother with a course when you've been a detective for years?'

A fair point from a kid with wisdom beyond his eleven years. It still didn't feel right. 'I also don't have the equipment yet.'

'You mean bugs and disguises?'

Bennet laughed and decided to let it go. 'You're right, I don't need stuff like that. Well done, Joe. This is very good work. Thank you.'

He was still concerned, but when he later got a text from the woman who'd called Bennet Investigations, he dampened his doubts. There was nothing against the law about helping this woman with whatever she wanted. And she could be his first testimonial when he finally got the business authenticated and running in first gear.

Plus, Joe was right: Bennet had years of experience running a murder squad and he doubted many legit private detectives had such a résumé. Investigating was what he did, all he did, all he knew. He was no sham or cowboy.

'You told that woman I want a hundred and fifty pounds a day. How did you come up with that number?'

'Your police wages,' Joe said. 'I remember you said you get

fifty-five thousand a year. I just divided it by days in a year. Is it not enough? Are you going to take the job?'

Bennet couldn't bring himself to say no. Skills and experience aside, he had the one requirement to be found in anyone who wanted to investigate: curiosity. He was dying to know what kind of problem the woman needed help with.

CHAPTER NINE

The address was on a housing estate in Hackenthorpe and Bennet found himself on a section of the A6135, where he pulled into a car park of a pub called The Birley to check his map. His destination was half a mile east. This close, he was suddenly a little nervous. He'd never gone to a 'job' alone before.

His attention was caught by a small white van that turned off the main road and drove past the side of the pub. It said CRIME SCENE INVESTIGATION on the side. This was Sheffield, Liz's territory, and the van made him curious about the case that had dragged her away from him earlier. He rang her.

'I just saw a forensics van go by. Anything to do with you?'

'I'm Sheffield, remember, not Barnsley.'

'No, I'm in Sheffield.' He didn't want to mention he was going to see a potential client, even though she knew about his plans to open a private investigation business. It was too quick, too soon, and would reek of desperation. 'Just visiting someone.'

'Where did you see the van? If it was near Frecheville, then it's mine. I just called the forensics in for another go over my crime scene.'

He'd seen Frecheville on the map. 'Yeah, that's where I am. Birley Moor Road, near a pub called The Birley.'

She was surprised. 'The Birley is just down the road from me. Like two hundred metres. Who are you visiting? Ask him or her where they were Saturday night. I might close this case today. Hey, come on up, I'll meet you. It's the community centre.'

He left the car park and went up the side street, across a junction and quickly found the community centre on Churchdale Road. The forensics van was in the car park and he saw Liz's vehicle too. She was standing by it.

He parked by her car and got out. 'Where's Joe?' she asked.

'I dropped him at a friend's for an hour.' He noticed her suit was creased. 'You sleep dressed last night?'

Her smile vanished and she self-consciously smoothed her jacket. 'My furniture is at my husband's house. My bedsit's empty. Long story. And a long few days.'

Had she stayed at her husband's house? He felt she'd see his jealousy if he enquired, so he nodded at the community centre. 'What do you have here?' he asked.

Murder of a homeless man, she explained. He went missing three years ago but under suspicious circumstances. Now his corpse, dead all that time, was back at the same spot, head caved in by a car baby seat. The body had been called in by an anonymous male from a phone box nearby, and this person hadn't yet come forward. At that location there were no usable fingerprints and the touch DNA was a mixture from myriad contributors, some of it degraded over time, so the lab was still working on it.

They'd fast-tracked other DNA, though, and now knew that

the skeletal remains belonged to one James Breakspear, thirty-five, in the system for a theft conviction.

The 'nook' bore evidence that another homeless person had been living and sleeping there. They'd found a complete DNA profile for this person and usable fingerprints, but she wasn't on record.

'She?'

'I believe it's Clara Breakspear. James's sister.'

'His sister? You're saying this James Breakspear went missing from here, and now his sister lives here, and suddenly his body's turned up, and she's now missing?'

'It gets stranger.'

The forensic post-mortem had been performed on Sunday evening. The C-7 neck vertebrae had a fracture consistent with a sharp-edged weapon. The fracture edges were smooth, unhealed: perimortem damage. The skull fracture edges were stark white against the yellow discolouration of the rest of the bone: post-mortem damage.

Bennet said, 'So he was killed by a stab wound to the back of the lower neck. And years later the skeleton had its skull smashed in.'

'Very good. You should be a detective.'

'And you a comedian.'

'Bizarre, eh? It gets weirder still. A baby seat for a car was used to smash James Breakspear's skull.'

'This car seat – was that already at the scene, do you think? Not exactly something someone would carry around.'

'Unsure. She didn't have a baby when she was registered with a homeless shelter called The Cat and Mouse a year ago.'

'Cat and Mouse? Nice name.'

'It was a pub that was converted into a day centre and kept the name. Anyway, if she'd had a baby since that's unregistered, there was no evidence at the crime scene that a baby lived there.

Perhaps she found the baby seat. I suppose it could have been used to keep items off the ground, like a table. Maybe she's so skinny now she can sit in it. We just don't know yet.'

Bennet checked his watch. It was already passing seven o'clock. His client had said between seven and seven thirty, so he had a few minutes. 'Any good news? Any suspects?'

They had a few potentials, but only one warranted a decent look. Breakspear's theft conviction had been from back in June of 2016, just over a year before he went missing. He had been arrested for stealing strawberries from Eastfield Farm in Tickhill.

Instead of bringing his container of picked fruit to the shop to be weighed and paid for, he'd fled across the field, towards the A1(M). The manager's young son, also out picking, had followed and watched the pair get into a car parked on the shoulder of the northbound lane. He'd gotten the registration and that was traced to a fifty-seven-year-old man called Hubie Jones.

A former prison officer, Jones had been convicted of, amongst other things, GBH with intent. With a dodgy record, he'd been sentenced to two years while Breakspear got only a slap on the hand. Jones served nine months and was released just two weeks before Breakspear went missing, and perhaps he held a grudge because he blamed Breakspear for his arrest.

'We went to Jones's house,' she said, 'but it's empty and his neighbours say he's known to be away often, sometimes for weeks at a time. We have no clue where he is, so we'll have to wait. So, now you know pretty much what I know. What's your gut feeling on this one?'

He gave her a stare. 'Are you asking to make me feel better? I did that with my dad, remember?'

Bennet's father had been a murder detective and had often quizzed Bennet about his cases to offer help. Bennet played along because he knew his dad missed being in the game. He suspected Liz was doing the same. After all, it was no secret he'd quit the police only because of childcare issues and a growing unease at being away from his son so many hours a day.

'I knew you'd think that,' she said. 'But I just want an opinion.'

'You know the crime, not me. What's your take?'

'If Clara Breakspear is responsible for her brother's body turning up, she could be on the run with a child. There could be a killer hiding with her baby. Or there could be a dead mother and child out there. I just don't know yet. I've brought in this CSI to have another sweep of the area, just in case we missed something. The only blood we found so far was the stain on the wall, so we're not even certain Breakspear died here, or even if he died the night he made that stain.'

'I know how dedicated you are to the job. But did you have to come here just for that? I mean, I'm glad to see you again, but is this an acting DCI's task? You should have posted a DC here.'

She shrugged. 'We might find a bombshell that blows this thing wide open. This is a bizarre puzzle I'm desperate to solve.'

Bennet had to admit this case was just the sort of thing he'd have loved. And yes, he was jealous as hell.

CHAPTER TEN

The client's house was clean, tidy, respectable, unlike its owner.

The woman who answered the door of the semi-detached that evening was in a nightgown barely big enough to cover her extra-large frame. It was yellow but stained brown in places and there was soup not yet dried on the collar. She gave him a look like he'd turned up to evict her. She was about thirty-five, he figured.

'I'm Felicity. You're the private eye?' He nodded and she said, 'Come on in, and get those shoes off.'

He obeyed and was led into a living room as smart as anything on show in a furniture store, and a far cry from the owner's attire. Felicity sat on a sofa, behind a small table she'd dragged close to eat her soup from. He sat and she slurped the meal, spilling more down her collar. He'd already noticed a clear bin liner on the floor with what looked like a handbag in it. And nine or ten sheets of plain A4 paper laid across the length of the radiator under the window.

After a few seconds, he got the impression she might not say a word unless prompted. So he asked what she wanted him to do.

She pointed her spoon at the bin liner. Bennet took out the handbag. She nodded as if to say, look inside. He saw it was empty except for some loose little items of junk, crumbs, and a single receipt stuck to the side. There was white staining. Probably mayonnaise, given his client. He figured he was expected to look at the receipt so pulled it free, but it ripped and left the adhered half behind. It was a Tesco receipt. Simple food items. Nothing on there that stood out.

'Not the receipt. See that nasty white stuff? That's his sperm, the sick bastard.'

Bennet literally dropped the bag and stepped back. As a murder detective, he'd handled all manner of items far more terrible than this, but he'd always worn gloves. He felt disgusted.

'That's lovely, Felicity. Any chance you could have just told me this before I... Why am I here?'

'This is why you're here, isn't it?' she said as she reached into a pocket and pulled out paper cash and thumped it on the table. 'I mean, you're not here as a favour. That's three hundred. Your exorbitant call-out fee and one more day's pay. Cos I don't want this taking more than one day.'

Bennet sat without touching the money. He took a breath to get his attitude right. Maybe he'd be just as obnoxious if someone had ejaculated into his wallet. 'I don't know if I'm taking the case yet. Tell me what you need.'

She angrily flicked her spoon at the handbag. A dab of tomato soup flew and landed on it. 'I met a man online last night. Through one of those dating apps. What, you think that's wrong? You think I'm scummy or something?'

Good Lord. 'I said nothing of the sort.'

'But you're thinking it.' She jabbed the spoon at the wall her property shared with the neighbour's house. 'Just like that bitch next door. I'm scummy because I wanted a man from the internet. Well, I work hard all week, and I don't have time to go to wherever people go to find people. So what's wrong with the internet?'

'Nothing. I said nothing, Felicity. Please finish the story.'

So, she'd chatted to a man and they'd agreed to meet Sunday evening. They'd gone to the roller disco. It was the school summer holiday, so why couldn't she stay up late? And those people who think she can't skate because of her size, well, they were just morons. She skates quite well, thank you.

A pause. Bennet realised she wanted a response. 'Yes, you can skate. Yes, you can stay up late. Ignore those fools. So, last night, man from internet, roller disco...'

'On the dating site his name was Jacob Bressler. Doubt it's real. He said he didn't have any ID, so he'd have to go in the disco under my membership as a guest. He was a nice man. Tall, handsome, smart, polite. We met outside the disco but then he suddenly says he doesn't want to go in. I thought he might just want to go back to mine and have sex, so I asked him. And he said yes. What's wrong with a woman making the first move? Why is sex on a first date such a big no-no? Who's got the right to say that makes me scummy?'

Again she glared at him as if he'd made such accusations, and again Bennet regretted coming here. 'Women can make the first move. They can do first-date sex. Please carry on.'

Jacob didn't have a vehicle so she drove them both back here. She should have realised something was up because Jacob had eyed up her handbag when they met, and he'd refused to kiss or hug her, and when she left her handbag in the car after getting home, he told her to bring it inside. Said it might get stolen. But that wasn't why he was bothered, was it? He had an ulterior motive, didn't he?

'I don't know. What happened then?'

Jacob told her to get in bed while he used the bathroom. But he didn't use the bathroom, did he? He slinked downstairs, got her handbag, and did his nastiness. And she came down and caught him.

He had the bag over his dick, both hands around it, moving himself inside it. She yelled at him, but the slimy bastard just started going faster, trying to finish. Nothing stops you men when you're seconds from shooting a wad, does it?

She paused. Actually paused for an answer. He nearly told her to *hurry up and finish*, then realised how bad that would sound and opted for *what happened next?*

'I tried to hit him, didn't I? But he lobbed my bag at me and ran. I threw a soup bowl at him, but it missed. He just ran out the door and down the street. Isn't that the freakiest thing ever?'

She probably wanted an answer to that question, but he didn't oblige. 'Let me just get this straight. He didn't assault you. He didn't steal anything. All he did was, let's say, abuse your handbag?'

She nodded, but not before tipping her bowl to her face to finish the soup and wiping some off her chin and nose with the collar of the dressing gown. 'And that bastard needs to pay. He's the scum, not me.'

'Pay how? Why didn't you call the police if it upset you that much?'

'Pay with a pound of flesh, that's what he needs to do. I have brothers, they've done time, they're bad boys, and they'll smash him up when they get hold of him. So I want you to find him.'

'That's why I'm here? You want me to find this man so your brothers can assault him?'

'And it better not take more than a day either.'

Bennet got to his feet. 'I can't take this case. And I have to warn you that vigilante justice might get you in trouble. Call the police. Or just get a new handbag. Goodbye.'

As he headed, fast, to the door, he was careful to look back. She still had that soup bowl in her hands, and the last guy to walk out on her had had one thrown at him.

CHAPTER ELEVEN

Before leaving the community centre earlier, Liz had mentioned to Bennet that she was looking for someone to help shift her furniture. He offered. She had seen the upset look on his face upon learning her gear was at her husband's house.

So she'd made sure to mention that she'd slept alone in her new, empty bedsit, hence the cricked neck and creased clothing. And baggy eyes, because some idiots making noise out on the street had woken her a couple of times. He'd asked if her husband would mind if she turned up with another man.

'He's got no say. And he knows you're just a work colleague.'

Just a work colleague. She'd seen that sting him a little too. But in a way that was good. He was handsome and single, but it would be a bad idea to start dating him. She was certain he liked her sexually, although he'd never made a move.

On Tuesday morning, after another awkward evening sleeping on a bare floor in an empty bedsit, she met him at his house. True to his word, he'd borrowed a van from a neighbour, and they drove her to her former home with Joe sitting between them.

She'd called Dan's mobile and her ex-husband had offered to take the morning off work to help. She'd refused, and he'd said he'd leave the door unlocked while he went to work.

But he was home. His tradesman's van was in the driveway and when she looked in the back window, there was all her stuff. Enough to fill the attic room at her sister's flash house, but seeing it all in the back of a vehicle made her realise how little she actually owned. She had unofficially let Dan keep just about everything when she walked out on him.

She tried the front door and found it locked. So much for sneaking in to find the key to the van. She knocked.

Dan answered with a smile, which he lost when he saw Bennet's van at the kerb and Bennet watching. Dan had made an effort, with neat clothing, combed hair and a fresh shave. His girlfriend's car wasn't here. She hoped he hadn't spruced himself up for her benefit.

'Why is my stuff in your van?'

'I thought I'd help you move into your new place. But you have help. New boyfriend over there?'

'Not your concern.'

'I left my girlfriend, in case you were wondering.'

Hell no. 'Sorry about that. If you unload it all onto the lawn, I'll get it packed.'

'Too much hassle for you. Why don't I drive it down and you and the new Mr follow?'

She didn't want him to know her address, but his idea made sense. 'There's a backyard. You can leave it all there. Follow us.'

During the drive, Liz didn't take her eyes off the wing mirror.

'You think he wants you back?' Bennet said.

'I don't want to think about it.'

'Strange, isn't it? That the people we come to despise most are the ones we used to love most of all.'

She gave him raised eyebrows. He shrugged. 'Just being weird. Ignore me.'

The bedsit was on Retford Road in Woodhouse Mill, a former pit village in the east of Sheffield. The housing estate she lived on the outskirts of had been farmland half a century before. Her new home was above a chip shop just metres from an iron railway bridge, which ensured that when trains weren't rattling her windows, drunken customers downstairs would. She felt low. How many other high-ranking police officers lived in such squalor?

They turned off Retford Road and accessed a wide alley round the back and stopped behind a BMW that she knew belonged to one of the chippy owners. Dan's van stopped behind. He came to her door.

'Quaint. Tight for space, I imagine. But a bedsit will do if you don't plan to have friends round. Although make sure your car doors are locked.'

He knew damn well she had no friends, having vacated social time in favour of her career. But he had a point about the area. The alleyway was littered with trash and broken glass. The chippy owner's BMW had a personal wheel clamp on it, even though it was daytime. As her landlord, he'd warned her about leaving valuables on show if she parked here overnight. There had been a problem with druggies hanging out, although they hadn't made a show in a few weeks.

Dan started to unpack the stuff and carry it through a gate, to lay in a junk-filled backyard. Her rear door was accessed by a flight of iron steps, and it was going to be annoying to get all her stuff up there. But it beat letting him see inside the bedsit.

After they'd watched him pick and carry the first load, Bennet said, 'Unfair to let him do it all.'

She reluctantly let him help Dan. She wound up her

window because the two men talked as they heaved and she didn't want to hear it.

Joe said to her, 'My dad is feeling lonely. I think he might have been waiting for Mum to come back to him. But Mum is dead. He needs someone new. You two like each other.'

Very blunt. In anyone older, she would have blushed. 'He's a good friend. Let's talk about it later. Not now.'

Joe nodded and returned his attention to a game on his phone.

When the job was done, Dan came to her window. She thanked him, but wouldn't look at him. 'Call me if you need anything else,' he said. 'Or just a chat over a pint.'

'Thanks again. Bye.'

When he was gone, Liam, Joe and Liz carried her stuff into the bedsit. She took items from them at the door to carry inside, because she didn't want them to see the interior. Every cupboard door in the kitchen was loose, the wallpaper was faded and peeling, and the carpet looked as if every army since the Akkad had marched across it. When the last item was done, and the boys were leaving, Liz called Bennet back. He stood on one side of the threshold, she the other.

'I always avoided dating you because you were a police officer. You know I had a bad experience with a colleague. But even though you're out of the force, I don't want to spoil our friendship.'

He seemed embarrassed. 'I never said anything about us getting together.'

'I know. But just in case.'

'I get it. Just friends.'

Her phone rang. It was one of her team, who said, 'You

might want to head in early, boss. Hubie Jones just handed himself in. He said he just heard he's wanted and not happy about it. Been out of the city all week, apparently. And he came with a solicitor.'

So now they had the man who'd gone strawberry robbing with the murder victim found outside the community centre in Frecheville. It was a little worrying though. If killers handed themselves in, it was more often than not with an admission. Those claiming innocence usually had to be found.

She told Bennet duty called. 'No hard feelings about what I said?'

'The friends thing? Nah. I always knew that.'

Poor guy. He looked so nervous. Usually they'd part with a cheek kiss, but such would feel inappropriate today and she left him with a thumbs up.

As she pulled into the car park at Woodseats Police Station, she saw a man and a woman arguing by their vehicle. He was in the car, she standing by his open door. Curious, Liz parked close so she could catch their conversation. She'd seen this sort of behaviour before and knew exactly what was going on. The woman wanted the man to visit the station; the man was reluctant to.

As Liz walked past the arguing couple, ear cocked, the woman saw her ID lanyard and stopped her.

'You police?'

'Yes,' Liz said. The nosey part of her would love to hear their story, but time was pressing. 'I can't help you. You need to go to reception please.'

Liz continued past. Behind her, the couple continued arguing.

'Jason, we didn't come all this way for nothing. See, the police are nice, just like that woman.'

'But I wasted their time, they'll be angry.'

'You reported the body and without you they wouldn't even know yet–'

Liz stopped dead.

CHAPTER TWELVE

Hubie Jones and Jason Smith. Two men with possibly vital information. Two men who might be a killer. Liz got her pick of the two. Each man was in a separate family room and she poked her head into both. She asked a simple question:

'Do you like this hot weather, yes or no?'

Puzzled, both men said yes. Liz repeated the format, but the next question was:

'Do you know how much trouble you're in?'

The man who'd claimed to find the body, Smith, sagged his shoulders. The man most likely to have put it there, Jones, tensed his.

Question one had been colourless, designed to establish a baseline so she could better analyse the response from question two. Good for determining who might lie and who could be stubborn. Jones, the strawberry thief, was going to be the tough cookie. Smith, despite his reluctance to be here, was probably going to roll over and cause no headache.

In the hallway, between both cells, Liz told a colleague, 'I'll take Jones.' She liked facing the tough cookies.

Both men were interviewed at the same time, in separate rooms, by two-person teams. Afterwards, the four detectives met upstairs in the incident room to discuss the results.

Liz had been right: Smith had admitted everything without trouble, and provided his alibi checked out, he was completely innocent. The officers conducting his interview had a smooth sail.

On Saturday night he'd been at a barbeque, with ten witnesses to prove it. He lived just half a mile away from the community centre and that Sunday morning had arrived to attend the poetry reading. He looked for a place to have a sly piss before going in, because the toilet in the centre was broken, and found the body.

He panicked and ran to the phone box, reluctant to use his mobile because he knew it could be traced. He knew the police would want a face-to-face interview and they'd have to investigate him, and he was dead set against that. His wife had eventually convinced him to hand himself in, although he'd gotten cold feet at the last moment.

He was released, but he wasn't happy, and now the detectives learned why he'd been so averse to raising his hand. The simple fact that police had questioned him would set tongues wagging, and there were personalities in his neighbourhood who'd assume he was guilty. Now, Jason Smith wanted officers to knock on his neighbours' doors and tell everyone he was innocent. He wanted it announced at a press conference.

In fact, he wanted praise for his assistance in trying to solve a murder. He refused to leave until the police agreed. Jason Smith became the rare creature who posed a bigger problem for police after release without charge.

Meanwhile, Hubie Jones had dedicated himself to creating a problem in the interview room. He'd paid a visit, so he wasn't under arrest and his unofficial chat was conducted in one of the family rooms to promote the idea that he was simply helping with enquiries. Despite this, he no-commented his way through the first few minutes. What he did say was done via a prepared statement read out by his solicitor.

Hubie Jones claimed he'd been staying with his ex-wife and kid in Shropshire for the last week. He admitted knowing James Breakspear. A pair of former junior football players, they'd met six or seven years ago at a homeless hostel, before Breakspear chose to live at the community centre. When Jones was caught for stealing strawberries, he hadn't blamed Breakspear in any way. It was his car that got spotted in a hiding place he'd picked. His own fault.

By the time he'd finished his sentence, Breakspear was long gone and Jones hadn't seen or heard from him since. He had nothing to do with the man's disappearance and was sorry to know his old friend was dead.

'Did you know of his sister? Did he mention her?'

No comment.

'Don't mess about, Hubie,' Liz said. 'Fight that habit. Kick and scream to prove you didn't do this. Do you want me to ask you if you killed James Breakspear? Because if I do, and you no-comment that instead of denying it, how's that going to look? Shall we try it? Hubie Jones, did you kill James Breakspear?'

Jones gave a little snort-laugh. 'Nice. Okay. Yes, I knew his sister. Yes, he mentioned her.'

'That's better. What do you know?'

'Not much. I know she had big things planned in her life and James figured he might drag her down. So when he was kicked out of their home, he stayed away. Did that to give her a chance. They were pretty inseparable before. But they lost touch.'

Inseparable? Liz had gotten quite the opposite impression from Clara three years ago. But she recalled a line uttered by the woman: *If he cared about me, he would have been in contact.* Perhaps Clara Breakspear's apparent lack of care about her brother had been a product of bitterness at being abandoned by him.

'And was Clara upset that he left?' Liz asked.

'Yeah, probably. But he never spoke to her again, so I don't know. He used to watch the house, he told me. For her own good. He did that for years, every few weeks or so. He'd sneak around there and just watch. Just to make sure she was okay. I think he did that until she was twenty and left home herself. So about four years or so.'

'He was kicked out at sixteen?'

'Sixteenth birthday, that's what he said. So, yeah, he was homeless for like half his life. I don't really know much about it. She got on with her life and then he got on with his. The way I just told you all this? That's basically how he told me. Now you know as much as I know.'

'Did you know Clara is homeless too?'

That shocked him. From his interaction with the police and the court system, he'd known she had started her own successful hair salon business while still a teenager. It was around that point that James Breakspear ceased watching her. She was clearly going to do all right in life. 'So after that she was out of the picture. What happened to her since I had no clue of. Homeless? How'd that happen?'

Liz wasn't here to answer questions. 'We believe she's been sleeping rough round the back of Frecheville Community Centre. Exactly where James was living before he vanished.'

Jones was in disbelief. It looked real. 'This is all messed up.'

'It gets worse. She might have a baby. Know anything about that?'

'No. There was no baby by the time James stopped watching her. Don't know anything about that. You need to talk to her people, her friends and stuff. Or check hospital records or something. I'm the wrong guy. I never even met her.'

'Her people haven't had word in nearly two years. Her friends were solely work colleagues and they drifted apart after she quit her profession. We can't find anyone who knows anything that can help us.'

'And you've just hit another brick wall. I'm getting tired of this now. I know nothing, and that's all I'm saying. But you didn't bring me here for my expertise. You think I had something to do with Breakspear's murder. So arrest me for that or let me go.'

'Christ on a bike.'

Liz was in Allenberg's office on the top floor of Woodseats Police Station. Liz had just outlined her case so far for him, and he wasn't happy.

Most murder victims were slain by someone they knew, and these cases mostly got solved quickly. Stranger-on-stranger kills by far took up more ink in the unsolved files. Until this update, the super had rested his hopes on Clara Breakspear being culpable, but Liz had stated her doubt.

Yes, Clara had been living in the very spot where her brother's decayed skeleton reappeared. Yes, as Bennet had said, *the people we come to despise most are the ones we used to love most of all.* But she had been a successful businesswoman and out of contact with her brother way back when Liz had found a bloodstain behind Frecheville Community Centre, and they now knew James Breakspear had been dead by then.

For certain Clara was someone with vital information, and she might have been living with her brother's corpse for some time, but Liz would bet the house she wasn't a killer.

To make things worse, one of Liz's team had telephoned Jones's ex-wife and she'd confirmed that Jones had been staying with her for the last week and had returned to South Yorkshire today. She'd also offered the names of the ten witnesses who would swear that while someone deposited a skeleton behind a community centre in Frecheville, Jones was cooking sausages a hundred miles south-west.

If this alibi was validated, they were out of viable suspects and could be in for the long haul. Liz shared her super's worry.

'We need a press conference,' he said. 'This afternoon. I'll get it arranged as soon as you leave here. Let's get pictures of Breakspear and his sister out there and get her found. Hopefully she'll admit everything.'

He was still banking on Clara then. But Liz had a bigger concern right now. 'And who's going to lead the press conference?'

He smiled. 'Well, you're the lead detective.'

'I really should get DC Donaldson. He worked the bloodstain three years ago and he knows as much as I do.'

'Don't worry, I know you're terrified of the cameras these days. You're sure this Donaldson can handle it?' She was. Certain. 'I still want you there in case there's questions he can't answer.'

Liz nodded. It was true that Donaldson had good knowledge of the case – the whole team did, of course – but he was expert in only the aspects he'd been tasked to work. He didn't have the scope Liz did. However, he soon would. Because Liz was going to sit him down and talk his ear off to make sure there would be no 'questions he can't answer'.

CHAPTER THIRTEEN

F ive mornings a week MIT 2 had a Team Ten, which was a team meeting to discuss the Breakspear case, recent findings, and tasks for the day. On Wednesday morning Liz began by telling her audience about a phone call prompted by yesterday afternoon's press conference – at which Donaldson had performed beautifully and kept the spotlight off her.

The call had come from a cousin of Clara and James Breakspear living in London. He said that he'd not even known of James's death and was shocked to learn that he'd died three years ago. More so than knowing his body hadn't turned up until recently.

The cousin's sense of shame intensified when he admitted his side of the family had somewhat disowned the Breakspears. Clara and James's mother, Maggie, the caller's auntie, had been kicked out of home at an early age, just like James. She had moved from London to Sheffield and been mostly forgotten. The caller had heard about a pair of kids, but had met them only once. This was at a family funeral in 2001 when the siblings were young teenagers.

Maggie and her sister, Mia, the caller's mother, had never

been close, but they spent an hour chatting at the funeral. It was from this short meeting alone that the caller had gleaned all he knew of young James and Clara Breakspear. Maggie had had nothing but praise for her Clara, and bitterness towards James.

Clara was obedient, kind, thoughtful, and eager to acquire a healthy career. James was the direct opposite. Cruel, selfish, and a criminal. Apparently he'd been a keen footballer and had played for a junior league, but high hopes of a sports career had evaporated by the time he was ten.

He'd started hanging out with the wrong crowd, all older children who introduced him to fun ways to make illegal money. Being small, he could fit through windows the others couldn't, climb drainpipes that wouldn't hold his bigger comrades, and he quickly became a tool used to do their bidding. He was often in trouble with the police for street violence, muggings, burglaries, you name it. Instead of a future kicking footballs, he looked set to kick his heels in a prison cell.

The caller had heard no more about the family except for a single postcard Maggie had sent a few years after. In it she admitted kicking James out of her house and had no idea where he was. Clara, she said, had left home to pursue her career, and Maggie had decided to relocate to Scotland to start anew. 'When I get settled,' she promised, 'I'll invite you up.' There had been no invite and no further contact. The caller did not know where Clara was and had no further information. He was very apologetic and hoped for a reconciliation one day.

The team discussed other aspects of the case and then Liz delegated various tasks. Afterwards, she turned her attention to another major case her team was dealing with.

It was the rape of a twenty-nine-year-old female schoolteacher on Monday night in Hackenthorpe. She had been jumped while walking across a field to reach her home. The attacker had penetrated her, but not with his penis. Instead, he had taken a hairbrush from her handbag, wrapped the bag around the handle of the brush, and forced the makeshift item inside her. He had made one thrust and fled.

There was no description because the attacker had worn black clothing and a black mask. Witnesses had heard the teacher yelling but nobody had seen the attackers. So far, the only CCTV they had was from the main road fifty metres from the scene, and the rapist hadn't been shown. There was no biological evidence and no physical evidence to get excited about. Her ex-boyfriend hadn't yet been cleared, but he wasn't a likely suspect.

With nothing new on this smaller investigation, Liz could do no more than tell everyone to keep at it and then she ended the meeting. Detectives and police staff sauntered away to coats and phones and computers, while Liz sat at DCI Bates's desk and grabbed a map.

CHAPTER FOURTEEN

The man who worked for the Senior Management Team of Barnsley Metropolitan Council left his office at close to midday and lunched at a café down the street. Bennet parked across the road and sighed. He'd watched the town hall all morning, just sitting in his car. As a detective constable he'd been on numerous stake-outs, but he'd been after criminals, trying to prevent future crimes, and that had meant something.

This task, despite the money on offer, seemed like a big waste of his time and sucked at his soul. He hoped the councillor would go off and try to rob someone, just to give today some meaning.

It didn't happen, but the councillor did finally do something that allowed Bennet to end this thing. The middle-aged manager was in the café just long enough to order a takeaway meal wrapped in foil, which he ate as he drove west out of the city. Annoyingly, he drove right past Churchfield Police Station, as if to wind Bennet up: *that's where you should be, pal, not following me.*

Bennet looked at the station to see if he recognised anyone coming or going, but he saw none of his team. If he'd caught them piling into cars and racing away with an armed response team, that would have really pissed him off. A year ago he'd been the coolest cucumber on the shelf, but these days he constantly sweated the small stuff.

The councillor drove two miles, turned off the main road, and fed his Vauxhall into a car park outside a tall block of grimy flats. The remains of a burned-out car were nearby, like a sign telling all that they had definitely not just entered Shangri-La.

A car was parked by the entrance doors, and the councillor made a beeline for it on foot. There was a short conversation through the driver's window, then the councillor put a hand through for two seconds. Afterwards, he darted into the tower block, gone.

Bennet also crossed the car park on foot, aimed for the entrance doors, but the guy in the car yelled out, 'Hey, what's your business here?'

Bennet approached the car. The driver was about twenty, tattooed, with a face only a mother could love. Cauliflower ears were a dead giveaway that this guy practised combat sports. There was a fob in his hand, surely for the entrance doors: he'd let the councillor in.

'Maybe it's not business. Maybe I'm visiting.'

'Visiting who? I know everyone in there and everyone they know and I don't know you.'

'Ah, but do you know everyone that they know knows?'

'Get lost, pal, while I still have some patience.'

'Maybe I want to visit the same person as that man in the suit you just let in.'

The thug gave Bennet a long look, trying to decipher him. If he came down on the 'threat' side of the fence, Bennet would probably get his own cauliflower ear. It didn't happen. 'Maybe that person's busy right now and you can wait over there somewhere.' He waved his key fob. 'And it's a hundred to get inside.'

'I'll go get my wallet.'

But Bennet didn't fetch his wallet. He got in his car and made a call. To the woman who picked up, he said, 'I have your answer, Mrs Harper. Technically, no, your husband isn't having an affair. But he's visiting a prostitute.'

He expected her to be emotional, and she was, but not in the way he thought. No grief, disbelief, tears. Instead, she started raving about her husband, threatening him, cursing the day he was born. Bennet barely heard because he saw the car parked by the doors start to come his way.

Instinctively, he reached to a pocket for his warrant card, but of course, it was no longer there. Instead, he told the woman he'd phone back, killed the call, and loaded the internet.

When the thug pulled up alongside, driver's window to driver's window, Bennet showed him the phone. He'd loaded a picture of himself with the police and crime commissioner. He'd received a commendation for bravery that day, for saving a bank robber from a crashed car, but the newspaper article was five years old.

'That's me. A copper. So either go away or be arrested.'

Again the thug gave him a decoding look. Thirty seconds later, Bennet drove away sans cauliflower ear.

Forty minutes later, Bennet knocked on a door. When Mrs Harper answered, she was red-eyed from crying. He followed her into the living room, where she handed him his fee. The cash was in an envelope, which made the transaction seem a little dirty.

As he put the cash in a pocket, she suddenly darted forward and planted her lips on his. He moved away. 'Revenge? That's not the way to fix this problem you have.'

Mrs Harper deflated and started crying again. 'You should leave then.'

He was happy to, although she followed him and, on her doorstep, said, 'Do you like this job? Getting paid for ruining people's lives?'

'No,' he said, honest. 'I used to try to make people's lives a little bit better.'

'Should have stuck with that,' she said, and slammed the door.

CHAPTER FIFTEEN

At ten that evening Liz parked on St Philip's Road, at the rear of the Medico-Legal Centre. She had swapped out of her suit and into jeans, a T-shirt and, most important, trainers.

The low red gates into the car park were shut, so she climbed over and approached the red-brick building. By a pair of red fire doors was a large, wheeled bin.

The centre, which contained coroner's courts and a mortuary, had opened in 1977. Liz had been here many times to talk to pathologists and witness autopsies, some of which were now done by CT scan and negated the need to cut open bodies. In fact, the centre had been the first in the UK to employ this digital software. Inquests were now more common since the serial killer and doctor Harold Shipman killed over two hundred of his patients. Nobody wanted so many death certificates signed off by doctors alone.

This was the first time she'd been here after hours. She climbed onto the wheeled bin to access the low roof of the annex. And saw what she'd hoped. A rotten blanket and the detritus of a homeless person's living space.

She sat to wait. An hour later, she heard noises and someone climbed onto the roof. Skinny with very short hair, grubby tracksuit bottoms and an equally grimy jumper, the person could easily have been mistaken for a male, yet it was a female. The woman standing before her was a far cry from the image in Liz's memory, but she knew she had the right person.

Despite having lived rough for a time, Clara Breakspear didn't look any older than her thirty-one years. The girl looked shell-shocked and Liz's heart went out to her, not least because she'd lost her brother. Clara had had a major turnaround in her life, going from popular businesswoman to unwanted and homeless in the space of a couple of years. But how?

Liz showed her ID badge. 'Don't run. I'm a police officer. Clara, this is very important. Have you got a baby somewhere?'

Clara didn't run, but she stayed by the edge of the roof, sideways on, ready to jump if this scene turned to her dislike. In a repeat of three years ago, the woman's eyes scanned Liz, head to toe, as if once again surprised a pretty young woman could be embroiled in the dark and stressful world of murder detectives. 'No, there's no baby. But I know why you're asking.'

'Do you remember me?'

'No, I don't remember you. Are you one of the ones who moved me on?'

She must have meant a night when she was sleeping rough and the police had told her to find another location. Liz moved closer, but carefully. 'No, that's not me. I was the one who talked to you at your home when James went missing.'

Now she seemed to relax a little. 'Yeah. I remember you. I didn't kill my brother, if that's what you think.'

'I don't think that. I know you didn't. He's been dead three years. But you might know who did.'

'I don't know who killed him.'

'But I think you were there, behind that community centre, when his body was placed there.'

Clara glanced behind her, at her escape route, but remained in place. 'I'm not going to a police station. I can't help you. I didn't see it. I was... I woke up at...'

She started crying. Liz gave her a moment.

'I won't go to a police station. And if you come closer I'll run. I can live anywhere, as I'm sure you've guessed.'

'I know. But you want to stay here. Near your brother.'

Clara said nothing for at least a minute. She sat on the low parapet, one leg either side, as if still ready to run. She had the jitteriness of one who'd seen a lot of conflict during her time on the streets. She stared at the roof, as if able to see right through. To her brother's corpse. 'He was just a skeleton.'

'I know.'

'But I recognised him. That T-shirt he made. They told me all about it.'

'Who did?'

'The people. The people on the street.'

Liz took a step closer. 'You spoke to other homeless people about him? Did you look for him?'

She laughed, but it wasn't mirth. 'You have no idea. How did he die? Has there been an autopsy?'

'Yes. I'm afraid it looks like he died of a single stab wound to the back of the neck.'

Clara swung her dangling leg over the parapet and sat facing Liz, no longer determined to run. 'How did he die? I mean, did he suffer? Was it quick?'

Liz wasn't sure. The only blood they'd found was the stain on the wall. That at least suggested James Breakspear had remained in place after the attack. But it gave no clue to how long he might have taken to expire.

'Yes,' Liz lied.

Clara cried again and wiped her face on her grubby top. 'I am pathetic. I can't even pay for his funeral, and no one else will. What will happen to his body? Will it just be thrown in the rubbish?'

'No, of course not. He was found in Sheffield so Sheffield Council will take care of it. They will want you to take responsibility, but you can't be forced. However, there are options for you if you *do* want to arrange the funeral. You can get financial help. There are charities that help with funding. If you don't want to take responsibility or can't, he'll have a public health funeral. He will probably be cremated. The council will have control of the funeral, and it will be a cheap, basic affair, I'm afraid. But you might be able to have a say about certain aspects of it. Decorations, for instance. You might be able to take his ashes.'

She cried again. 'I am so pathetic. I should have helped. When you came that first time. But I didn't. I just didn't want an upset to my life. I had a good life back then. It was easier not to think about my brother. And I was angry at him for leaving me.'

'I understand. And there's no reason to believe you could have prevented this. But now you can help. I need you to give me some answers.'

'About that night. I know. But I'm not going to a police station.'

Liz would try to get the girl into an interview room at some point to make her statement official. Not tonight though. But she needed what the girl knew as soon as possible.

'Talk to me first. No recordings, no police station. But not here on this roof. Will you come with me? And I don't want you to sleep here tonight either.'

'I have nowhere else to go.'

'For tonight you do.'

CHAPTER SIXTEEN

There wasn't much in Liz's bedsit, but she had a kettle and to Clara that made it The Ritz. Liz made tea while the younger woman tried out the sofa Liz had bought from Bluebell Wood Children's Hospice shop across the road yesterday. She eyed the sofa somewhat suspiciously, as if wary of the promise of comfort.

Clara had refused the help of a family liaison officer, but had eventually agreed to tell her story at a police station tomorrow morning. Liz's team already knew Liz had Clara and would be ready to receive them. But Liz planned to get a head start.

As they sat and ate fish and chips from the shop below, Liz said, 'Let me be honest. I'm eager to solve the case. Desperate, in fact. In your head could be the answers, even if you don't realise it. It's going to be hard for me to wait until tomorrow.'

Clara ate fast as she was hungry and unused to such splendour. But she paused, put down her cutlery, and leaned back in her creaky wooden chair. She didn't wait for a question. She started talking.

'James was kicked out of our home when he turned sixteen, on the very day of it...'

Her brother had been such a troublemaker and their mum had planned to evict him since he was barely a teenager. Having worked with someone with a child with autism, Clara believed her brother had been on the spectrum. There was never a diagnosis, but she'd read up on the condition and was certain.

Their mother, Maggie, had never wanted a boy child, so Clara had been the one she lavished attention on. What little interest she gave her kids, that was. She had always taught them to work for themselves, not a boss. Their mother took the route of prostitution, but Clara planned to get her own business. She worked in a hair salon when she left school, saved and studied, and when she was twenty, she and another girl there bought the place from the owner and moved in upstairs. They turned it around and it made good money for a few years.

She had always figured James was watching her until she left home. Sometimes late at night she'd spot movement outside the front of the house, across the street, and sometimes she'd find a discarded soft drink can in the backyard, as if James had slept there. Such little details were no real proof, but the feeling that he'd been present couldn't be shaken. He'd always promised to take care of her, and perhaps watching the house at night was his method.

Reliving the past made Clara cry. Liz gave her time, but pushed for more.

Clara got on with her life, years passed, and when Liz turned up in 2017 with news that James had possibly been hurt, she saw it as a way of breaking free finally. No more having to worry about him. Because worry she had, at least for the first few years. After she left home and their mother moved away, Clara never again got the sense that James was watching her. She'd told herself he'd found a new life, perhaps even had a family by now, and that was enough to satisfy her. Had she really believed it? No. But ignorance had been comforting.

And then Liz arrived with bad news. A week or so after the detective's visit with a story of a bloodstain matched to her brother, Clara had a dream. Or a sleeping memory, for she had replayed some of the good times they'd had together. The times when he had saved her from bullies, or from drowning one time, and she had begun to miss him all over again. No longer did the idea of his having a new family seem believable; now she feared he needed her help.

When she contacted the police, James was already officially a missing person – Liz admitted here that this was her doing – but there had been no progress. So she did her own investigation.

At first she started to use an hour or two on a day off to call homeless shelters in Sheffield, to no avail. The next step was to visit Frecheville Community Centre every other night, but there was no sign a homeless person had been sleeping there. Then she started driving around the streets, looking for him.

The escalation was quick and a month after he went missing, she was cutting off work in order to search. She would scour the streets and talk to the homeless. Some promised to call her if they heard anything, some marked known haunts on a map, and others blatantly lied to her about having seen him. She paid out a lot of money for this help, but it all came to nothing.

Her work started to suffer. Two months into this mission, she was sleeping in her car in homeless areas, watching and hoping he'd show. A month after that, she sold her share of the salon and rented a city centre flat in order to be closer to the action. The following six months were a bit of a blur, but she eventually ended up accompanying a homeless man around the city, like a tour guide. He educated her on street rules and took her to various places, and soon she became an expert.

The natural next step, for someone so knowledgeable about the world of the homeless, was of course to get her feet wet. So she got rid of the flat and started sleeping rough. She'd given up her job, her home, her car, her friends, and had paid thousands for help. Before she knew it, there was no going back.

A year after that visit from Liz, Clara too was homeless and penniless, sleeping in all weathers and eating leftovers, just as her brother had for so many years. She had a close homeless friend call Daisy whose side she stayed by. She gave up trying to find her brother.

She and Daisy survived on the streets for another year, before finally deciding to visit a homeless shelter. She found The Cat and Mouse, which offered services for the homeless between ten in the morning and four in the afternoon. She would sleep rough with Daisy, then visit the centre to eat and wash her clothing.

Then, six months ago, Daisy died in her sleep. Feeling lost, Clara abandoned the day centre and Sheffield city centre altogether. Without a close friend, her mind returned to her brother and she made a home round the back of Frecheville Community Centre. It was the last place James had been known to sleep and this was a measure of comfort. Somehow, it made her feel close to him. Sleeping where he had called home gave her pleasant dreams about him. With luck, he'd one day return for real.

And he did, on the night of Saturday August 15th, 2020.

Clara needed a break here before tackling the next part of her story. She wanted a bath, which Liz ran for her. The tub was coarse with painted-over rusted sections, but to Clara it was a world of comfort. Liz, meanwhile, paced impatiently.

She gave Clara some of her old tracksuit bottoms and a jumper, and then the younger woman was ready to continue her tale.

On that Saturday night, in her sleeping bag behind the community centre, she was woken by noises. She saw a dark humanoid shape in a corner, standing over a mound, smashing at that mound with a large item. She saw little more than silhouettes, but half an hour later learned the truth. That weapon was a car baby seat. That mound was her brother's skeleton. That figure was his killer.

'An hour later?' Liz said.

Clara nodded. 'Because I ran. I didn't know anything other than a man was effectively in my home. So I ran. And when I came back later, I found out the truth. I recognised the T-shirt people had said he wore.'

'What happened then?'

'I ran again. I didn't know what else to do.'

'Why didn't you call the police?'

'For what reason? James was dead. So someone could be arrested? That's just for you police, or for the public. I didn't care about that. So what if his killer went to prison – that wouldn't ease my pain. I had stayed at that community centre in the hope James would come back, and now he was dead and I had no reason to be there. I just wanted to get away. Who would want to stay in a place where your brother's body was dumped?'

'I understand. Did you see the man's face? Recognise him, anything about him? Did he say anything?'

'I didn't see the man, not really. He was just normal. Not fat or tall or whatever. Didn't hear his voice. I just know he was dressed in black, with gloves and a mask.'

Liz questioned her some more, but the only additional information she got was that Clara thought the man's clothing was a one-piece. Just like the type of protective suit forensics people wore. But black, not white.

Soon, Clara visibly deteriorated under the rain of questions and Liz reluctantly changed the subject. The women chatted like old friends until Clara fell asleep on the sofa. Liz got her murder book and lay on the bed, mind suddenly returned to the Breakspear murder and whirling with a thousand questions. She started making notes.

The protective suit reeked of pre-planning. Nobody walked around in such an outfit, so the killer probably had a car, backed up by the car seat. He'd need one for transporting the body.

But why use a car seat as a weapon, even against a skeleton? Practically, it would involve two journeys to the community centre nook since the seat and the body couldn't be carried at once. Perhaps the baby seat had a direct connection. Could James be a father who'd abandoned his child? Had he hurt someone else's young son or daughter?

An hour later, her head began to ache. This was a massive puzzle and Liz felt she was missing something vital, and simple, without which her brain would just go haywire and become lost in wilder theories. She had to take pause, sit back, wait for more information. But it was hard.

She'd sat back three years ago when she'd found a bloodstain, and that had been a massive error.

CHAPTER SEVENTEEN

L iz's door was opened by a thirty-something woman who was wearing Liz's jumper, but Bennet didn't have a clue who she was. Without a word, she took the box of knick-knacks he carried and vanished into the bedsit. He closed the door behind him. She sat on the sofa and rifled through the ornaments he'd brought.

'I'm Clara. Liz is letting me stay here a while. Are you Liam? Where's your little boy? Are these for Liz? Where did you get them?'

Clara. Sister of the man found at Frecheville Community Centre. He noticed her hair was coarse, but otherwise she looked fresh and bubbly for someone who'd been living rough.

And she wasn't in a police cell. God, he was suddenly desperate to know what was going on, but it wasn't his place to ask, and certainly not here, within sixty seconds of meeting this woman. 'I am. He's in the car. They are. Priceless family heirlooms handed down from my great-great-grandfather. Where is she?'

'Shower.'

Now he heard it. The bathroom was off the kitchen and he went to the kitchen door. 'It's me, Liz, I brought you some cheap junk to fill this place with.'

'I'll be out in a minute.'

He sat at the dining table, which was just a foldaway picnic table near the bed. On it was a little purple-covered notebook. He knew it was Liz's murder book of notes. He still had his own back at home in which he'd written his thoughts and feelings and tasks regarding every murder case he'd investigated. Now never to have the final pages filled in, alas.

He flipped it open. Clara said, 'Not sure you should be reading that. Although you're in it. You had a big case together last December. She thought you hated her at one point. She tried to hijack one of your cases.'

'Maybe I did at first. Can't remember. So you read it?'

'Shocking, all those crimes,' she said. 'So many murders. And rapes. And bank robberies. She should publish this.'

'It's not finished yet.'

'She's going to solve my brother's murder. He died three years ago.'

It seemed like the perfect chance to start firing nosey questions, but again he held his tongue. She said, 'Liz told me I will be here alone on Saturday night. She's going to ask you out for a drink. Are you going to go? I want to watch TV naked. I haven't lounged around naked for years. So you need to go out with her. Get some condoms just in case, but take her to a hotel.'

He was lost for words. Liz exited the shower at that point, which was a saving grace for all of two seconds. Until Clara said, 'He says yes to going out Saturday. And he'll buy condoms.'

Liz and Bennet couldn't look at each other, which made Clara start laughing.

Woodseats Police Station's family rooms were colourful, with comfy chairs, tea-making equipment, and a window overlooking the car park. Despite the fact that Clara's interview would take place here, to be formally videotaped, her earlier high spirits had vanished and she walked up the stairs like a woman heading to the gallows. Liz had agreed to conduct the interview, alone, to make Clara comfortable, even though grieving relatives were usually dealt with by specially trained members of her team.

As soon as she'd sat down and the door was shut, Clara threw Liz a curveball. She had already answered myriad questions about the murder of her brother, but so far hadn't once asked how the investigation was progressing. Now, rather sternly, she said, 'I want to know what you know so far, before we start. What leads have you got? What suspects? I need to know that you people are doing this right and know what you're doing.'

This about-face in demeanour made Liz stumble over her first few words. 'Er, nothing, we – I mean, we don't have a suspect yet. Not a viable one. I'm sorry. But we're working hard and my team is highly experienced.'

'I hope you aren't hoping for some eureka moment from this interview. I don't know anything beyond what I already told you last night. If you need my help, then this is going to be one of those unsolved cases.'

Clara had first appeared as withdrawn, scared. Once in Liz's bedsit, she had lightened up and a joking personality had even been exposed. Liz put the woman's current defensiveness down to the formal surroundings of a police station. She stood up and brandished her phone.

'I need to video this interview, Clara, but we don't have to do it here. There's a café across the street. I need a bacon roll. Let's go.'

Clara jumped to her feet, and Liz saw a new brightness in her eyes.

CHAPTER EIGHTEEN

On Saturday, August 22nd, Bennet got his former team member's sister to babysit while he went out with Liz in Woodhouse Mill. She picked him up and drove him back to her area, then a third of a mile along Retford Road, just across the River Rother, to a pub called the King Royal that sat next to a patch of wasteland. There was a weekly darts tournament at the pub, which she fancied entering.

She wore a short skirt and a T-shirt and looked a little like a cheerleader. She didn't often get to let her hair down like this and wanted to make the most of it. But she wasn't drinking and had her work clothes in the car. The on-call rota for MIT 2 had five DCIs, working a week each on rotation, but it was her turn to leap when the murder hotline rang.

The family-run pub was very homely. Outside, on a letter pegboard on the wall were the drinks prices, meal of the day, and the first names of the Yard family members next to their photographs. There was also a dice showing a three that had been fashioned from number 1s and full stops.

Inside, the daughter of the owners, a twenty-something in a wheelchair, was working the bar, and her two big, handsome brothers were darting around and making conversation. One, Andrew, was the reigning darts champ and eager to recruit people to test him in the tournament. When he approached Liz, Bennet wasn't a fan of the way Andrew's eyes lingered on her legs.

Mrs Lynn Yard, their mother, regularly got on a microphone to advertise food and forthcoming attractions, including karaoke tomorrow night. Liz loved the place and figured it was somewhere she might call a second home if she got time. She needed new friends.

After she went to the bar, she handed Bennet his second pint, sipped her second bottle of water, and said, 'I'm sorry for the remark about seeing you only as a friend. We both knew that and it didn't need saying out loud.'

'That's fine. Don't worry about it. Anyway, how's the homeless skeleton investigation going?'

She could sense her remark – about a remark – had stung a little and he wanted to change the subject. 'Slow progress. Nothing really new since I last told you.'

'Feels weird now I'm a civilian. You would have told me before.'

She laughed. 'I'm not hiding anything. Or maybe I am because I don't want to make you jealous.'

'Jealous? I have lost dogs and cheating husbands to deal with, so why would I be jealous? No boss, no red tape, no budget concerns.'

'You keep telling yourself that.'

A little while later, while Liz was battling a nineteen-year-old girl in the first round of the darts tournament, something curious happened. The darts master, Andrew Yard, rushed across the lounge. Those who caught something urgent in his stride – including Bennet – watched in surprise as he slammed the heavy oak front door shut and slid a bolt.

'No bastard leaves,' he roared. The music suddenly shut off. On the other side of the room, his brother, Rodney, locked the rear doors leading into the beer garden. 'Everyone damn well stays put.'

From another door that probably led outside, Lynn Yard walked across the room, talking on her mobile, and crying. She vanished through a door behind a curtain.

The room buzzed with a curiosity that amplified when two young men wanted to leave but were blocked at the door by Andrew. Liz approached him and showed her warrant card. 'What's going on?'

Andrew grabbed her arm. She let him. As he almost dragged her towards the back door, she glanced at Bennet and realised he was thinking the same thing. She said nothing.

With the front door now clear, one of the two men who'd tried to leave slid the bolt back. Bennet stepped up, pushed the man's hand away, and re-engaged it. Then he slid between them and the door.

'He said no one leaves.'

The guy got close. 'Get out of the way, pal. We're meeting people.'

Bennet shook his head. The young man tried to push him aside, but he pushed back. Bennet was older but bigger, and the guy didn't get physical again. Around the room, what had begun as marvel had turned to disfavour. Someone yelled out that nobody could stop them leaving. Others demanded to know what was going on. People started coming towards the door, as if ready to barge it open.

Liam held his position and addressed the room, loudly. 'This whole pub is now a crime scene, and you're all going to have to talk to the police. So nobody goes anywhere just yet, and anyone who tries gets a night in a cell.'

Andrew led Liz into the beer garden, to a gate in the low wall that accessed the wasteground between the pub and the river. Some hundred or so metres ahead, Liz could see the moonlit water; the space between was jet black.

All he'd said during the short journey out of the building was, 'It's my dad,' and she'd asked no questions. She didn't have to. Now, seeing where he planned to take her, she pulled him up.

'Stop. Don't go out there.'

He had his hand on the gate. His voice was shaky, but suddenly angry. 'What? My dad, he's–'

'Just stop. Fetch me beer trays, as many as you have. Go now.'

The urgency in her tone convinced him. He was back thirty seconds later with a high stack of round plastic trays. Liz opened the gate and threw one down. Then she stood on it, trampling weeds flat, and tossed another. 'Stay back,' she told him, and dropped another tray.

Using these stepping stones, she created a path deep into the weed-infested wasteland, leading the way with her phone's torch. Twelve trays in, the light caught a mound some ten metres ahead. Seeing it lit up, Andrew, back at the gate, yelled in grief.

Liz made a call to a number she knew off by heart, although she'd never before had to ring it. When it was answered within three rings, as it always was, she said, 'It's me. Get the team down to the King Royal in Woodhouse Mill. I've got a body.'

CHAPTER NINETEEN

Until the police arrived, Liz and Bennet coordinated the restless crowd. Everyone had to be kept calm, while also effectively kept prisoner. Nobody was allowed to use the toilet in case they dumped evidence. This operation was aided by the dead man's family. His sons continued to block the exits, while Jade, the wheelchair-bound daughter, continued to try to promote a typical atmosphere by working the bar.

Most people seemed to accept their lot and a kind of calm prevailed. But then a drunken idiot who had misunderstood the scene tried to leave and turned nasty when he was rebuked. His friends joined in. Bennet was halfway to the mob when Lynn Yard got on her microphone and, her voice broken, said,

'There's been an assault outside and nobody can leave yet because the police have to speak to everyone. Haven't you been listening?'

Uproar from the mob.

'I understand some of you have other places to go, people to meet. But this is the way it's going to be. Since you're so insistent on leaving, you must have something to hide. You two will be questioned by police first.'

That got the message across. The mob quietened.

When uniformed police and members of MIT 2 arrived and secured the pub, Liz found a moment to head out to her car. Police had strung tape across the car park entrance, so the area was clear, but it was a Saturday night and there was a throng of nosey partygoers just outside the cordon.

Feeling like an animal in a zoo, she kept her head down, got in her car and transferred it to a gloomy, quiet corner, where she wouldn't be observed changing into her suit in the back seat. Afterwards, she got her forensics whites and Nikon camera out of the boot.

Boeson hadn't arrived with the other members of her squad, but as she returned to the pub, she saw his vehicle arrive along with two forensics vans. There was an awkward moment when her DS's car tried to slide under the police tape across the car park entrance before a uniform could lift it. The tape caught a windscreen wiper and snapped, and members of the drunken onlookers apparently read this as an invitation. They cheered and flooded into the car park.

Boeson jumped out of his vehicle, yelling, and fell little short of barging the partygoers right back out onto the street. When order was restored and the tape ends had been tied, the DS and DCI headed into the pub.

CHAPTER TWENTY

B ennet understood the rules and was happy to wait, although he didn't like being shut out from the investigation. It just wasn't something he was used to and it was made all the worse because he was right in the thick of it.

After he'd given his story and a voluntary DNA swab to an officer, he looked towards one of the back windows. The curtains were closed, but he could visualise what was happening out there in the dark wasteland. Liz would be analysing the crime scene, soaking it in and developing early theories. He wished he could be out there.

He saw her appear in the back porch, where she stripped off her forensic whites. A detective led her through the lounge, talking in her ear. As a kid Bennet had always wanted to be able to teleport and have X-ray vision and invisibility, but right now he would have picked the power of super hearing.

Liz spotted him, gave a thumbs up which he returned, then headed through a staff-only door. Once relieved of crowd control duty, the family had vanished through the same door and were upstairs. Liz was probably going to interview them. Teleportation would have been a better superpower right now.

Bennet had met Boeson a few times, so he waved when he saw the man return from out back. The DS approached and Bennet said, 'Soon as you're done with me, I'd like to get out of here.'

'To dump the murder weapon, you mean?'

High curiosity negated a return joke. 'Do we know what the murder weapon was yet? What do we know so far?'

'Can't talk about that, mate, as you know. You been seen to?'

'Statement and swabs, all done. But I'll get mobbed for information if I stroll out the front.'

Boeson nodded his understanding. He whistled over a uniform and gave him orders to escort Bennet through a side door, which put them on a little patio shielded from front and back by trees. Once there, Bennett moved through the dark, bypassed the car park, and emerged from the trees onto Retford Road, thirty metres from the crowd. No one loitering at the entrance to the car park had seen him exit, so he walked towards, through, and away from the crowd without issue.

Gawkers were still strung out along the pavement overlooking the wasteland, although a row of trees prevented anything but a glimpse of portions of the area. He joined four young women whose taxi had stopped to let them out for a nosey. They had found a good spot.

He could see a sliver of the crime scene, which was roped off and bright under portable floodlights. Forensic scientists and plain-clothes detectives buzzed around while uniforms hung back and watched them work. But the body had already been covered by a tent to shield it from eyes and weather. He so wanted to be down there. Invisibility sure would have been welcomed at this point.

Instead, he turned away. Even if he'd still been a DCI, he wouldn't have had this murder. This was Sheffield; he was Barnsley. He saw that the parked taxi driver was impatient to get the four curious young girls back into his vehicle, but they were too captivated by the genesis of a major news story.

Bennet hopped into the car, a twenty-pound note leading the way. This reminded him of an ancient event: a night out partying with his college mates; getting turned away from a nightclub and his so-called pals going right on in without a care; cutting the night short with a bus-ride home, alone, effectively ousted from the party.

'Barnsley,' he said. 'And don't ask me what's happened here. It's not my business and I know nothing.'

CHAPTER TWENTY-ONE

'Less than an hour?'

'Oh yes,' the Home Office pathologist told Liz. He dabbed a gloved finger in a small pool of blood captured in the dead man's upturned palm. It dripped from his glove. 'Still wet, see? I reckon they found the body just moments after the attack.'

Despite the corpse and the numerous living present, the place felt serene. The river and the trees by the main road and the grounds of the pub created a private area. The night fogged out those watching from the outskirts. If not for the myriad drunken voices yelling from by the road, she could almost convince herself there was nobody else for miles.

To some this was the sort of atmosphere that could unnerve, but she would take a dark wasteland over a daylit street anytime. She almost didn't want to go back inside that pub and face all those stares. It kept her heartbeat steady and allowed her to think more clearly.

That said, the peacefulness almost sent her into a daydream, realised only when the pathologist's next words snapped her back.

'Hang on, there's something in the mouth.'

She leaned a little further into the tent. He shone a penlight into the dead man's open mouth and tried to pluck out whatever was in there with tweezers. He grunted. 'Damn. No, won't come. Tight in there. Something big. Looks yellow and black. You'll have to wait till I get this chap on the table.'

'First thing tomorrow?'

The pathologist tried again with his tweezers. 'Hell no. Tonight. I need to know what this is.'

CHAPTER TWENTY-TWO

Now that she had confirmation that Paul Yard, fifty-nine, had been dead less than an hour, she could waive any suspicions that one of his family had killed him.

All four had been hanging around the lounge during that period. Each had left the room periodically for this or that reason, but only Jade had been seen out back by patrons and she was in a wheelchair. A pair of family liaison officers had been assigned, and so far these ladies had found nothing suspicious in the behaviour of the Yards.

Now Liz wanted to chat with them. Most murder victims had some kind of association with their killer, so it was imperative to get a full background check on Paul Yard to see if someone he knew, even years ago, had had reason to end the man's life.

Paul's wife, two sons and daughter told the same story. Paul had been upstairs working on his finances and had come down a staff stairwell to exit out the back and walk their dog, Maisy. Intriguingly, this had been a nightly habit for months. Walk the dog on the wasteground at eight until nine. It would be worth finding out who knew this routine.

Jade Abbott, the daughter, said she'd been in the beer garden to collect glasses when Maisy returned, scrambling over the low fence, her white fur streaked with her owner's blood. Patrons in the beer garden confirmed this, although none of them had seen the blood on the dog.

'I felt so weak,' Jade said. 'I knew my dad was hurt out there. That's why Maisy ran back. But the wall... the weeds... I knew I couldn't get to him. God, what if I'd been alone here with him tonight? I mean, it's happened before. Last week he took Maisy into the wasteland early one morning and the pub was closed and no one else was here. What if he'd been hurt then and called out for me, and I could see him in the grass but not get to him because of my damn legs?'

Drawn by a yell from Jade, Andrew had rushed into the wasteground, led by the dog, which had stopped and whined at a dark shape lying in the weeds. It was too dark to make out the face or clothing, but he knew it was his dad. He also knew enough from TV cops' series not to get close and to keep witnesses – and possibly the killer – at the scene.

'I knew someone had hurt my father. Right then I knew our only chance to find out who and why was the police. There could have been a stranger roaming that wasteland, but the killer could also have been in the pub. I knew the police would have to talk to all customers, and it would waste time if they had to do that by appealing to them in the news and visiting homes. So I locked the pub down.'

Rodney Yard, who at twenty-four was younger than Andrew by three years, was a marketing director just like his brother, but didn't have his capacity for calm.

'I'll kill the bastard who did this,' he said.

Lynn, the dead man's wife, was still in shock and hardly able to speak. But she showed that she, like Andrew, knew a little about murder investigations.

'A hundred thousand pounds. Announce it. If someone's got information, if someone knows who did this, that's what we'll pay them. A hundred thousand pounds. This scumbag will have a wife like me or kids, and they can quit their crappy little job and live a life of luxury. You announce that, Detective Miller. Do a press conference. If someone shops this bastard, they get a hundred thousand pounds.'

Jade Abbot was married to a café chain CEO, her brothers were high-paid marketing directors, and the pub was owned outright by Paul and Lynn. There was no doubt the family was rich and had clout. And were probably used to getting their way, as Liz discovered when Rodney pulled her to one side and said,

'Ten grand. I know you've probably got other murders on your books. Maybe people more important than my dad. Well, there's ten grand in your pocket if you put my dad at the top of your list.'

'Mr Yard, I'll pretend you never said that. And never say it again. I will give this case the highest priority, as I do for all my cases.'

Ultimately her time with the family put her no closer to knowing the killer's identity. Paul Yard didn't have known enemies, he hadn't upset anyone recently, and the only people who'd benefit from his death were already rich. The family members would endure tougher interviews over the coming days and there were many other names to interrogate for answers, but Liz doubted she would learn much more about why Paul Yard had been slain by day's end.

CHAPTER TWENTY-THREE

The body and the pathologist had just left, and Liz's exhibits officer, an Asian lady called Bandera, had accompanied them to the Medico-Legal Centre to watch the post-mortem. Liz's boss, Bates, often watched autopsies to get real-time updates, but it wasn't Liz's thing. Plus, she wanted to work the area.

She headed out front. By now the late hour had thinned the crowds and only a handful remained at the cordon across the car park. She took a photo of the faces lined up, watching her, and recognised a battered red baseball cap.

'My book would benefit from a quote by a celebrity detective such as yourself,' Barry, the crime nerd, yelled out. He had binoculars and a notepad, like a birdwatcher. He wore a jacket over pyjamas, as if he'd been asleep when he heard the news. But how had he heard?

Liz walked closer. 'Do I have to raid your house looking for a police scanner, Barry?'

Barry pointed at something past her. 'Are you not going to dust that for fingerprints? The menu board? That dice?'

She didn't turn to look. 'There's nothing to see here, Barry.

Why don't you go home and rewrite one of the older chapters in your book?'

She turned and walked away. 'There was a dice at the other crime scene, that's all,' Barry yelled after her. 'On the noticeboard at the community centre. That had a three on it as well. You saw that, right?'

'I saw that, Barry. It means nothing. Goodnight.'

Knowing Barry was watching, she didn't stop as she passed the pegboard menu beside the front door, but she took a good long look. She'd seen this dice image earlier, but only now registered that the plastic number 1s and full stops used to craft it had been lifted from other places on the board. The pub owners hadn't been responsible. There seemed to be no reason for that dice to be there.

She veered off and headed towards her car, casually. When she drove towards the cordon and an officer lifted the tape to let her out, Barry watched her carefully. She hoped he didn't suspect what she was doing. He'd just love to write in his book that he'd helped solve what could be two connected but seemingly random murders.

The little sod was right. Liz could hardly believe her eyes.

The wall-mounted poster board outside Frecheville Community Centre had a little square of paper, about the size of a CD case, in the bottom corner, and on it was a sketch of a dice showing three dots. The paper was askew, one corner hidden by the frame, and when she took a closer look, it was apparent that the item had been slotted inside without the door being unlocked or opened. A sliver of the corner poked out.

She hadn't told her team about this in case Barry was full of shit, but now she called Boeson and ordered him to instruct forensics to bag the pegboard menu at the King Royal. She wanted the dice analysed for biological evidence. When he asked why, she said,

'And send forensics to Frecheville Community Centre. I've got one here as well.'

'No shit?'

Boeson said he'd get right on it, but Liz couldn't wait. She had her own forensic collection kit in her car and now retrieved it. She taped off the area around the board, donned protective equipment, and took a wet and then a dry swab of the side of the board, where someone might have touched it to insert the paper.

Nearby was her phone, video recording the whole process. She also took high-quality photos with her Nikon. She was tempted to grab the exposed corner of the dice paper with tweezers and try to haul it out, but didn't want to damage it. The whole noticeboard would go to the lab.

Afterwards, she remained nearby to await the scientists and tried to get a grip on what they had here. Unless the two dice were a bizarre coincidence, the murders were connected and they could have a double killer on their hands. Someone to whom dice, or the number three, meant something. Someone propelled by either a mission or a bloodlust. Someone who'd struck on consecutive Saturdays and might not yet be done.

CHAPTER TWENTY-FOUR

W ay past midnight, Liz sent the last of her team home to sleep, but didn't follow her own advice. She drove to the station to work in her office – hers only while DCI Bates was off work, of course. She was trained to use HOLMES 2, the Home Office Large Major Enquiry System and wanted to see what it could throw up about 'dice'.

The digital storehouse contained a welter of details from investigations undertaken by all the police forces in the UK, and could display links between them, rather like a Google search.

It sounded faultless, but the sheer size of the system could overwhelm. Manageable results might be obtained from a search for, say, a satanic symbol carved into a victim's forehead. But if all you had to go on was a stab wound, or a white car, the list was going to be so vast as to be useless. If a user could add search elements such as a description of a piece of CCTV or a time frame or a shoe size, the field could be narrowed further.

After the murder of James Breakspear, the system had been interrogated for, amongst other things, 'baby seat', but hadn't provided much help because that bizarre weapon could be a *single peculiarity*. This was a term DCI Bates had coined to describe a feature of a crime that had massive significance, yet was so personal to a perpetrator that no one but he or she understood it. In other words, Liz might need the killer to explain why he'd bashed in a skeleton's head with a baby seat.

Now, she had 'dice' featuring at both killings. That made it a signature, and there was a good chance it had featured if the killer had attracted police interest before. If an officer at a burglary in some remote village years ago had seen a dice chalked on a wall and decided, well, why not mention it on the computer, she could hit the jackpot.

She got lots of hits and a reminder of the vastness of the system. An old murder at a casino, something to do with loaded dice. A threatening phone call to a man later slashed up, in which the caller had said, 'Roll the dice and take a chance'. The slaughter of two dogs, described as diced. And more. Dozens more. Too many. But overlooking a crime that seemed irrelevant could backfire disastrously, so she made note of these cases for one of her team to look into.

In a final effort, Liz tried to restrict the range by combining the dice and the baby seat, and did get a single hit from the unsolved files. Alas, it was a parental kidnapping in which an officer had noted the toddler was snatched from his 'dice-pattern baby seat'. Still, who was she to rule out some kind of loose but important connection? It would have to be checked out.

She was too tired to do more. She should go home, make sure Clara was okay, but she needed to be back here in the morning and leaving didn't seem practical. Bates always kept a blanket in the cupboard in the corner of the office. She would fetch that and get some sleep on the floor.

Instead, she fell asleep in her chair. Her last thought before it happened: I hope the morning brings good news.

It would.

CHAPTER TWENTY-FIVE

She was just drifting off when Bennet called. He told her he'd got home fine and couldn't sleep, but she wasn't fooled.

'Lies, man, lies. You just want to know all about the murder.'

'Oh, no, I'd forgotten about that. But if you need a sounding board.'

Actually, she did. They'd played this game many times and it was always helpful. So she told him the murders of James Breakspear and Paul Yard had a connection: dice illustrations found at both scenes.

'Wow. Could be a disgruntled better,' he said. 'I'd check to see if the community centre had a craps night that the two victims attended.'

'Or a casino they both went to, although Breakspear was homeless. A croupier who lost big and lost his job?'

'Or they cheated at a game involving dice. Remember the sand from our other case?'

He was referring to the big investigation they'd worked on last year, which had involved a *Dead Cold* revenge murder. 'Possible. Possible. But let's get serious. I think this is about the

Egyptian game of Senet. It's the oldest known board game and uses a form of dice.'

He liked it. 'So, an Egyptian killer? Could be why the first victim was a body that had been dead three years. That hessian T-shirt he was in was cloth for mummification.'

'No,' Liz said. 'Obviously you're tired because you're overlooking Skara Brae. It's a stone-age settlement in the Orkney Islands. Bone dice three thousand years old have been discovered there. I think our killer found these ancient bone dice and our two victims stole them, and he's seeking revenge.'

Bennet grunted. 'Your detective skills are slipping, Liz. Isn't it obvious we're dealing with disdyakis triacontahedron? The hundred and twenty-sided dice. A firm called the Dice Lab made these using 3D-printing. Our victims are involved in a patent dispute.'

'Did you read that right? Diskeewhat? It's obvious you're looking dice up on the internet.'

'Oh, and you're not, Mrs ancient Skara bones?'

They both laughed. Bennet said, 'Okay, it's late and I'll let you go. Get some sleep. And solve this thing quickly so we can redo our failed drink.'

After the call, Liz again debated going home, but chose against it. This time it wasn't a practical reason. That place just didn't feel like home.

So she fetched Bates's blanket from the cupboard, put it over her, and played a movie on her phone using the station Wi-Fi. She grabbed the pad of plain paper that Bates used to craft his aeroplanes and tried to make a handful. She was asleep before completing the fourth.

CHAPTER TWENTY-SIX

The MIT 2 detectives had all seen DCI Bates sleep in his office overnight, but nobody put that down to anything other than job dedication. Because he had a steady marriage. Liz had a pending divorce and housing problems, and of course everybody would assume this was why Liz had stayed the night. So she slipped out for breakfast before anyone arrived.

She had spare stockings in the car and hoped these would fool her team into believing she wasn't in the same outfit as yesterday. Whether it worked or not she never knew. Not a word was said when she returned.

Team Tens were not normally a feature of a Sunday, but she called one to outline the results of the post-mortem. The pathologist had called her with his findings while she waited in the McDonald's drive-through.

Samples from the body of Paul Yard, found dead near his pub, were yet to be analysed, but the pathologist had a cause of death. 'The item in the throat,' he had said. 'Suffocation. And I got it out. Want to guess? Black and yellow and made of rubber.'

She had had no patience for games. 'Don't keep me on tenterhooks.'

'Football.' He had waited for a shocked response, which she gave.

'A cheap PVC football,' he continued. 'The whole thing too. Sliced open, folded, squashed into a manageable size, and forced into the victim's throat. There was teeth and gum damage from this action. I tell you, this wasn't some popped item found at the scene and forced down the throat. No way would it have fit unless it was properly folded, which would have taken time. Someone specifically prepared this. I mean, a whole football. Never seen anything like it.'

The pathologist had clearly thought the football was a major clue, or it had provided him a break from monotony, but Liz hadn't been as impressed. Sure, there could be a football connection that blew the case wide open, but she was doubtful. She wasn't even sure the item had a specific importance to the killer. She'd never come across *two* singular peculiarities.

When her team heard about the football, they were on her page. But, it had to be investigated. The PVC football would go into the HOLMES 2 system. Sales of such items would be traced. A connection between footballs and their list of interesting people would be sought. But these actions were secondary to the day's main task: finding a link between Paul Yard and James Breakspear. James Breakspear had played football for a junior league, but that seemed far too tenuous to be a real connection, so others were sought.

With luck, the two dead men would have a common enemy and Liz could make an arrest quickly. Answers about dice and baby seats and footballs might thereafter be revealed, or never be required.

Tasks handed out, Liz ended the meeting and drove home. She needed to get changed and find out how Clara was doing.

The first sign that something was wrong was when she found Clara's spare key on the interior doormat. The room looked normal, nothing trashed or obviously missing. She moved into the kitchen to make sure everything was the same, and it was here, on the cooker, that she found the note. It was very blunt:

DIDN'T WANT TO INTRUDE ANY MORE. WILL BE AT THE END OF THE PHONE YOU GAVE ME. WILL BE HONOURED TO ANSWER A CALL BEARING GREAT NEWS. THANKS FOR EVERYTHING.

Liz had to commend Clara's tactic. The wording suggested that a call from Liz would surely be about the capture of whoever killed Clara's brother. Anything else would greatly disappoint. She had guaranteed that Liz wouldn't phone to seek another interview or to ask meaningless how-you-doing questions.

Liz was a little disappointed that Clara saw her only as a police officer, not a friend. It was, of course, silly to consider them friends, given what had brought them together. It was just that... the homeless woman was the only female Liz had hung out with socially for a long time.

Hopefully, Liz would be able to make that 'great news' call soon.

CHAPTER TWENTY-SEVEN

Early in the afternoon, while waiting in a lunch queue at the café across the road from Woodseats Station, Liz saw one of her female DCs rush in, and she knew something big had happened. She realised she'd left her phone back at the station.

She left her position in the queue – next to be served, annoyingly – and they spoke beside an empty table. 'The same profile is on both dice,' the DC said. 'Billion-to-one match.' Liz sat at the table to absorb this.

Tests had been fast-tracked on the dice drawing found at Frecheville Community Centre, and the plastic pegs used to fashion a dice on a menu outside the King Royal in Woodhouse Mill. Getting DNA from them was something Liz had figured too good to be true. Now, they had a full crime-scene profile, the best result possible, but optimism wasn't useful in this job. 'But he's not in the system, right?'

'Sorry,' the DC said. 'But it's still great news.'

'Is it? Close your eyes until I say otherwise.'

Puzzled, the DC did so. A few moments later, when prompted, she opened them and saw Liz holding up something. It was a product barcode. Liz pointed at a stand of nine or ten condiments on the table. 'Read these lines and numbers and tell me which condiment it's from.'

The DC refused to play. 'Look, boss, I understand where you're going with this. But I still think it's good news.'

The court-standard odds of a billion-to-one meant the crime scene DNA was definitive. Whoever had left it had handled both dice. Absolutely. As evidence, DNA beat any witness statement, any piece of CCTV, any fingerprint or fibre. It was the ultimate conviction tool, but without a subject profile to match it to, this fabulous technology was useless. They had no description, no name, no address. All they effectively had was a barcode.

The only shining light in Liz's opinion was that the DNA pointed towards a single man. She'd been worried that, even given the dice connection, they were dealing with two killers. Now it appeared they had a possible serial killer on their hands. Bad for public worry, but easier for detectives and prosecutors.

The DC had also brought Liz's phone, having heard it ring in her office. Two minutes after the DC had left and Liz had again made her way to the front of the food queue, it rang.

'Good news about your case,' Bennet said. 'I might not have access to police databases, but I'm allowed to use the best tool in the world. Google.'

He sounded convinced and she needed cheering up. 'You did it, or Joe?'

'Joe. He's the computer whizz, I admit. Anyway, I told Joe all about the dice connection, although I was careful not to give too much away. I got him to look for other crimes. And he found one.'

Once more Liz stepped out of the queue to chat privately. 'Go on, shock me.'

'There was a dice mentioned on a website called Mumsnet. It's a forum for mothers to talk about whatever. Anything and everything. Joe found a post from a woman moaning about what happened to her poor, blind daughter, who's seven.'

He explained that the crime, unreported to the police, had occurred on Mundella Place, near Mundella Primary School, which was just four or five hundred metres east of her station. It had occurred on Sunday August 9th, exactly two weeks ago.

After he'd outlined the 'crime', Liz said, 'Highly bizarre. Nothing like my murders, and a Sunday instead of Saturday, but the dice angle makes it one that certainly needs looking into. I'll go chat with the mother. Well done. Or well done to Joe.'

'*You'll* go chat with the mother? Take a breath, Liz. Anyone can do that job. That's not the kind of legwork a DCI should be doing.' He paused. 'And it doesn't even have to be a detective. Just someone with interview skills will do.'

His concern for her stress levels was genuine, but she knew he was also fishing. Like her, like all detectives, he loved investigating clues, working snippets of information, and completing a jigsaw that put away a bad guy and relieved a grieving family. And for years he'd had the power to go out and follow those clues or tell others to. Now he was hunting missing cats. She decided to do him a favour.

'You're right, I shouldn't be doing it. But I've currently got all my people on other tasks. Hang on, I've had an idea. You're a private detective now. How about South Yorkshire Police pays you to go have a word with the mother? The crime wasn't reported so it's not a police matter anyway. You can find out what she knows and pass it on to me.'

'Actually, yeah, I could do that. Sure thing.'

She grinned at his play at innocence. 'But by pay, I mean I owe you another drink. Our last one was interrupted.'

'Sure thing again. I'll go find the mother today. Now.'

'I'm sure I don't have to tell you this, but keep the dice angle quiet. It's something we're keeping back for now.'

'Sure thing for a third time.'

She knew she could trust Bennet to not only keep a secret, but also to take care not to let something important accidentally slip out. But a few hours later the matter was moot. Because someone sans such professional care had opened his big mouth.

CHAPTER TWENTY-EIGHT

Barry the crime nerd had spoken to a local online newspaper, and at midday they ran the story of two connected murders just a week and three miles apart. They even sent a cameraman to Barry's house and Liz was appalled to watch a video of him talking about how he had spotted the dice connection and had had to point it out to detectives. He even mentioned Liz by name and said he was upset that she hadn't thanked him. The article hailed him as a super armchair sleuth, able to fathom what the police couldn't.

Filmed at home at a computer desk loaded with files and hardbacks, he did as much as he could to plug his own upcoming true crime book. Apparently, he'd had sleuthing abilities since he was a kid, and knew how to tell a great story. He wrapped up the interview with a plea to camera:

'To the police, if you're watching. I offer my services to you, free of charge. And I'm not just talking about this crime. Any crime, any police force across the country. Just pay my expenses, travel me down there, and I'll help solve whatever crimes you're having problems with.'

The interviewer seemed to believe him, or played along. 'You certainly have showed an affinity for crime busting. Have you anything to say to the police right now that could help?'

'You want a supercop to draw him out, Ms Miller,' Barry said, staring at the camera. At her. 'One officer who becomes the face of the investigation. You've been on TV and the killer will have seen you. You need to either say you understand the killer, or cuss him down as pathetic. Be his only friend or his ultimate nemesis. That way he might contact you. He'll feel you're someone he can bond with, even as enemies. Contact me if you need to know more, Ms Miller.'

Barry had clearly learned the 'supercop' trick from books and TV, yet was passing it off as his own insight. Liz wanted to punch the TV, and not just because he'd uttered her name.

Keyboard warriors bought every soundbite and South Yorkshire Police's social media was bombarded in equal measure by requests for updates and claims of incompetence. Within an hour of the story breaking, Liz's super, Allenberg, called from home.

Only at his most frustrated did sarcasm rise to the surface, so she knew immediately that he was reeling from a media blitzkrieg. She'd seen a newsvan and three reporters outside the building and knew force headquarters over in Tinsley was getting similar treatment. So of course the news bloodhounds would also target the homes of off-duty high-ranking officers.

'How much would it cost me to plant traps all around my house, Liz? Drop everything, forget the murders and robberies and all that, and get me bear traps. Hundreds.'

'I need the odd reminder why I wouldn't want your job.'

'But I get to fob my problems off on my team leaders. Like this one. I want you to send some uniforms to my house to block these people. And then – and this is direct from the chief constable – I want you to liaise with Jane and...'

She didn't need to hear the rest. She knew he was referring to Jane Turnbull, the force's main communications and media officer. He wanted Liz to work with Jane to downplay the dice connection and reassure the public that everything was being done to catch the killer. Standard operating procedure, of course, but the media officer was big on making sure the important faces in investigations got seen to promote sincerity.

In other words, instead of Jane reading out a statement from the police, she'd want Liz to directly answer questions, on camera. Not good.

After the call, Liz had an idea. She called Jane and outlined it. The media officer agreed, but was probably swayed by Liz's claim that she would just stumble over her words if forced to stand in the press room and talk to a throng of reporters. Jane gave her the number of a trusted reporter and Liz made that call.

She left him a voicemail saying she'd like to update him, alone, on the current state of the investigation. It was effectively an exclusive, so she knew she wouldn't wait long for a reply. Job done. Back to the important stuff.

With the dice out the window, she needed something else she could keep secret and use to verify a confession, if they ever got that far. She chose the popped rubber football that had been sliced, folded, and stuffed down Paul Yard's throat out back of his own pub.

The remainder of the afternoon involved fielding phone calls. First up was a familiar voice.

'This new murder. That old TV star. Has it given you any clues to help catch my brother's killer?'

Clara Breakspear, who had heard about the new murder and clearly hadn't been able to wait for a call 'bearing great news'. Liz wished she had, because there was nothing positive to impart. 'No, I'm sorry, Clara. It's still early. These things can take time. I'll call you as soon as we know something. I promise. How are you keeping?'

'So no suspects?'

Every case had its interesting faces, but elevating someone to the status of 'suspect' was no small deal. Of the dozen or so who'd warranted further investigation regarding the murder of James Breakspear, nine had so far been cleared and the others were still no more than potentials with little cause for optimism. Liz couldn't risk giving this girl hope and was forced to boil it all down into a simple, concrete, 'No. Sorry.'

'Fine. I'll wait for your call. I have to go.'

Clara hung up.

Liz immediately loaded Google on her phone. Half a minute later, she was looking at an online newspaper story about the murder of Paul Yard.

The article mentioned that in 1990, Paul Yard had appeared on an episode of series one of *Troubleshooter*, a BBC reality TV programme in which a prominent businessman helped struggling firms. Paul Yard's pre-King Royal venture, a nightclub, had been featured. Liz picked up the desk phone and called an extension. A detective constable appeared in the doorway a few moments later.

'You want to see me, ma'am?' he said.

This was the detective charged with looking into Paul Yard's background. Liz hated reprimanding staff and she was a little nervous. About what was to come. She told him about the article she'd just read, and was surprised to learn he knew about it. 'But I didn't know,' she said. 'Why didn't you tell me?'

'That he was on some reality TV show thirty years ago? Hardly relevant.'

'When we ask for the public's help, we tell them to call in with any information, no matter how irrelevant it seems.

Nobody mentioned this to me. In future, I want to know everything, okay?'

'Okay. I'm sorry. I'll go look into it more now. I just didn't think it mattered.'

'No, leave it, you're probably right. I'll have a look myself.'

Once he'd gone, she wanted to rush out and apologise. But she didn't. Relevant or not, he should have told her everything he knew about their murder victim. It made her worry about what else people had held back or missed.

The incident room's phones had been buzzing non-stop. Despite relying heavily on public help, none of her team answered these calls with confidence. Cranks and jokers and those trying to frame enemies were common, but fairly easy to dismiss. It was the deluded do-gooders who caused the biggest headaches. Ninety-nine per cent of this information was useless, but every single piece had to be investigated.

If there was something that might evolve beyond the useless, low-level staff would pass it up a rung, and if on that level it was deemed worthy of more interest, Liz would hear about it. Sometimes that could be days or even weeks after the initial call.

Sometimes not. In the late afternoon, as Liz was preparing to head out for food, one of her staff bypassed the chain of command and banged on her open office door.

'Our teacher rape from Monday, in Hackenthorpe. She just called because she heard about the dice connection.'

Liz grabbed her handbag and groaned. People had been calling in all day about crimes involving dice, and suspicious people they'd seen with dice, and bizarre hypotheses about the relevance of the dice. 'Don't tell me she's got a theory as well.'

'Not a theory. A dice. She says there was one left in her backyard.'

CHAPTER TWENTY-NINE

Mundella Place was a stubby dead-end street along the side of Mundella Primary School. Facing the tall, bland flank of the school were six houses in three semi-detached properties. Each was behind a slanted lawn so steep that the upper windows were barely above street level. Bennet had emailed the author of the Mumsnet post, one Lisa Bennet, strangely, and she'd supplied an address. He knocked on number four.

The thirty-something woman who answered seemed to recognise something 'detective' about his appearance. But he wasn't going to lie.

'I'm not police. I'm a private detective, but the police did ask me to speak to you.'

'Right,' Lisa said, frowning. 'When I saw that dice thing in the news today, I figured they'd eventually have to take me seriously. But I guess they haven't. What are they going to do about what happened to my Lilly? Nothing, I bet. They just want clues to catch this killer.'

The dice angle had been in the news? Had Liz released that

information? 'I can't speak for the police, I'm afraid. But I'm here to help. Why don't you tell me what happened?'

Lisa relaxed a little and invited him inside. He sat on an armchair and she took a second armchair that was facing it across a coffee table with a built-in radio that was playing low classical music. The home was clean and neat except for children's toys scattered around, just like his own.

'I'm sorry for my attitude,' she said. 'I was just upset because the police have done nothing. But I understand. It wasn't exactly a major crime.'

'Your Mumsnet post said it wasn't reported.'

'I called the police and they took two days to send someone. I just told this pair of officers not to bother. If they take two days just to come get my story, they're hardly going to use the big guns to solve it.'

'I understand. But now what happened to you could end up helping to solve a real major crime. I'm not saying the murders and what happened to your daughter *are* connected, but every piece of information helps. Tell me what happened.'

On that Sunday afternoon, August 9th, Lisa's daughter, Lilly, and her friends had been playing Kerbie out on the street. Lilly had been blind from birth, but she was the Kerbie master.

'I don't know that game,' Bennet said.

'Oh, it's very old. My dad taught me it when I was a kid, back in Nottingham. Two people stand facing each other across the road. You throw a football at the opposite kerb. If it bounces back and you can grab it without stepping in the road, that's a point and you get another go until you miss and then...' She gave him a stare, then a smile. 'I see by your face what you're thinking. How can a blind girl play Kerbie?'

'No, I wasn't thinking that at all.'

She laughed. 'Sure you were. Everyone does. But it's okay. My Lilly's got muscle memory better than most because she's got no eyes to help her. She's the best at Kerbie.' She lost her smile. 'But what she didn't see was the man.'

Lisa got a little emotional as she described how a man in a hoodie had approached the children. Because it was a dead-end street with only a handful of residents that all knew each other, the kids had assumed he was lost. When he'd stopped in front of them, they'd assumed he wanted directions. But he hadn't.

'He snatched Lilly's teddy bear right out of her arms. Then he put a big dice in her hand. She was happy at first, because she didn't know what it was. But it was big and fluffy and she liked it. That's because she didn't know what he'd done to her teddy, even though her friends were upset when it happened.'

What he'd 'done' was squirted the bear with fluid from a little bottle and set fire to it. He'd then dropped it in the street before running away. He'd clambered over a wall at the end of the street and vanished into the school grounds.

'Have you still got the dice?'

'Yes. I know, for DNA and fingerprints and stuff. But I washed it. Lilly wanted to keep it, but it had been touched by that vile man. Also, one of the children said the man was wearing gloves. Plus, I can tell you right now that only two of the houses here have CCTV, and I've watched the tapes and you can't see much detail. Definitely not a face under that hood he was wearing. Sorry.'

Lisa left the room to fetch the dice. It was red foam, about the size of a standard Rubik's cube. The dots were depressed and green. There was a little piece missing out of one edge. She handled it by two fingers, as if to preserve evidence. He displayed the same care when he put it in a clear plastic food bag he'd brought along, but he knew forensics would have a problem. The dice stank of bleach.

'I don't suppose you have any clue if a certain face was showing when he handed it to Lilly?' he said.

'No clue. Lilly might. Wait a sec.'

She fetched her daughter from the backyard. Lilly was cute as pie, with spirally blonde hair down to her waist and a Spiderwoman outfit. She was led in by the hand, but walked with a confidence borne of knowing the outlay of her own home inside out.

'Here he is, Lilly,' Lisa said. She sat on the armchair again, but Lilly climbed onto the coffee table, kneeling there, facing Bennet. He couldn't see an obvious problem except for rapid eye movement. He complimented her outfit and asked his question: did she know what number was on top of the dice when the man handed it to her.

Based on the direction his voice came from, Lilly shifted a little to be fully facing him and put out her hand. He realised she wanted the dice and must have been told he had it. Bennet removed the item from the bag and touched her palm with it. She took the dice in both hands and started to turn it this way and that.

When she stopped, she had it in the palm of her left hand, index and thumb of her right plucking at the curve where a piece was missing from one edge.

'Like this. I pulled this bit out by accident when I was trying to suss what it was.'

Bennet stared. If Lilly was correct, then the man had handed her the dice with two dots on the upper face. A two, not the number three present on the two dice from the murder scenes. Was that significant? Had the man done it intentionally? Was it random? Another three would have hinted at an obvious connection, but now he didn't know what to think.

He felt further from the truth than he had before he'd asked the question.

CHAPTER THIRTY

'I'd rather he got away with rape.'

'You don't mean that,' Liz said.

She was in the teacher's living room on Stoneacre Avenue in Hackenthorpe. The woman was tall and very slim, almost skinny, and looked a lot older than her thirty years. What had happened to her was hardly going to slow her visible ageing process.

Her name was Alice Carter and she hadn't been eager to meet Liz early that evening. Immediately after her rape last Monday, she had screamed for justice, but in the six days since, she had changed her tune. Despite calling about the dice, she was reluctant to talk to Liz, but the detective managed to talk her way indoors. Even so, Alice was adamant she wanted to let the whole thing go. She hadn't even mentioned the dice yet.

'It would be nice to see a culprit get convicted, but the stress isn't worth it.'

'We can make things easy for you,' Liz said. 'Don't worry about that.'

They were in the kitchen. Alice had offered to make tea, but she had stopped by the sink, kettle in hand, and was staring out the window, her back to Liz.

'You think that's my only worry? I went through a humiliating assessment by a Forensic Nurse Examiner and questioning by support workers and then police. I just wanted to get it over with, but that wasn't the end of it. Oh no. The Sexual Assault Referral Centre is at Hackenthorpe Lodge on Occupation Lane.' She turned to face Liz. 'That's only half a mile from here. So people will know, won't they? People in my community. They'll know I was raped.'

'It's confidential, so–'

'Oh, sure, but people are human, aren't they? The support worker there, she has a child at my school. Can you believe that? So what's to stop her pointing me out to the other mothers and talking about it? Nothing. People gossip. Are you saying you never told police stories to a friend or your husband or whoever? It's right on my doorstep, so people will find out.'

'Nobody at the referral centre will gossip, Alice.'

'And what if you do arrest someone? I'd have to point him out in a line-up, repeat my story for all these strangers at a trial. And what if the rapist's family wants revenge? He'll deny it and they'll believe him, and they'll want to get back at the lying woman. It's just not worth it.'

'You called me here, Alice. About the dice. You do want this man caught and convicted. And that's what I plan to do.'

Alice filled the kettle with water, but then just stood there with it. 'I know, it's why you're here. My rapist could also be a murderer. There's a dice connection. If the same man left the dice, he's killed two people, right?'

'If there's a connection, yes. But we're not certain of anything yet.'

'Then a man who's killed two people will go to prison

forever, won't he? If he's charged with two murders, you don't need a rape conviction as well.'

Liz saw where she was going with this. 'The Crown Prosecution Service likes safety nets. Multiple charges in case some fall through. But if we get enough evidence to hit this man with two murders, then, yes, the rape charge could be discarded and you won't have to attend a trial. Is that what you want? Although I should stress again that there's no guarantee your attacker and the killer are one and the same.'

She seemed to relax. She put the kettle on its stand and turned it on. 'Then I'll help you. But you can tell the CPS people I want no part of it. I don't need a case-closed stamp on what happened to me. I just need him suffering in a cell. So I'll help and you can send this bastard down for two murders. Now follow me.'

Alice led Liz upstairs, into a back bedroom used as a gym. At the window, both women stared out. Alice's backyard had a high wooden fence and a picnic table on the lawn. Beyond her property was a green area with trees lining one side. A path snaked through the grass, past a veterinary clinic's car park, and onto the main road some fifty metres away.

One of her DSs had taken the case, so this was Liz's first look at the crime scene. She knew the victim had got off a bus on the main road, Sheffield Road, and walked through the car park to reach the path. There, in the dark, just metres from her back gate, a man in a mask had erupted from the trees and snatched her.

He'd taken her bag, emptied it out, wrapped the leather around the handle of a hairbrush, and penetrated her with it, just once. After that, he'd fled. From appearance to disappearance: twenty-nine seconds. In less than half a minute, Alice Carter's life had been ruined.

Alice pointed to a stone border by the back fence. 'He used those stones to draw a dice.'

Liz was shocked. 'You mean in your backyard?'

'Yes. On the grass. It was about five inches in size. I saw it the next day. I just swept the stones away because I had no idea it was connected. Not until I saw the dice on the news. I just thought a kid had done it. Maybe it was.'

'Do you remember the number on the dice?'

'Yes, a five. Five stones. So does that mean the killer has now killed five? Or attacked five people? Killed four and left one alive?'

Others had made a similar assumption about the dice, that the killer was counting his murders, but Liz had discounted that theory from the outset: the first two dice had been threes. Now she had a five and everything had just gotten muddier. Was it possible the numbers had no significance, only the form of a dice itself? Or was the killer rolling a dice to achieve these numbers? If so, why? She might never know unless the man himself explained.

'Alice, we just don't know what the dice numbers mean. But we don't believe he's killed four or five people. And he made no attempt to murder you, so you really shouldn't worry about him coming back. I very much doubt he will. And we're not certain it's the same man, like I said. I really need you to try not to let this worry you.'

Alice nodded. 'Look, if you want to print the stones or swab them or whatever, I put them back round about in the middle. So if you scoop up all the stones from the middle, you'll probably get them.'

'I'll do that.' And she'd get forensics to swab the gate and check the lawn for footprints. 'Alice, you told my investigator that nothing interrupted your attacker. I have to ask you again if you're certain.'

'You mean because he... only did it... put it in me once? Because he ran away so quickly? No, nothing.'

'No dog barked? No light came on in a house? There wasn't a shout, or someone walking nearby, or a car backfiring?'

Alice tutted. 'No, I explained this already. There was nothing. You don't think it's him, do you? The same man?'

'I didn't say–'

'Because he might have panicked and that's why he ran? But why would he run if he wasn't interrupted? Why would a man who's killed two people suddenly get cold feet about a rape? That's why you think it's not him, isn't it?'

'I want a clear, full picture, that's all. Please don't read too much into it.'

Alice put her forehead on the window. 'I find myself wanting to sleep with men now. Is that strange? I thought I would abhor sex and men. But my sex drive has gone up. It should be the opposite. Do you think I'm subconsciously putting others between me and him? Is it wrong? Or is my mind just doing faulty things because it's breaking? Am I going insane?'

Liz didn't know how to answer that, but Alice gave her no chance anyway. 'Can we just end this now? Can you just leave, please? I don't want to do this any longer.'

In her car, Liz called the sergeant heading the Carter rape and asked one question. She hadn't wanted to scare Alice by asking it of her. When she had the answer, she hung up and took a moment to let everything sink in.

Before this visit, she had had no idea the attacker had been in Alice's yard. He could have assumed one of the nearby houses was hers, but the detective had just confirmed that Alice had had nothing bearing her address in her handbag. The attacker couldn't have known for sure.

Yet he had. He'd been in her yard. So he knew her, or of her, or he'd watched her before the day of the attack. That fact erased the notion of chance. The man who'd killed Breakspear and Yard had then targeted Alice Carter, and she hadn't been a random victim. What if all three victims had been carefully chosen, perhaps because of a connection to dice or each other?

Just as important were two other questions. Who else might he have attacked? And who would be next?

CHAPTER THIRTY-ONE

When Bennet relayed his findings in the burned teddy bear crime, Liz put out a message for the whole MIT 2 team to return to the incident room. Being a Sunday, most were off and came in civvies, some of them with families waiting in cars outside because activities had been interrupted. She started the meeting with an apology for dragging everyone in and then overviewed what Bennet had learned and what she'd found out from the teacher in Hackenthorpe.

She put a pin in the giant map of Sheffield pinned on one wall and outlined the crime. Mundella Place, lower east of Sheffield. The burning of a teddy bear stolen from a blind girl. Sunday August 9th. Dice number: 2.

The next pin, two-point-seven miles east of the first. Frecheville Community Centre. The deposition of homeless murder victim James Breakspear. Saturday August 15th. Dice number: 3.

The third pin, east of the second by one and a quarter miles. Hackenthorpe. The rape of a young teacher called Alice Carter near her home. Monday August 17th. Dice number: 5.

Pin four, north-east of the third by two miles. Woodhouse Mill. The murder of Paul Yard near his pub, the King Royal. Saturday August 22nd. Dice number: 3.

Liz addressed the room. 'There appears to be no clear MO, but what do you see from this?'

Someone said, 'Our perp is moving east across Sheffield, and then upwards.'

A DC called DeVille said, 'And it seems he's escalating. Arson, rape, now murders.'

Someone else countered that last statement. 'Except that the rape was between the two murders.'

Deville shot back: 'We don't know Breakspear was his murder. All we know is he dumped the body. If he didn't, we have our perp burning a teddy bear, dumping a corpse, raping a woman, and then murdering a man. That's escalation. Unless you think body dumping is worse than rape?'

'You're suggesting he found Breakspear's corpse? Highly doubtful.'

Others joined in, taking sides, and Liz had to step in. When calm was restored, she moved on.

'The baby seat used to crush Breakspear's skull could have been found nearby, although his sister claims it wasn't at the scene. The hairbrush used in Carter's rape could have been employed simply because it was in the victim's handbag. The PVC football stuffed down Paul Yard's throat could have been lying around in that wasteland behind his pub. The teddy could have been grabbed off the blind girl because they're fluffy and easy to catch fire.

'But I don't buy it that these were impulsive weapons employed at the crime scenes. A baby seat is bulky and awkward, even if you're only attacking a skeleton. The PVC football had to be cut and folded to fit down Yard's throat. The teddy bear was squirted with lighter fluid before being set alight. Our perp knew where the rape victim, Carter, lived, and this suggests pre-planning.

'Pre-planners don't rely on the hope that suitable weapons will be lying around where they intend to offend. Just as the dice link the crimes, so might the weapons. It could be something frivolous or insignificant, but if there's connective tissue, no matter how thin, let's find it. Let me give you an example. The rape victim bought the hairbrush used against her at a local B&M. That store also sells lighters, rubber footballs, and even car baby seats.'

Liz reeled off three names and gave those staff the task of establishing 'connective tissue'. Start with the B&M angle, she told them, just to rule it out. They'd never sleep at night if that example link turned out to be on the money and they'd laughed it off.

Liz moved on. 'Environment. Is our perp a marauder who operates close to his home, or a commuter who lives outside Sheffield? If he's close, is he becoming bolder and moving outwards from his comfort zone, which might put his residence somewhere east of the crimes? Is he becoming more confident and braving locations closer to home, which would put his lair somewhere west of our crime scenes?

'Are the short distances between his targets because the perp has no vehicle? Or is he located outside Sheffield and travels here for work, or because he has family? Following the discovery of the teddy bear crime, we now have to add Mundella Place into the mix.'

She picked another detective to undertake the task of contacting their go-to geographic profiler with their new information.

'Next, victimology. Let's continue to look into the

backgrounds of our victims, and now we have to add Lisa and Lilly Bennet from the teddy bear burning. We need to find out what they and their neighbours know and review any CCTV evidence.'

She jabbed a finger at two more detectives, their task to visit Mundella Place and start asking questions.

'And finally, the dice connection. I think the burned teddy is intriguing. If our boy can set fire to a little girl's toy, he can do something else seemingly insignificant. Escalation might not be a factor. He could murder one week and steal sweets the next. The list of dice-related crimes in the files is large and until now we've discounted them based on location and date and other factors.

'We can't do that anymore. We have a recent spate of crimes, but Breakspear at Frecheville says otherwise. I don't doubt our perp killed him, but I do doubt he went offence-free for the following three years. So we'll start with that window. Any and *all* crimes with a dice angle in the last three years. No matter how trivial and unrelated a crime seems, it needs investigating.'

A murmur of dismay ran through the group. Someone voiced its collective opinion: 'The numbers will be massive.'

'It gets worse. The teddy bear crime wasn't reported. Maybe others haven't been. So we're not just talking about reviewing police files. And not just Google and social media either. This task is for everyone. Talk to friends and neighbours. To informants. Get the word on the street. Listen to the grapevine. I'm talking about good old-fashioned policing like our mums and dads did. But no rousting bars.'

The team started to get to their feet, ready to head back to work or home, but Liz said, 'Just one more thing I want us to consider. Don't worry, it's not another task. Just a thought I want to share.'

Everybody sat. Liz said, 'The rape of Alice Carter is the third offence chronologically, but it just reeks of insecurity. The rapist used a hairbrush wrapped in the victim's own handbag, and he penetrated her only once. Sounds like he was disturbed, right? Except he wasn't, according to the victim and the neighbours we spoke to. And if he was nervous, on edge, how did he find time to create a dice of stones in her back garden, either before or after the offence? I get the feeling he was obliged.'

She waited for someone to ask, so she could explain. 'What if he set out to rape, but he didn't really care for it? Like he had to check it off a list? Perhaps he used a hairbrush because he couldn't bring himself to penetrate his victim woman with his fingers or penis. Perhaps he used the handbag as a kind of padding because he thought that would hurt her less, either physically or mentally. What if he penetrated her just once, to make rape official, and then he left?'

'Like a task?' someone said. 'You mean he might be using the dice to choose victims or locations?'

'Not implausible. The dice could well be nothing more than a calling card to make sure we connect the crimes. Our killer could be after a dice-related nickname. It could be something personal to him that we could never work out. It could be a red herring to make us do this very thing – sit around and waste time seeking answers.

'But what if the numbers on the dice do actually mean something? If he isn't picking victims with dice rolls, perhaps the numbers are part of a code. Even something as simple as words decided by their numerical place in the alphabet? The dice rolls are 2, 3, 5, 3. B,C, E, C might not make much sense, but it could be incomplete and there might be a further aspect to any code that we don't yet know. We're not in the guessing game, but keep a code in mind. Any ideas, bring them to me.'

'Maybe we'll know more when we get another number,' someone said.

Liz agreed, but with a heavy heart. To get another number, another clue, their killer would have to strike again.

CHAPTER THIRTY-TWO

When Liz entered Bates's office on Monday morning, one of her police staff knocked on the door. The woman was one-manning the phones and she'd just received a call about a crime involving dice, which had occurred yesterday morning. Apparently the police had investigated it, but no mention had been made of 'dice' in the reports, so there was nothing in the system.

Like with Alice Carter, the teacher who'd been raped, the victim had seen the news about dice and called it in. She'd waited until Monday morning because she thought the detectives would have weekends off.

'I wish,' Liz said. 'Does it sound legit?'

'It's in Beighton,' the staff member said with glee.

Liz left the office and stood before the large Sheffield wall map. Beighton was a mile to the right of the rape of the teacher in Hackenthorpe, continuing that journey east. It was also a mile and a half south of the murder of Paul Yard at the King Royal in Woodhouse Mill, so now they had a relatively straight line with a spike.

Although they were dealing with tiny distances, which

meant a clear pattern was hard to affirm, it did seem as if their offender was moving from west to east, hence the staff member's glee. That spike, though, was a curiosity.

Liz grabbed one of the paper aeroplanes she'd made yesterday, stepped out of the office, and threw it. Bates had a quirky way of delegating some mundane tasks: launch a plane and whoever it hit got the job. A couple of the team had desk fans to help deflect the planes. Liz's plane did a rapid loop the loop and came down onto her shoulder. Thankfully, nobody saw this lame attempt.

Rules were rules, she figured.

The location was a place called Polished Pooches, a pet grooming and kennelling service on Sevenairs Road, across from Beighton Community Hospital. The large front window had pictures of dogs undergoing various services, but the animals all looked like toys. Liz stepped into a reception and stated her business. The receptionist called for the manager – literally called, as in out loud from her seat.

The manager appeared so quickly she might have been awaiting the shout behind a door. She was a young Indian woman in a knee-length smock apron so thick it reminded Liz of the body armour she sometimes wore on raids. Her name was Jigi. Once she knew why Liz was there, she led the detective into a room where she was tending to an Irish wolfhound. The room was clinical and grey. The grooming table had a crossbar which the dog was attached to by a lead so short Liz figured he'd probably hang himself if he tried to leap down.

While she trimmed and polished the dog's claws, Jigi recounted what had happened on Sunday morning.

A man had turned up at Polished Pooches and claimed to have been sent by the owner of a Kerry blue terrier, with orders to take the dog to another salon. Jigi hadn't been in at that time and had left her assistant in charge. It immediately struck the assistant as strange because the dog owner, a biomedical scientist, had left the clinic perhaps a minute earlier. She had admitted her terrier every Sunday morning for months while she visited family.

The assistant had wanted to phone the owner, but the man had kicked up a fuss, and the assistant had foolishly let him walk out with the terrier. When she subsequently informed the owner, she discovered the man had lied. But it was too late: he was gone.

The assistant had sent someone to search the streets and the dog was indeed found, tied to a bus stop half a mile away. It was fine and there was even a business card for Polished Pooches folded in its collar, as if to alert people as to where to return the dog.

But also on its collar was a folded piece of paper with a dice illustration.

When Jigi got in later that morning, the police had already been and taken a statement and gone. They hadn't taken the notes for fingerprinting or even checked the CCTV, which Jigi had watched and claimed showed a man who was careful to hide his face. The assistant said the police hadn't seemed that bothered because the dog had been found, unharmed.

'But when I saw the news about the dice, I knew it was important. Do you want me to fetch the piece of paper?'

Liz did. When Jigi returned with it, Liz saw a simple piece of lined paper with a dice drawn in pen. The number was another three.

Three threes, a two and a five. One burned teddy bear, a raped woman, a dumped body, a murder, and now the kidnap of a dog. What the hell was going on?

CHAPTER THIRTY-THREE

On Wednesday the 26th, Joe packed again. He'd loaded a suitcase at least five times, Bennet noted, and had always had to unpack again because he needed a certain piece of clothing or his pyjamas. This time Joe didn't take the risk and left the job until his dad said it was time to go. So Bennet had to wait half an hour.

They had roughly two hundred miles ahead of them, to the hamlet of Capel in Tunbridge Wells, where Bennet's father, Ray, lived alone, his wife long having passed away. Bennet rarely saw the old man, who'd met his grandson only a handful of times and not at all this year so far, so they'd stay until Sunday afternoon.

The three of them would fish, barbeque, play games. And when Joe was in bed, the two elder Bennets would doubtless play a game in which Liam would try to tell his dad he really didn't miss the police, and Ray would try to convince his son leaving had been a bad idea and he should go back. Despite knowing a telling off was coming, Bennet was looking forward to the trip almost as much as Joe was. He needed a break.

CHAPTER THIRTY-FOUR

On Saturday morning Liz opened her front door to get rid of the smell of oil and chips and fish from a busy night at the chippy below her bedsit. She was sitting on the bed, combing her hair with her back to the door, when she heard a voice.

'How's things, Liz?'

She spun to see Dan standing outside the door. He was wearing jeans and a shirt and was freshly shaved. She hoped it wasn't for her benefit. She rushed to the door to block him in case he stepped inside.

'Good,' she said. 'I'm just off out to work. I'm in a rush. What do you want?'

He pulled out his phone, accessed the internet, and showed her a photograph. She recognised the subject. It was a window illusion painting of a peeling wood frame overlooking a beautiful Gothic church set against one wall of a leafy canyon, with a bridge connecting it to the other side. Dan had bought the painting when they moved in together, and for years it had hung in the house she had last year moved out of even though they had a joint mortgage.

She had loved the painting, especially when in the bath. She would create a finger-frame to block out everything except that painting, pretending she was actually in a room in that gorgeous part of the world. She had never even known if the church depicted was an actual place.

Next, he showed her another picture. It was the same church, but this time it was a real photograph. 'I found it,' he said. 'It's the Las Lajas Sanctuary in Ipiales, Colombia. It was built after a deaf girl saw the Virgin Mary and–'

Liz snapped out of her memory and cut him off. 'Why are you telling me this, Dan?'

'I thought we could go. I have savings. You always wanted to.'

She had indeed. Staring at that picture, day after day, had made her eager to know if that gorgeous landscape was real and where it was. And it had given her a yearning to visit.

But that had been a long time ago, or so it felt, and everything had changed since then. 'We? Dan, we've split, we're over, so why would you want to go on holiday with me?' She didn't even wait for an answer. 'We're not getting back together. But while you're here, let *me* show *you* something.'

Her phone came out. Not a picture for Dan's perusal, but a voicemail message she'd gotten about a week ago.

A female voice said, *'Hey, you don't know me. I was Dan's girlfriend. I say was because I dumped that cheating bastard. You can have him back. Take him back so he stops hassling me.'*

Dan tried to laugh it off. 'I didn't cheat on her, I just got bored and dumped her.' His tone sounded sincere, but the guilt was all over his face. Liz reached for the door, but he used a foot to block it from shutting.

'Let's just go for a drink, Liz. See what happens. You're being childish.'

'Get lost, Dan.' She tried to kick his foot away, but he elbowed the door fully open.

'Are you shagging that copper, is that it? You found someone better?'

He grabbed her arm. She thumped his fingers to free the grip and pushed him out of the doorway. 'Touch me again and that's assaulting a police officer. I'll put you in a damn cell.'

He visibly calmed and tried another tactic. 'Won't be the first time you put me in handcuffs, eh?'

That was a memory she didn't want. Disgusted, she slammed the door in his face. It thudded from an almighty kick, shocking her. 'You damn bitch,' he yelled, 'I'll get you for this.'

If he meant to follow through on that threat, it would be another time: she heard his feet thumping down the metal fire escape. She doubted he posed a genuine danger to her because Dan had never been violent towards anyone. Then again, the people they'd been way back had seen a dynamic change and she didn't know the man she'd once married.

She should call the police, just in case, but was worried how it would look. Instead, she opted to get out of the house. She wasn't due in to work for a few hours, so she decided to go swimming. Hopefully, Dan would calm down and realise how foolish he'd been.

Always likely to be called away at a moment's notice, Liz had purchased a waterproof phone so she could receive calls while swimming. She got a call as she was doing lengths of the pool and tugged the device out of her bikini top.

'Someone just called the station and reckons he's got information about the murders,' Boeson said. 'No name, but he wants to meet you. He said you'd be silly to refuse. I tried that chat-up line many times in my youth.'

The pool was pretty busy and many eyes watched her. She

kept her voice low. 'Me? He asked for me by name? Is he at the station?'

'No. He wants to meet outdoors. And I think he must watch too many crime films. He asked for you to come alone.'

CHAPTER THIRTY-FIVE

The seventeenth century Bowden Housteads Woods, on the edge of Handsworth, were sliced into three major sections: Sheffield Parkway cut through horizontally, and the bottom half was bisected vertically by Mosborough Parkway. The housing estate where Liz was to meet the unknown informant was nestled against the patch of woods in the crook of the inverted L created by the two major roads.

Richmond Park Rise ran alongside the woods; where it cut a sharp turn there was a break in the houses for a path into the trees, and it was here, by a sign for the woods, that the nameless informant wanted to meet. Liz parked about fifty metres away and scanned the area, especially the houses.

The informant had specified only 'this morning' instead of giving a specific time for the meeting. That gave the impression he wouldn't mind hanging around, which in turn suggested he lived on this estate or close. Every street had a car with undercover officers in it, watching who moved here and there. Two cars were watching hers. There had been no time to organise armed cover, but Liz had been supplied with a taser.

Just in case. It was hard not to suspect something a little sinister about a meeting by some woods.

She couldn't see anyone watching from a window or garden or lurking in a parked car. And nobody was by the sign on the path into the trees. If somebody was watching, they would likely wait for her to reach the sign before making an appearance. She drove closer. Soon, she spotted something on the sign. Something that wasn't part of it.

She got out. She could hear the traffic on the Sheffield Parkway, just a hundred metres north beyond the woods. To her left, west, was silence because Mosborough Parkway was twice the distance. The traffic noise, and a scattering of residents going about their business, calmed her a little. But her DS, Boeson, who was back there with binoculars, wasn't as trusting. His voice crackled in her radio earpiece.

'Watch what you're doing. Snipers out there. Japanese holdouts and you look like an American general's daughter.'

'I'm fine,' Liz said. She had no idea what Boeson was talking about, but she understood he was worried about her safety. This was highly irregular, but she'd insisted. She approached the sign. Now she could clearly see the piece of paper stuck to the metal and the outline of words written on the other side. With a final look around, she plucked the paper away and turned it over.

Capital letters in pencil said, DCI MILLER MEET ME AT PARKWAY MAN ALONE. She read it aloud for the listening police.

Her earpiece crackled again. 'What the hell is Parkway Man?' Boeson said.

'I know,' she whispered. She pulled her phone, loaded Google Maps, and found it. Parkway Man, who the locals knew as Iron Henry, was a three-metre high statue of a topless steelworker wielding a sledgehammer. She'd seen it once while driving down the Parkway. Now, her map told her it was just a hundred metres away across a thin slice of the woods.

'I'm going in.'

'No you're not. Just wait for people to get closer.'

She knew which people he meant. Just in case she got sent into the woods, officers had been placed on a bridge over Sheffield Parkway and two bridges on Mosborough Parkway. Including the officers here on the estate, it meant she was covered from all sides.

'No. Have them hold their positions near the bridges.'

'That's not a good idea. We don't know who's in there or what they have planned.'

'What they have planned is probably to run if they see coppers creeping through the woods. I don't want what could be vital information getting away. Look, I've got a taser. I'm going in. He asked for me, and I'm going.'

She wasn't about to admit that she also felt a little bit of a rush.

She walked along the path, into the gloom as trees enshrouded her. The path split and she took the right fork, towards the Parkway. Nobody around, although she could hear a couple of kids somewhere. Iron Henry was just a few metres from a wire fence alongside the road, sideways on but with his head turned as if to stare at traffic. At times he'd been dressed as Superman, Father Christmas and a Hallowe'en ghoul, but today he wore only trousers and a coat of bird poo.

She could imagine the statue was a scary sight at night if you didn't know it existed. As she got close, she saw something attached to his chest. It was another sheet of paper. She looked around, but saw no one. No informant waiting. No police lurking in the trees. Despite the traffic taking the Sheffield Arena exit of the Parkway just metres away, she felt loneliness closing around her like a fist. But it didn't sway her intention here. She tore the paper away, turned it round.

And saw a dice drawn in felt tip. The number was a six.

There wasn't much tree cover this close to the road, but the noise of passing trucks on the Parkway covered the footsteps of whoever ran at her. She heard his approach too late, and what sounded like a bell, and turned his way, then felt a terrible fire in her head as something slammed into it.

CHAPTER THIRTY-SIX

The call came late on Saturday night. It was DS Boeson with bad news. When the call was over, Bennet approached his son and father, who were out in the garden, sitting in deckchairs beneath a gazebo. Joe was trying to show his grandfather what TikTok was all about.

'We have to go home,' Bennet said. 'Liz has been attacked and she's in hospital.'

Bennet's dad knew little about Liz other than that last year she'd tried to jump aboard one of Liam's investigations, and he'd considered her a distraction. Bennet hadn't mentioned her since so there had been no reason for his dad to alter his opinion. Hence his puzzled expression and the response, 'Okay. Right. Well, nothing you can do for her, is there? And it's too late to go visiting. You can see her tomorrow.'

But Joe had hung out with Liz a few times, and he liked her. He also read the lack of care in his grandfather's voice. 'No, I get it, Granddad. Dad likes her. They might start going out. She babysits me sometimes.'

Ray didn't look convinced, but he and Joe exchanged a look

that said they'd been scheming. 'Joe's not been fishing properly yet.'

'No,' Joe said. 'So it's too early to go. And too late. It's nearly my bedtime.'

Bennet told himself off. What was he thinking, trying to drag Joe away at this time of night? 'We can go first thing in the morning.'

Grandfather and grandson exchanged another look. Ray said, 'Joe tells me his new school doesn't start till September 2nd, which is Wednesday, and the morning is an inset period. We thought he could stay until Tuesday evening. I'll bring him back. Even if he's up late, he's not at school until the afternoon. You've done nothing but work and look after Joe for years, so you could do with some time alone too. Joe isn't yet a master fisherman either. How's the boy going to be the best in the world if he doesn't practise?'

The elder and younger Bennets almost looked pleading. The two guys before him could do with some extra bonding time. There was no other family Joe saw and his mother had been murdered nine months ago.

'Okay,' Bennet said. 'I'll go first thing in the morning. You can drive down with Joe on Tuesday and stay over, and head back on the Wednesday.'

Grandfather and grandson high-fived each other.

CHAPTER THIRTY-SEVEN

'Yes. Those hundreds of thousands of poor sods who didn't get whacked over the head.'

'Glancing blow. Surprised you felt it,' Boeson said.

Liz walked slowly to her hospital-room window and stared out. Blinking still made her vision blurry for a few moments, but after that all was fine. In her reflection she saw the bandage on the side of her face and touched it.

It was early Sunday morning. She'd been knocked unconscious and had come round as police officers flocked to her. She'd sat on the ground and waited for the ambulance, which buzzed her to Northern General Hospital with a police escort. There, her wound was cleaned and she was given an MRI to check for blood clots and brain bleeding, of which there were none.

If any kind of surgery were needed, it would only be a cosmetic procedure to her ear. The blow from the blunt object had caught her flush on the side of the head and been dampened a little by her earpiece. But the cable of the device had split her ear and the wound had required stitches. Her face was bloated and bruised on one side. She wouldn't look good for a while, but it could have been so much worse. Still, it was hard to accept the claim that she'd been lucky.

She had no symptoms of brain trauma except mild runny eyes and it wasn't deemed that a stay in a neurology unit was needed.

Last night she'd insisted on leaving, but the hospital staff wanted her to wait and speak to a neurosurgeon, although they couldn't say when that would be. They'd reckoned they'd misplaced her clothing. Her assessment of the missing gear: hidden at the behest of her superintendent, who damn well knew she'd try to make a run for it at the first opportunity.

As proof of his interference, he'd personally visited, wished her well, and ordered her to stay right there in that bed until the neurosurgeon said she could do otherwise. He'd also orchestrated some protection just in case her attacker decided to try again. Uniforms were lurking outside her room and would probably be on her tail for days to come.

The neurosurgeon had arrived late Saturday night and his assessment of her took little time. He deemed her fit and well, but just to be sure wanted to see her again the next morning. Within minutes of that meeting, as she was again demanding her clothes, her super called and ordered her to stay until after that next meeting. It was all a massive conspiracy.

In the end, she had fallen asleep while plotting her escape and had woken twenty minutes ago when Boeson arrived. She was desperate to leave and get back on the case, but the neurosurgeon wasn't available now until the early afternoon. One attempted murder to add to the killer's tally, and this time they had police officers as witnesses and a crime scene as fresh as you could get. She needed to be out there, hunting him.

However, the bastard had left no evidence. No footprints that could be attributed to the killer in that oft-walked area. Officers had invaded the streets around the crime scene like an army, but nobody yet questioned had seen or heard a thing. No prints or DNA found on the dice note or the Iron Henry statue, or on the weapon he'd used.

Boeson hadn't managed to visit last night because he'd been busy working this new twist to the case. He'd hoped to bring her good news, hopefully an arrest, but all he'd managed to do was create a depressing start to the new day.

However, they did have one, vital piece of information, and what a corker it was. If a baby seat and popped football were strange weapons, then the one used to attack her could be labelled downright bizarre.

A 12 volt Bosch car battery weighing over thirty pounds.

According to the two kids who'd saved her – and who she'd heard nearby in the woods – they had ridden their bikes into the area and spotted a man and a woman. They had described the man as white but wearing all black. They had no idea of his age, but he wasn't a kid.

They'd said the woman was lying on the ground and the man was bent over beside her, about to lift a black box. The car battery, which he must have dropped after swinging it into Liz's head. In all likelihood he'd been about to hoist that heavy weight high and drop it for the kill. The thought chilled her. If those kids hadn't pedalled into that area at that moment...

Staring out the window, Liz soon got her mind off what ifs and focused on the investigation. 'Why a car battery?' she said aloud, more to herself than Boeson. 'That's even more unwieldy than a car seat. He would have had to carry that round.'

'Perhaps you should lie down,' Boeson said. 'We'll probably need more time before we can work this out.'

'What about the Iron Henry statue? Was that just a place to put the note, or is it relevant in some way? And why a number six?'

'Don't know, boss. Best not to worry about it until you're out of here.'

'Also, the woods are, what, three miles or so north-west of Beighton, where we had our perp steal a dog last Sunday. Bang goes the theory that he's moving east? What's that all about?'

This time Boeson didn't answer. He knew she was just speaking aloud, and aware that she probably wasn't in the right mind for serious discussion yet.

'What if the man who attacked me isn't the man we've been hunting? What if this is simply a personal issue?'

That he responded to. 'You sound like you have someone in mind.'

She turned to him. Her head was still woozy, but she felt she was thinking clearly. And she'd been consumed by a name ever since last night. She gave it to Boeson.

'For real?' he said. 'Why him?'

Liz gave Boeson a quick rundown. 'So go get him and let's see what he has to say.'

Like her, Boeson liked legwork and wasn't about to pass this task along. He pulled his phone to arrange an arrest team, but he also headed for the door.

'I could be wrong, Boeson, so do this fast and loud, but also gently, right?'

'Fast and loud and what?' he said, then vanished before she could answer.

CHAPTER THIRTY-EIGHT

This was a two-time killer, rapist, attempted murderer and teddy bear burner, an elusive phantom who could kill again and flee the country in the time it took to get an arrest warrant. So they didn't bother. An arrest team converged on his address within twenty minutes of being supplied his name. 'We're coming for you,' someone shouted a moment before a battering ram smashed into the front door.

Cops piled in and surrounded a guy who'd just got out of the shower. He was in the kitchen, wearing just a towel and making coffee, and he sprayed milk everywhere when the door blew open.

Not a single armed officer amongst the team though. No one would ever admit it to the professional standards department, but nobody on the raid thought their target was the aforementioned ghost. He'd be in and out of custody in no time. They were here to teach the guy a little lesson.

'She's a lying bitch, whatever she said,' Dan yelled, dripping milk as well as water. By now he was on his belly with his hands behind his head, all unprompted. You learned a few things by being married to a police officer.

'Up and get dressed for a little ride,' Boeson told him.

'This is bullshit. I'll be making a complaint. The job centre's going to have a whole new influx of unemployed bozos claiming benefit soon.'

'If it's a mistake, we'll clear it up at the station. Clothes, pal, sometime today.'

All eight officers escorted him into the bedroom and watched him dress. Dan's nerves were shedding fast. He grinned and pointed at the bed. 'You know, there was a time when your boss used to love moaning like a banshee right there. Before she became sour.'

Someone ran ahead to open the van, and then he got in the driver's seat and elbowed the horn for five solid seconds as Dan was led out. Dan wasn't fooled.

'Nice. For the neighbours, right? Liz told me about that trick.' And then, mocking: 'Oh, how will I ever live this down?' And, finally, loud: 'My bitch ex-wife set this up. Elizabeth Miller, South Yorkshire Police.'

When one of their own got hurt, it rattled some officers' minds and Boeson was a little clumsy as he helped Dan into the back of the van. Rubbing his head where it had hit the top of the vehicle, Dan took a seat and Boeson slammed the cage door.

CHAPTER THIRTY-NINE

Just after midday, Bennet walked into Liz's hospital room. He stepped into the bathroom, and there she was, wearing just bra and knickers and trying to comb her hair to hide a bandage over her ear. Their eyes met in the mirror just before he turned his back.

'Sorry,' he said. He saw her murder book on the overbed table.

'You're a grown man, you've seen half-naked women before. Are you okay?'

'That's back to front. The patients in hospital get asked that question.'

'I'm good. And about to leave, finally. The neurosurgeon has just been, declared me fit to leave. And magically the staff found my clothing five minutes later. I'm just trying to hide this bandage because I need to pop by my sister's.'

'She doesn't know?'

'I don't need that hassle from her. It'll be my fault in some way.'

He heard the rustle of clothing and knew she was dressing.

Still with his back to her, he flipped open her murder book. 'Talking of hassle, I heard your husband got arrested.'

'God, I know. He threatened me, and then I got attacked.'

Bennet absently flipped through the murder book. 'Surely it wasn't him.'

'Doubtful. But I had to rule him out. Maybe I overdid it a bit, knowing the boys would kick his door in. I regret that now. He'll tell all and sundry I did this because he wouldn't take me back, you just watch.'

'Well, at least he'll keep his distance from now on.'

Bennet flipped the book to the final few pages, just to see some of Liz's most recent notes. And saw something that stunned him: 'HACKENTHORPE TEACHER RAPE.'

'I could arrest you for that, civilian scum.'

He turned to face her. She had only put her shirt on and it was unbuttoned, so most of her skin was on show. But now he didn't care. He held up the book. 'Teacher rape in Hackenthorpe last Monday? I was in Hackenthorpe on Monday to see a teacher. Or I assume that was her job since she said something about having more time over the six-week holiday.'

She stepped forward until they were just feet apart. 'I remember you said you were on a case, when we met at Frecheville Community Centre. Are you saying it was the same woman?'

He started reading the notes, seeking more information. 'Well, my teacher said it happened on the Sunday before, the 16th. She said she met a man and invited him back and he did something nasty to her handbag. But she never mentioned rape.'

'Invited him back? No. And this was definitely rape with a handbag. And it was on Monday the 17th.'

'With a handbag? Raped *with* a handbag? Not that he raped her *handbag*?'

'Raped her handbag? I'm getting confused. A teacher from

Hackenthorpe was raped on Monday the 17th and the assailant used her handbag to do it. As in, he wrapped it around a hairbrush and used it to penetrate her.'

Bennet massaged his forehead. 'Now I'm confused. My client was also a teacher from Hackenthorpe, and that place isn't exactly massive. She said a guy ejaculated into her handbag. I'm wondering if my client called you and upped her story because I said no to her case. Except the dates are different.'

'My victim seemed legit. She went for a rape examination. There was definitely a rape with an object. Thin woman, quite petite. Same one?'

Bennet's jaw dropped. 'Not unless she lost ten stone overnight.'

While Liz dressed in front of him, Bennet said, 'The other day I asked Joe to do the pots and all he did was a couple of jugs and a saucepan. He tried to chalk one by showing me a dictionary definition of *pots*. It didn't include plates and cutlery. But in Yorkshire we say pots to mean all cooking items. I made him redo them.'

She paused with her shirt half-buttoned. 'The crimes attributed to my suspect have all been on weekends. Including the bizarre event with your client, whose handbag was abused. But the rape of the teacher, Alice Carter, occurred on a Monday. The very day after he'd abused another teacher's handbag. Two teachers, both from Hackenthorpe. Why the two crimes? Could the second one be because he'd failed to do it properly the first time? Was the Monday rape a... *redo*?'

Bouncing ideas off each other gave them momentum. Bennet said, 'Your suspect was supposed to rape a teacher with a handbag in Hackenthorpe, but he found a way to avoid actually raping a woman by taking that line literally. And on the following Monday, he was forced into a redo. Like Joe with the pots.'

Finished with her shirt, Liz started to slide her trousers on. 'But if Joe had chosen to do the pots, he wouldn't have found a loophole. If he was making the rules, he wouldn't have had to redo them.'

'Your suspect isn't making the rules. He was challenged on his loophole and forced to complete his mission correctly. Like Joe.'

'Forced by someone he has to obey. Our suspect isn't alone in this. Someone is forcing him to commit these crimes.'

CHAPTER FORTY

'Why are there rules?' Liz said.

'Is it some kind of twisted challenge? A dare? But how do the dice come into it?'

Liz was fully dressed now. She sat on the bed while Bennet paced. 'To choose the victims, or the location? From a list?'

'Possibly. Perhaps one man places the dice picture in a location and the other has to commit a crime there. You were sent to those woods, remember, and it could have been anywhere.'

'You think my attack was part of it?'

Bennet stopped pacing and stared at her. 'There was a dice on the Iron Henry statue. Perhaps they included you because you're leading the team hunting them, so you're a threat. We've seen it before.'

So true. They both knew officers who'd been injured because they were close to busting up an organised crime group. It didn't deter the police from their job, but it messed with their logistics and sapped manpower. Even if it caused only a slight delay in the fight against crime, it was worth it to the crooks.

Here they both fell into silence. Theorising could help

untangle things, but it could also muddy the waters. The truth was they just didn't know what was going on. The reality could be something so simple they'd missed, and far from what they thought. The twisted mission of the killer or killers might remain unfathomable unless they confessed everything.

Bennet said, 'There's something else to consider. The Monday rape was a redo of the crime the day before, so we discount that day. What we have is a crime every Saturday and Sunday. Except that the first we know of was the teddy burn at Mundella Place...'

Liz jumped to her feet. 'Which was Sunday the 9th. So there could have been a crime that we don't yet know about that occurred on Saturday the 8th. I already have people looking into such a thing, but now we can narrow it down. The crimes seem to have been moving east. Now we can focus on Saturday the 8th in an area west of the Teddy Burn, as you call it.'

'Glad to be of help.'

She could see his distaste, knowing the investigation was getting wings – without him. 'And you can help some more, since you're a private detective now.'

'Déjà vu,' Bennet said. 'Is this where you tell me all your people are busy and... yeah, you know.'

'Do you want the job or not? And, no, I'm not doing it because I think you miss the chase. You already have a foot in the door and can achieve answers quicker.'

'You're talking about my teacher client, aren't you? You want me to go back to her and get more on this bogus Jacob Bressler? See if there's a dice?'

'I can give it to a constable if you're not up to the challenge.'

When Liz had collected all her belongings, they left the room. Liz pointed out the officer guarding her doorway and told Bennet her boss was just overreacting by posting security. She didn't expect Bennet to side with him.

'No, he's right. You're in danger. You need to be careful.'

'If my attacker indeed was our perp, he'd be mad to try coming at me again.'

'Not if he's forced to. Haven't you thought about this? You were supposed to die. That was the plan.'

She *had* thought about it. The perp had left a dice at the scene of her attack. If he'd been on a mission to kill her, then he'd been unsuccessful. He might have been tasked with a *redo*.

CHAPTER FORTY-ONE

Memory loss was another symptom of head trauma. Liz and Bennet got outside before she realised she didn't have her car. It was probably still up near where she'd been attacked. She'd already called Boeson on the way out of the hospital to tell him to look into insignificant crimes, possibly unreported, in the lower west of Sheffield on Saturday the 8th. She'd had to call back and asked for a lift. Bennet had offered, but she'd told him to be on his way to visit the teacher whose handbag got abused in Hackenthorpe.

Boeson pulled into the ambulance drop-off zone forty minutes later. 'The super's just found out you're not going home. He's not impressed. I didn't tell him I was picking you up. I got your car moved to the station. I just hope the officer I sent didn't use that back seat with his girlfriend.'

'Nice. I'll call the super sometime.'

'Good. And he also said not to try to lose your escort.'

The officer who'd been outside her room had joined another in a car parked nearby. Two men, watching her. This pair's offer of a lift had also been refused, and she'd told them to remain out of sight if they were determined to follow her around all day.

'Also, your husband is going to make a complaint about you. I gave him an IOPC complaint form from the Treasures, to buy you some time.'

She smiled. Boeson's glovebox was known as his Treasures. In it he kept all sorts of police paperwork designed to make life easier. When people wanted to complain about the police, the quickest way was by contacting the relevant force directly. A longer route was going through the Independent Office for Police Conduct. Phone, email or online form were the speedy ways to contact this organisation, but they also had a post office box you could mail a hard copy of the downloadable complaint form to.

Boeson had a number of copies of the form for when people threatened to complain about him, or his team, or any other coppers. He'd edited out the parts containing a phone number and email address, to increase the chances of a complainant quitting because of all the effort involved.

Finally, just to delay the determined moaners, he'd changed the postcode district from M33 to M333. Perhaps morally and professionally a bit lacking, but it was hardly a crime itself and Liz saw no problem with it. Many complaints were bogus and their investigation wasted valuable time.

As they started driving out of the hospital grounds, she asked, 'Did you find any crimes for Saturday the 8th?'

'Plenty. I've arranged a team of uniforms ready to hit the streets. Here's the list.'

She took an electronic tablet from him and scanned a spreadsheet. A fact at the top startled her. 'My God. Five hundred and three 999 calls to SYP on Saturday the 8th.'

'Yep. The commissioner needs to slap faces with that the next time people moan about the police precept in their council tax.'

The spreadsheet was part of data to be submitted to the

police and crime commissioner and he needed only statistics, so there were no details of the subjects or results of those calls. But the crime numbers would give them everything they needed.

The list was broken into the boroughs and she concentrated on Sheffield. Two hundred and twenty-one emergency services calls had been made in Sheffield on Saturday the 8th of August. Of these, only ninety-seven had earned a crime number. These were supposed to be allocated to every crime that got called in, but sometimes the reports were bogus or erroneous or so ludicrous they got labelled 'no further action' before a reference number could be generated.

Liz clicked a button to sort the new, edited list in ascending chronological order and next discarded those crimes she felt were too early in the day – none of those attributed to her killer had occurred in the morning. Forty-five got bounced. Christ, a lot of ne'er-do-wells had been active early that day.

Fifty-two crimes remained. Next, she filtered out postcodes that were too far from ground zero: south-west Sheffield. It left just fifteen, which was a manageable number. Of course, they couldn't discount the others on the list, even the ones that hadn't warranted a crime number. But the fifteen contenders were a good starting point for a woman full of impatience and energy.

She jabbed one with a finger. 'We'll start with this one right here, right now.'

The first port of call was a house next door to St Chad's Church in Woodseats, about three quarters of a mile south-west of Teddy Burn. Four women and their eight kids chattering on the pavement outside didn't bat an eyelid when Boeson's car pulled up. But they fell silent, staring, when another plain car, three patrol vehicles and a forensics van crowded the pavement.

The silence didn't last long. As Liz, Boeson and two detectives from the second plain car piled through the garden gate, one of the women, in a bathrobe, turned to the house and yelled,

'Don! The fuzz! What the hell have you done?'

A man appeared at the door before Liz could knock. His face was a mask of shock. Before he could utter a word, Liz showed him her warrant card.

'DCI Miller, South Yorkshire Police. I understand you reported a slashed tyre on Saturday the 8th?'

He still looked shocked, as did the women watching. All these cops for a slashed tyre?

CHAPTER FORTY-TWO

The door of the house in Hackenthorpe was opened by the same woman, wearing the same stained nightgown.

'Hello again, Felicity,' Bennet said to the overweight teacher. 'I thought I might just take your case after all.'

His mention of her 'case' took the puzzlement from her face. She flicked a hand. 'Oh, you had your chance, babe. I'm not fussed anymore.'

'That's fine. However, I'm kind of here on police business now. The man who did something nasty to your handbag might be connected to another crime and I need to ask you some questions. The name Jacob Bressler is fake, like you said.'

Given the name by Bennet, Liz had already run it through the Police National Computer, to no joy. No Jacob Bresslers fitting their guy had been found on Google or the electoral register, either. There was no proof yet it was fake, but they were dealing with a cunning and careful criminal.

'No questions,' Felicity said. 'I've forgotten about him now. And I'm busy.'

She tried to shut the door, but he blocked it. 'I really need to come in and talk to you. We think the man might have left a dice somewhere here.'

She looked puzzled. 'What dice? What are you – no, look, I'm not fussed. I don't want to report a crime. Be on your way now.'

His mention of dice hadn't rung the woman's alarm, so she probably hadn't seen the news. He chose not to enlighten her just yet. 'It's important. You heard what I said about another crime, right? I've been asked to talk to you because it's a delicate matter. And there's delicate stuff in your house and I don't want you to lose your job if the police have to come here instead.'

Now she looked a little perturbed, but remained silent. Bennet said, 'I know you didn't call the police about this Jacob Bressler because you don't want them in your house. They might see those sheets of paper you like to dry on the radiator. I'm guessing you have a brother or a friend in prison that you write to. What drug are the sheets soaked in? Ecstasy? Diluted heroin? Spice?'

Felicity gave a nervous laugh. 'That's just silly. I spilled tea. I...'

'Why don't you just answer my questions, promise never to send *tea* into prison again, and help me get a bad man off the streets?'

Two hundred metres east along the same road where a tyre had been slashed, someone had graffitied the side wall of Bluewoods Spa with the words DIE TWICE. Local word had it as reference to the fact that the father of the spa owner had died in an ambulance after a heart attack, although luckily he'd been revived at the hospital.

The same gossip vine named a young thug called Davy as

the culprit because his mother had been banned from the spa. No one really cared anyway.

Until today. The singular for dice was 'die' and the 'twice' could refer to the number two, so Davy's parents' house got its door kicked in by riot officers. The family was having Sunday dinner in the dining room and froze with their forks to their mouths when police flooded in.

The parents didn't have a clue what was going on, but Davy did, and he bolted out the open French doors. In the backyard he scampered up his little brother's slide and leaped over a fence, into the neighbour's property, where his bravado earned a sprained ankle. Four burly male officers who'd been waiting out back helped him to his feet, then Boeson grabbed an elbow to lead him home.

Davy, nineteen, tattooed to hell, was put on the living-room sofa with his parents. Liz approached them. She was bristling with ego and confidence. Entering a room behind a team of kick-assers under her control never got boring.

'David Leems, it seems you've been up to no good with a spray can again.'

Davy relaxed a little, making it clear he'd expected a comeback for a more serious crime. But, like his parents, he was utterly surprised. All these cops for a bit of graffiti?

CHAPTER FORTY-THREE

Bennet had planned to again use his commendation photograph to prove he at least used to be a police officer, but he didn't need to bother in the end.

Roller World was next door to Napoleons Casino on Livesey Street, just a couple of miles from the city centre. Sunday afternoons were for kids and as Bennet bypassed a rowdy queue and entered the foyer, the manager turned from a sign he was placing, smiled and pointed a finger.

'DCI Barnet, is it? No, Bennet.'

Bennet recognised him too. Three years ago the man had been a manager at a gaming arcade in Barnsley, and he'd called the police one Saturday evening because two men arguing over a fruit machine had fought. One had pulled a knife. The case had been pretty clear cut and the killer had been quickly caught. Bennet had later bought an outdoor trampoline off the manager.

Bennet didn't correct the manager on his DCI status. He said, 'Good to see you again. I'm here on some business and it would be great if I get a look at your CCTV covering the exterior. Nothing to do with your disco, so no need to worry.'

'Sure thing. Follow me.'

And he was in.

The teacher, Felicity, had said she'd met the man called Jacob Bressler outside the disco at about ten on Sunday the 16th of August. Three cameras covered the exterior: front, side, back. Bennet used the one covering the front doors and wound back time. The picture quality was pretty shocking and faces and general descriptions were going to be of no use. However, the teacher's large bulk was hard to miss when she arrived outside the doors to wait.

When the time code read three minutes to ten, Bressler arrived. He was tall and slim, wearing jeans and a bomber jacket and sunglasses. He had his head down and constantly scratched the back of his neck. They chatted outside for about two minutes, then left out of the bottom of the screen, reversing the route the teacher had taken to enter the frame – heading for her car.

Felicity had driven them to her home, so Jacob must have arrived by taxi. Bennet accessed the camera covering the side of the building, still on Livesey Street, and was rewarded at 21.56. A taxi pulled up near an area for bins and out he got, clearly averse to allowing the teacher to see his mode of transport. Here he didn't employ his neck-scratch trick to avoid the camera, but the grainy picture was his saviour.

However, Bennet was able to read the company sticker on the side of the taxi. Now he had a new line of enquiry and an itchiness to get moving.

God, he missed this.

CHAPTER FORTY-FOUR

Seven hours after it had begun, all fifteen possible volume crimes had been assessed and Liz was back at her station. It had all been a bust, but that was the majority of police work. You didn't hit the jackpot every time, and sometimes never at all.

It was nearly 9pm and most of her team had gone home. Liz was ready to follow suit when she glanced through her office window and saw a uniformed officer enter the sacred floor of MIT 2. He looked like he had something important to say, so she watched as Boeson intercepted him. Seconds later, Boeson virtually manhandled the uniform to her office door.

'Tell her.'

Liz leaned back in Bates's chair as the uniform rapidly spoke. 'It was on that date you're interested in, Saturday the 8th. I was in Gleadless Valley. I live there and I was just heading to work, and a lady pulled me up. She led me to another street. There was a black Range Rover parked out front of her garage. The window was bust and it had been hot-wired.'

Liz hadn't seen a stolen Range Rover on her list. 'Did you call it in?'

'No. The garage next door was wide open. That's where the car came from. I knew who owned it. He's a drug dealer in prison. He's had that vehicle vandalised before. He's got enemies, as all drug dealers do.'

'So you didn't report it. So what did you do?'

'It would have been a waste of police time. The drug dealer was hardly going to help us even if he knew who did it. So I just rolled the car back into the garage and shut the garage door. I knew his ex-girlfriend lived on the same estate so I knocked on her door and told her. I said she should tell him. So I basically left it in his hands if he wanted to call the police or not. And he obviously didn't.'

'Get to the bit we give a hoot about,' Boeson told him.

'Dice. There were two fluffy dice hanging from the rear-view mirror. One had come off and it was on the dashboard.'

'He thinks it might have been showing a number three,' Boeson said.

The uniform nodded. 'But I left it alone. I didn't touch it. So it should still be there. You can look if you want.'

'Oh, thank you,' Boeson said.

Minutes later, Liz, Boeson and the uniform were driving west, followed by others, including her protectors. It was just over a mile to Gleadless Valley.

The location was a set of five lock-up garages on the edge of Blackstock Road, which wound through a small estate surrounded by woods. Not long after Boeson's car and a second bearing detectives pulled up, two patrol cars and a forensics van arrived. The heavy police presence immediately drew attention. Behind the garages was a high-rise and myriad people appeared at their balconies. Nearby pedestrians either stopped to watch or moved closer.

Garage number two got its roller door lifted and Liz stepped inside. There was the Range Rover, its busted driver's window visible. Shelving on both sides of the garage contained all sorts of junk, from car parts to empty mobile phone boxes. Boeson told a couple of uniforms to have a sift through and see if anything dodgy popped up. Liz gloved up and opened the driver's door, while Boeson did the same on the passenger side.

The officer had been right. One green fluffy dice hung from the mirror and its partner was on the dashboard. With three dots face-up. It rested atop the curve above the speedometer and rev counter, and wouldn't have settled in that precarious position after a fall. Nor could it have survived movement of the vehicle.

Boeson used a finger to prod it, but it was stuck fast. He pulled it away to expose a lump of Blu-Tack. That explained things. Someone had deliberately positioned the dice.

The detectives looked at each other across the interior of the Range Rover. Each face said the same thing: this is a good find. Both stepped out of the garage and Liz sent in the forensic team to dust and swab and bag. She and Boeson found a quiet spot to discuss this finding.

Liz said, 'On Sunday the 9th, we had Teddy Burn. On Sunday the 16th we had the loophole rape of a handbag. On Sunday the 23rd we had the dog kidnapping.'

'So our boy will strike again today, with something else bizarre put to him by his handler.'

Handler. A good description. Yet wrong. 'But think about our Saturday crimes. This Range Rover vandalism on the 8th aside, we have the murder of Breakspear on the 15th. The murder of Paul Yard on the 22nd. My attempted murder yesterday. And think about locations. We thought our killer was moving east, but this Range Rover thing was the day before Teddy Burn, yet east of it.'

'I think I know what you're saying. Two starting points. Not a man and his handler, but two men committing the crimes, perhaps competing against each other. They're leapfrogging each other as they move east. But that still doesn't explain why your attack was way back west and north.'

'Perhaps because I am a threat. So, one takes Saturdays, the other Sundays. And Saturday man is clearly the more dangerous. He's not committing volume crime. Not anymore. He's killing people, or trying to, each and every time. And Saturday's coming. We're probably going to be handed another murder.'

'Or what you called a – what was it?'

'A redo,' Liz repeated. 'Of my murder.'

CHAPTER FORTY-FIVE

When Bennet called, Liz answered the phone by saying, 'Did you learn anything from the teacher?'

'I'm fine, thanks for asking.'

'Teacher. Now.'

'I got the name of the roller disco where she met the man who called himself Jacob Bressler. Roller World near Napoleons Casino.'

'Good work. Hopefully he's got a membership and he showed ID. I'll get people down there.'

'No membership. They never went inside. He's all over the CCTV, which is good, but the quality is bad and he's been careful. Can't see a face. The man arrived by a Dragon Cars taxi.'

'Couldn't help yourself, eh? But good work. I'll also get onto the taxi firm and—'

'The operator there said the taxi picked disco man up from Grimesthorpe, about four miles north of where all the crimes are happening. It was outside a washing machine parts and service place in a row of shops on Upwell Street. There's a bedsit above that shop. Number sixty-seven. Just like at your place, the door is at the top of a fire exit round back. I saw a woman in the washing machine place, but nothing from the bedsit so far.'

'Good. I can find out who lives there and–'

'No one is registered there according to the electoral register. But there was a letter hanging out the letter box, which I accidentally took and opened and read. It was a cold call from a car insurance company to a woman called Ms Chaya Modi. I think I found her on Facebook. Used to live in Sheffield, now down in London. She lists herself as a property developer. So maybe she owns the place and is renting it out. To someone not yet registered there.'

'That's a common tactic amongst those forced to rent bedsits. My landlord insisted I register as soon as possible. Sometimes people are hiding from debt collectors or enemies.'

'You mean for instance a woman who doesn't want her ex-husband to know where she lives?'

'Funny, aren't you?'

'If someone is living in that bedsit, our only chance to find out who is to sit and wait for him to return. Across the road is a small MOT service station with a forecourt that could be a good place to watch from.'

'I'd say I'll get people to sit there and watch, but I have a suspicion someone's already been doing that.'

'It would be great if SYP could reimburse me for two new front tyres I didn't need.'

She laughed. 'Deep down I expected as much, Liam. Any more surprises?'

'I'm all spent. I've been here a while now and seen no movement from within. But I looked in the kitchen window when I was round back and saw next to nothing. As in the bedsit looks empty. Could be our guy has already gone. I wouldn't really bother with a surveillance team. I'd kick in the door if I were you so as not to waste time. There could be vital evidence in there. Imagine it points to his next murder and that happens while we're standing around. It's Sunday night, remember. There's been a crime every Sunday so far.'

'Easy for a civilian to say. Besides, I already have my people watching for strange crimes.'

Liz segued into a rundown of what she had learned since they'd parted that afternoon. And she gave him her new theory about a pair of criminals competing against each other at weekends.

'Competing?' Bennet said. 'The one working Sunday is stealing dogs while his crony leaves bodies.'

'Well, Sunday man also committed rape. But I know what you mean. They're hardly trying to outdo each other. We're still missing vital pieces of this jigsaw.'

'And they could all be in that bedsit. You need to get in there. This civilian is going to bust into that bedsit if you don't want to.'

'But I'd have to arrest you for trespassing and criminal damage.'

'Would you put the cuffs on me personally?'

She laughed. 'I was only testing you. A while back I spent a week getting bored on surveillance in Spain, remember? I sent my man to get a search warrant the moment you gave me the address.'

Bennet did remember. She'd been away while he was looking for his son's mother. When he found her murdered. He felt old anger rising and it needed an outlet. 'Hurry your man up, or I'm kicking that door in.'

CHAPTER FORTY-SIX

Amongst his glovebox Treasures, DS Boeson had a stack of printed search warrant application forms downloaded from the Gov.Dot website, all partially filled in. He noted the specifics to this case, signed and dated it, and after dropping Liz off with Bennet, he drove to Sheffield Magistrates' Court at high speed.

Liz and Bennet took up a position at a bus stop near the garage and here Liz made a call to her super to organise a raid team. Once she'd outlined what she had and confirmed the search warrant was imminent, and her super had agreed to arrange backup, Bennet heard her tone shift.

'You know how a few years ago we faltered a bit with the BUSS scheme...'

That was all Bennet caught as Liz moved aside for privacy. He knew of the Best Use of Stop & Search scheme, which attempted to provide transparency for the public to reassure them that police weren't misusing their stop and search powers.

When the government introduced the scheme across all forty-three police forces, it was a big headache because officers now had to record and explain every stop and search undertaken. South Yorkshire Police hadn't given a stellar performance in this duty. But Bennet was puzzled as to why Liz was bringing this up to her super.

She ended the call two minutes later and returned with a grin. 'Done. You can officially come in with us.'

Now he got it. As reparation for a bad score on the BUSS scheme, SYP had made it a priority to offer ride-along schemes for the public, so they could witness first-hand how coppers behaved when out and about on duty. 'You guilted your boss into letting me tag along on this raid.'

'If you feel bad, watch from this bus stop.'

He smiled. 'We seem to have come full circle. Last time it was my investigation and you were the one trying to hitch onto it.'

'At least I was a police officer. So don't think we're even. You owe me. You know how bad I'll feel if you get hurt in there?'

'Because your boss will come down on you like a ton of bricks, you mean?'

She feigned puzzlement. 'Yeah. Why else would I worry about a madman killing you stone dead?'

'And they say romance is dead.'

He half regretted that final line, especially when it evoked no reply.

They continued to watch the house while pretending to await a bus. Still no movement from the first-floor window. No one came or went down the alley between the building and a car breakers, which was the only way to access the door to the bedsit.

Seventy-three minutes later, the raid team arrived. Boeson had returned ten minutes earlier, waving a sheet of paper out his window before he'd even stopped the car. In the interim, Liz took a call from the raid team leader to finalise the details. So, when the van reached the location, everyone knew what to do. Without slowing, the vehicle cut into the alley and Liz, Boeson and Bennet ran behind it.

The rear yard of the building had a low wall with a gap; the gate that had filled it was lying in the yard.

The washing machine place had a back door that was open, and two middle-aged women were sitting near it on empty beer kegs, smoking. They froze as the van screeched to a halt and padded men piled out and into their yard.

Bringing up the rear with Boeson and Bennet, Liz put a finger to her lips and moved closer to the women. The raid team took no pause and hit the staircase, moving slowly upwards so the iron contraption wouldn't rumble like thunder.

'Who lives above?' Liz asked.

'Don't know him,' one of the women said. 'Just work here. Just know it's a man. Hardly see him. What's he done?'

'Get inside and shut the door, and stay off the phone.'

The women scarpered. Liz headed for the stairs, Bennet right behind, Boeson leading them both. A somewhat armed officer stood each side of the door, one holding a heavy metal battering ram, the other with a chainsaw in case something else inside needed opening. As Boeson reached the landing, he tapped the shoulder of the guy with the ram.

'I'll have that, boyo.'

Liz moved through the gap created by the officers and rapped on the door. 'Police with a search warrant. Open up.'

It was purely routine so nobody could be accused of heavy-handed impatience. She doubted anyone was home and, even if they had been, she allowed little time for a vocal response, let alone a stroll to the door. She stepped back upon her final word, barely getting her leg out of the way as Boeson swung his ram.

It took the strike team just seconds to confirm the bedsit was empty.

It stank of bleach, which was something that always intrigued police. The bed was a single mattress on the floor, no way for anyone to hide under it. There were no wardrobes to lurk in. No sofa or armchairs to duck behind. Also, no fridge, no carpets, no TV. Food in the cupboards was minimal and all ready to eat or microwavable. There was a kettle with a scattering of teabags and sweeteners in a bowl.

It was one of only two bowls; the other was in the sink along with the bedsit's single item of cutlery: a camping tool designed to be a spoon, knife, fork and bottle/tin opener. There was only one cup. It was obvious that whoever rented this place had intended to stay here infrequently, and alone.

But the hollowness of the bedsit amplified its main feature. The laptop sat on a cheap foldaway desk like an exhibit, as if the whole residence was nothing but a box to keep it in. The detectives were drawn to it like moths to a flame.

'We are dealing with one insane, sick mother-effer,' Boeson said, as he bent down to pick up a plastic bag of rubbish beside the desk. He held it up. 'Charity collection bag used as a bin liner. We need to get this psycho off the streets as quick as possible.'

Liz touched the laptop's mousepad and the screen came to life. It asked for a password. 'Damn.'

'It's almost like these criminals don't want to get caught,' Boeson said. 'But leave this to me.'

CHAPTER FORTY-SEVEN

By evening's end, the media had gotten wind that the police were going in heavy-handed to routine police calls. At first they chalked it down to a panic to hit conviction targets, but it didn't take long for a connection to be made to the recent killings. That Sunday night a reporter coined a nickname that would stick: the Dicer. So far news hadn't leaked that two killers were involved.

The majority of the call-outs were from genuine folk who were surprised and happy to receive immediate responses to their mediocre grievances. Some people called in believing they were the killer's next victim, like the woman who fretted because someone had lobbed stones through her car windscreen and the holes created a diagonal line, akin to the three on a dice. Other reports resulted from the work of pranksters who'd drawn dice on walls, posted them through letter boxes, left them on car bonnets.

Every report needed checking, however. Manpower was down and in some cases only a pair of uniforms in a car got sent out. The shockwave was felt most in areas where a dice-killer crime wasn't expected. In the north of the city, people reported that they had been shot at by air rifle while walking down Cherry Street, location of the staff entrance to Sheffield United Football Club.

Only upon the fifth complaint, some four hours after the first, did the police finally send a car. That officer had a quick look and was about to give up when a pellet hit his arm. He subsequently arrested a thirteen-year-old girl with a pellet gun who was hiding in the bed of an open-back truck in the football club's staff car park.

Back at ground zero, southwest Sheffield, not everybody was getting the royalty treatment. On Guildford Avenue in Arbourthorne, a mostly council house section of the city, police were called by a man who claimed he'd been getting harassed all day. His story fit 'strange' to a T.

Early that morning, he'd been woken by noise through his letter box, which he figured he knew the cause of. It happened again later in the morning. In the afternoon, when he took a walk to the local shop, someone on a small black motorbike and wearing a hoodie rode by and did it again. And in the early evening as he left to go to work at a restaurant across from City Road Cemetery, the same hoodie jumped into his path and used the noisemaking item right in his face.

The complainant had no idea who was harassing him or why. His call brought two uniforms and a detective immediately to his place of work, but his claim that he'd seen no dice pictures soon wilted their enthusiasm. They told him there was nothing the police could do unless the noisemaker touched him or his property, and then they scarpered.

They'd soon be back.

CHAPTER FORTY-EIGHT

Forensics turned up at the bedsit, so Liz, Bennet and Boeson took the laptop out to his car. Boeson had a laptop of his own with a portable hard drive and flash drive attached. He sat in the passenger seat for more room and Liz took the driver's position. Bennet stood by the open passenger door to watch.

Boeson plugged the flash drive into the suspect's machine and restarted it, using F12 to access the boot menu. He explained his actions while he worked. And it was no super hacking trick. From the boot menu, he picked the flash drive instead of the internal hard drive and loaded a program called Windows Password Key.

This showed him all accounts on the computer: just the administrator. Within seconds, he had reset the administrator password. He removed the USB, restarted the computer and let it load normally, and then used his new password. And they were in.

'That can't be legal,' Liz said. 'Where did you get that program?'

'It's all over the internet. Nothing illegal about it. It comes with a warning not to mess about with other people's computers, so don't worry.'

Immediately a desktop icon drew her attention. 'Croak Catalogue. What's that?'

Boeson clicked it and a website appeared. The main page was a black screen with large white letters that said CROAK CATALOGUE and had an ENTER SITE button.

Boeson made a happy noise, which prompted Liz to say, 'You recognise it?'

'Not the website, but the web browser. It's the Tor browser.'

'Deep web?'

'No. The deep web is just parts of the internet that standard search engines can't reach. My Netflix account is deep web. Anything that requires a login. No, this is the *dark* web. Encrypted websites. You don't get here unless you have special software. You don't go down into the dark unless you want to avoid being tracked. And you don't play around down there unless you have serious protection, like a VPN.'

'Go ahead and show me this thing. Show me this dangerous underworld.'

'You joke, but it can be dangerous. Go down in the dark without knowing what you're doing, you'll get your driver's licence cloned and lose what's in your bank in no time.' Boeson started playing with the mouse. 'Croak Catalogue, it seems, is for gamers who want something a little extra. Just give me a minute here to nosey around.'

He updated Liz as he learned. On Croak Catalogue, players bet on celebrity deaths, using Bitcoin, a digital currency that, like gold, could be exchanged for cash or goods or services. The internet was rife with such websites.

The rules of the game were: you paid $100 and were allocated a team, each with fifty players. Each team member picked 100 celebrities from a pool of 5,000. Points were awarded based on that celeb's prospect of dying, with fewer points for those more likely to meet the Reaper. Healthy people and children scored the least, with older celebrities and those with risky pastimes, like racing drivers, worth the most.

At the end of each month, the highest scoring team won all the money in the pot. The winners then shared the pot according to who'd scored the highest.

Players could also add a cause of death to their picks, for extra points. There was an example that showed a ninety-year-old film star and OLD AGE, which added no points. The same guy attached to SKYDIVING added ten times his original score. You'd get less for picking a child star to drown in a swimming pool. However, the full list of celebrities and causes of death were available only to logged-in members.

Boeson clicked on the LOGIN button. It asked for a username and password. 'Damn. I was hoping our boy would have the autofill in place, so we could have automatically logged in. We're not going to be able to get into his account. Not on a super-secure site like this. But I'll get the tech boys to have a try. Let me see what other gems are on this thing.'

Bennet had been watching for a few minutes in silence, but now he had something important to say. 'Seems to me there could be a lot of money to be made if someone could influence celebrity deaths.'

Boeson laughed. 'Yeah, like kill a vegan by choking him on a leg of lamb.'

'Or choke a reality TV star with a rubber football. Paul Yard.'

Boeson stopped laughing. 'Hang on a sec...'

Bennet looked at Liz and said, 'You're somewhat of a celebrity, right? Because of this investigation and the one we had together last year.'

'Er, you might want to see this,' Boeson cut in.

Liz didn't even hear him. To Bennet she said, 'And James Breakspear was a junior football star.'

'I think we're on the same page,' Bennet said.

'Our killers are murdering minor celebrities in bizarre ways in order to win money?'

CHAPTER FORTY-NINE

Boeson snapped his fingers to get Liz and Bennet's attention. 'Same page, you say? Well, turn over for a surprise. Look at this.'

Bennet and Liz had forgotten the laptop as they discussed the merits of their new theory. Now, they returned their attention to the screen.

Boeson had clicked on another desktop icon. They saw a large, computer-generated treasure chest filling the screen. Next to it was a pirate flag with a skull and crossbones and the number four. Underneath the chest was a large button that said SPIN. The lid of the chest was open and rising from a mound of jewels were three swords, each with a square of parchment atop bearing a single word. Left to right the words were:

TRUMPET, STALK, CHEF

'It's a randomiser, like a fruit machine with words,' Boeson said. He took a photo of the screen with his iPad. Then he hit the SPIN button. Blurred words seemed to roll in the parchments, just like icons on the reels of a fruit machine. When the spin was over, three new words were displayed.

VEGETABLE, KIDNAP, PROSTITUTE

The detectives looked at each other. They knew what they had here. 'One weapon, one crime, one victim,' Liz said. 'This is how our perps are picking what they do, and what with, and to who.'

Boeson nodded. 'Now we know why some of the crimes are downright weird. And why murder is being mixed with low-key silliness no one is reporting.'

Bennet tapped the counter, which had shifted from four to five after Boeson's spin. 'Only four spins had been made before Boeson tested it, not eight. We've had eight crimes, if we include whatever is coming today.'

Liz knew what he was getting at. 'Both our perps don't live here. This one belongs to Sunday man. Saturday man lives somewhere else. And he's got another randomiser.'

'How do you know this is Sunday man's place?' Boeson asked.

'We haven't seen crime number four from him yet. But we will. And here it is.' She indicated the photo Boeson had taken of the previous spin, number four. 'Bizarre, but it seems at some point today a chef is going to get stalked by a trumpet.'

A few weeks ago such words would have caused laughter. Not today.

CHAPTER FIFTY

Knowing the laptop could hold the key to everything, Liz didn't want to let it out of her sight. A crime-scene technician bagged it and took it to his van, and she followed. While he stored it and chatted to Boeson, Liz and Bennet got some space to chat.

'I guess you don't need me now,' he said.

'Don't look so glum. We wouldn't be this far along without you. And there's nothing much more any of us can do now except wait for the tech boys to do their thing. You should get back to Joe. I'll keep you updated.'

'He's away, staying at his grandfather's for another few days. So my house is empty.'

She looked him up and down. 'What are you saying to me, hot-blooded male?'

He looked aghast. 'Not that. But I did think you might want to stay over for a few days. You don't like your bedsit.'

She put her hands on her hips, a feigned gesture of defiance. 'You think I'll fall for your tricks and you can take advantage of me?'

'No, no.'

She laughed at his panic, but quickly got serious again. 'This is because you think I'm in danger. Just like my super, which is why he's got uniforms following me everywhere.'

'We just shouldn't take the risk. If the killer knows where you live, and you're there alone...'

'Look, I'm not stupid, Liam. There was a dice at the scene of my attack. I could be part of whatever game the killers are playing. I could be unfinished business. But remember that when they did the other redo in the teacher rape, they picked a brand-new victim. They knew it would be tough to get the same woman. And they have to know I'm well protected now. Also, we don't even have proof they were responsible. The dice connection is public knowledge now. I could have been attacked by someone I put away years ago who thought it would throw us off the scent.'

Bennet nodded. 'I know. But it doesn't mean you should take risks.'

'I have no problem staying at yours, Liam.' She indicated the police officers watching them from a car. 'I have a security detail. You really want them to see me stay overnight at yours?'

'Why would I care? It's not like we'd be having sex or anything. I just don't like an empty house. Or to know you'd be in an empty house.'

'Then the answer is yes. I'll come round when I've finished up for the day. Buy a pizza. I'll be wearing a chastity belt, by the way.'

Bennet started backing off towards his car. 'So will I.'

When Bennet was gone, Boeson approached her. 'I told boyo we want a list of all the words on the randomiser's three parchment reels. He said he can get one of his team to reverse engineer the software. So pull it apart while it's running and see the code.'

'They're that good?'

'I asked the same thing and he got a bit offended. Gave me some spiel about how the Y2K thing twenty years ago had everyone panicking and the computer world realised there just weren't enough people who knew how to reverse engineer. So people got on it. Programmers who don't have at least a basic knowledge of reverse engineering aren't worth their salt.'

'So everyone was out to save the world, and it was nothing to do with big money from software piracy? Gotcha. How long will it take?'

'Not too long, he reckons. They'll run it through a debugger to get the binary code, those ones and zeros that computers talk with. That binary code gets passed through a compiler to get to what's called the source code. That's the stuff programmers deal with, nice actual words. The section of code dealing with what's displayed on the reels will have all the words in speech marks. Dead simple. If the tech guys don't have it done by tomorrow morning, I'll get a sword and we'll have a purge.'

'And what about the Croak Catalogue website? We need that account info.'

'They'll have a try to hack in, but don't hold your breath. As for the list, that's available to members. Dead easy. I'll download the Tor browser on my laptop, then become a member of the website. Maybe I'll even have a bet. What's the chances that Tom Cruise is going mountain climbing anytime soon?'

'Forget Cruise. Your first search is going to my name. Let's go do that now.'

CHAPTER FIFTY-ONE

T RUMPET/STALK/CHEF.

Now that she knew what to look for, Liz soon learned about the incident in Arbourthorne, and again the public got to witness a simple complaint result in an invasion of police. Someone had called ahead to the complainant's restaurant, the City Road Eatery, and he left work to meet detectives at his home. When he answered the door to four detectives and a search team, he immediately said,

'My God. You don't think this is the work of the Dicer, do you?'

He spoke to Liz inside. He was a sous chef, he confirmed that the villain had used a trumpet, and he'd been hassled all day, which constituted stalking. He claimed no knowledge of a dice being involved, but one of the officers searching the immediate area found a small one drawn with Tippex on the side of the shed in the rear garden of the chef's house. Bingo.

Liz went out for a look. The dice showed a four, which did nothing to help clarify what the hell these numbers meant. But now they had definitive proof the killers had struck again and forensics and a second search team were called in. It was soon big news and the once quiet residential street was clogged with gawkers, journalists and vehicles.

While he answered questions, the sous chef stared out of his living-room window, amazed at the crowd clogging the street. And a little happy with it.

'Jasper? Please?' Liz said.

The chef snapped out of his trance and turned away from the window. He looked at the four detectives as if he'd forgotten they were there. 'Sorry?'

'The bike the assailant rode?'

He sat on the carpet, back against the radiator under the window. 'Er, it was a BMX. Blue. Low seat. It had green tyres, I remember. I think it said Voodoo on the frame.'

Liz was writing that down when a search officer from the local station came in from the kitchen. The chef had already been informed that they had to rule him out as a suspect and needed to investigate his home. 'Voodoo? A blue Voodoo Zaka?' Everyone looked at him. 'Kid round here called Lukasz has one of those.'

Liz jumped to her feet.

―――――――

Lukasz Babiarz, eighteen, lived in the new housing development of Cutlers View, half a mile west of the chef's home. His mother was washing the outside of her front windows when a slew of law enforcement vehicles pulled up.

The officer who knew Lukasz had said the family was well-respected and that the kid was known to police as a victim rather than an offender. The family was Polish and had endured abuse at the hands of xenophobes since the UK left the EU at the end of January. 'No way that kid's involved in this,' the officer had said, and after a review of Lukasz's Facebook, Liz agreed. So only she and Boeson got out of their cars to talk to the family. Liz met the mother at the gate.

Maria Babiarz would allow her son to speak to only one detective, so Liz alone was led upstairs to his room. The teenager was shocked when his mother led her into his bedroom, where he was playing solitaire on a computer. She spoke to her son in Polish for a few seconds and then stood in the corner of the room. Lukasz turned his desk chair towards Liz, waiting.

Liz figured he'd been ordered to answer questions, so she began. She recorded the conversation on her phone. He was very polite and answered every question fast and in-depth, finishing each with 'ma'am'.

Back in Boeson's car, Liz filled him in.

'Lukasz said this morning he went bike riding down the long and winding Park Grange Road, racing trams. A hobby of his. As he was passing Guildford Avenue, a man in a face mask and a baseball cap and a black tracksuit stepped in front of him...'

The man offered Lukasz twenty pounds to do a job, and he handed him a bag with another face mask and a trumpet inside, and then told him an address. He wanted Lukasz to hassle the man with the trumpet, all day. The victim, the man claimed, was a pal of his and they often wound each other up. Lukasz figured it was a harmless prank and agreed.

'The face mask he dropped on the street afterwards. The bag got binned. The twenty-pound note has been spent, but he told me which shop. Unfortunately, Lukasz doesn't know if the man had a car. From what little of the face he could see, he thinks the man was young, not much older than Lukasz himself.'

Boeson sighed. 'Would have been nice to have those things.'

She knew he meant the mask, the twenty-pound note, the trumpet, and the bag it had all come in. Still, there was a chance. 'We'll get people on the road, searching bins, searching that shop till, looking along the side of the road for the mask.'

Boeson nodded and held up an evidence bag with a trumpet inside. 'At least the kid kept this. We can only hope.'

He didn't sound convinced and Liz wasn't surprised. Lukasz had been loath to put his mouth where another had been, so he'd scrubbed the mouthpiece with washing-up liquid before using it. Even if they did get biological evidence from their perp, they already knew his DNA wasn't in the system. Like Boeson, she didn't feel the trumpet would yield a jackpot. She could only hope the tech guys would strike lucky with the laptop found at the bedsit.

Otherwise, the next time their enemy left them a calling card, it might be at the scene of another murder rather than a harmless prank.

CHAPTER FIFTY-TWO

When Bennet opened his front door, Liz thrust a bottle of wine in his face.

She was still in her work suit, but she'd applied a little make-up to her cheeks and eyes. Enough to look better but not give away that she'd done it, he figured. He took the wine and glanced over her shoulder, at a patrol car parked by his own vehicle.

'I feel bad for your protectors. Should we invite them in and share this wine with them?'

Her answer was to step inside and shut the door. 'I hope you've bought that pizza.'

He had. They chatted in the living room while it cooked, and ate it in the backyard in the dying light. They also played chess on the giant board on the lawn. Liz told him about the day's progress in the investigation, including that Boeson had signed up to Croak Catalogue and found a complete list of celebrities and causes of death. No James Breakspear featured. No Paul Yard. No Elizabeth Miller.

'So that line of enquiry is a bust?'

'I'm not hopeful, but we still can't get into the website

account. The internet at the bedsit is pay as you go, no name registered. We did get hold of the bedsit owner down in London. She's still registered as living there. Her husband's in prison and thinks she's living in Sheffield and waiting for him. She's not. She's got another man, lives in London, and rents the place out without him or the authorities knowing. She gave us a name. But it wasn't helpful. Donald Trump.'

'What?'

'I know. She never questioned it. The bedsit was advertised in the classified section of a local newspaper. This Donald called her and the deal was done. There's no official lease and the rent is paid in cash, posted to her monthly. The key was behind a loose brick in a wall. She's never even seen him. No security bond or anything like that. He posts rent or she sends her heavies to boot him out.'

'That's the end of that then.'

The peace was broken only twice, by two phone calls. The first was from Boeson. She'd already told Bennet about the day's findings; now she updated him.

'No fingerprints or DNA on the trumpet except for those belonging to the kid, Lukasz, who got paid to stalk the chef. But the searcher in the bedsit just found an item lodged behind a radiator. It's a valve guard for a musical instrument – like a trumpet.'

'That bedsit stank of bleach. Our perp is careful. So finding that valve guard was a stroke of luck. Maybe he didn't hide it but missed it. DNA?'

'They got bodily fluids with a UV torch and fast-tracked it to the lab. They got a full offender profile. And it doesn't match the DNA found on the dice at the two murders.'

'Well, that's good. Now we know for certain there are two slimeballs committing these crimes. But you're not smiling, so I can guess the result when the profile was loaded into the system.'

She nodded. 'Not on file. Maybe one day everybody will have their DNA registered at birth, just to make my working day easier.'

'I'm sure the government is working on it with you in mind.' He sipped wine. 'Any theories about why your perps seemed to have changed direction?'

Her attack had been back to the west and slightly north. At first she'd put it down to a detour taken by Saturday man in order to get his biggest obstacle – Liz – out of the way. But today's crime had occurred in Arbourthorne and that was further west again.

'We've somewhat given up on trying to predict where these bastards will strike next,' she said. 'So far, all crimes have been in the southern half of the city, but we just don't know why they're picking the locations they do, and we have no reason to believe they won't utilise the whole of Sheffield next. Or move to another city.'

The next call was from Clara, who dispensed with niceties and said, 'I just saw a newspaper. That other man who was killed outside his pub. That man from the old TV show. There's a twenty-thousand pound reward for information about his murder. Is there a reward for my James' murder?'

Liz had been expecting this call, this question. But Clara had taken her time: the press conference at which the Yard family had announced the reward had been over a week ago. Where had Clara been all this time?

Liz said, 'Well, I'm sorry, Clara, but that reward was offered by the family.'

'So they have money. Good on them. I'm so happy. But the police sometimes offer rewards. Why not for my James?'

Bennet, clearly aware this was a delicate conversation, took a stroll into the house to refill their wine glasses.

'It's very early in the investigation, Clara, and we've still got leads to follow up. It tends to be when we hit dead ends that rewards are–'

'Something you only do when you hit a brick wall? Well, can't you tell your boss you've already hit it? I know rewards are offered because some people might not give up their information without an incentive. Well, why wait? If there's people out there you know won't come forward, give them that push now.'

'It's not up to me, Clara. We even told the family of Paul Yard not to offer money so early because it would overload the investigation with useless information.'

'But they have money and they did it anyway. And now people will be calling in about that murder, not my James's. You'll get more information and you'll investigate that killing more. He's more important than my James because he wasn't some homeless scum.'

'The murders could well be connected, Clara. If we solve one, we might solve–'

'Save it,' Clara snapped. 'I could beg. I'm good at that, aren't I? I beg or I don't eat. But begging wouldn't do any good here, would it? Look, don't waste your time talking to someone who doesn't mean anything. Go do the important thing and make the Yard family happy.'

'Clara, where have you been staying? Are you okay? Do you need help with–'

Clara hung up. Liz tried to call back, but the phone was turned off.

Bennet returned to the garden bearing wine. 'I got the gist of that. It's been a long day. Maybe you should turn that phone off. Why are you helping this woman?'

It seemed like a callous question, off-character. 'She *needs* help. Her brother's been murdered.'

'No, I mean *you*. Why are *you* helping her?'

'She didn't want an FLO. She's got no one else. I feel bad for her and... I don't know.'

Bennet sat and Liz took a glass of wine from him. 'You're an acting DCI now, Liz. I was one, so I know what it's like. Although I was a bona fide DCI, not a watered-down version.'

She knew he was kidding and gave him the finger.

'My point is, you shouldn't be at the end of every phone call, and you shouldn't be killing yourself by taking on all and sundry. Slow down, okay? I've been where you are and I know the early parts of a new case make you feel the adrenaline buzz. You feel like you have to do everything at a hundred miles an hour. I also know it helps to pause and think sometimes. Time is a blessing, so drink heartily.'

'Some craggy old detective tell you that nugget?'

'Maybe. My point is, give your brain some downtime. It helps. And don't sweat the small stuff. And for God's sake delegate some of the lesser tasks. I bet you make your own coffees, don't you?'

She laughed. 'What, I should abuse my power and have someone fetch my drinks?'

'You should never get a chance. People should be bringing you drinks without being asked. And they shouldn't be coming to you with stuff that's beneath you. Get Boeson to earn his stripes by filtering some of the crap out so you only hear the juicy stuff. They'll be telling you the station toilets are blocked next.'

She playfully slapped the grass. 'Right, watch this.' Liz sent a text and then turned her phone off. 'Done. Boeson is the man now. I am officially unavailable until tomorrow morning.'

The rest of their conversation dipped into anything and

everything not work- or family-related, and they got through another bottle of wine by the time it was too dark and cold to sit outside any longer.

Back inside, Bennet said, 'By the way, you have my bed and I'll have Joe's.'

He tried to step past her, but she blocked him with her body. They stood just inches apart. 'Chess, Liam.'

He didn't create space. 'You want to play chess again? It's too dark now.'

'No. But we are two people who like chess, so we play it together, don't we?'

'Yes. Puzzled now.'

'I'm not committed to any other chess players and neither are you. No one has told us we can't play chess together.'

She took his hand, which was shaking because he knew where this was going. But he acted naïve. 'I don't follow.'

She was a little tipsy from all the wine. 'Some detective. I want to play again. I want you to take this queen. I order you, as a DCI.'

'I'm not a police officer. You can't boss me around. What if someone calls you about the toilets?'

'Then let's not waste time,' Liz said, and led him upstairs.

CHAPTER FIFTY-THREE

'I need a sword.'

Liz didn't get the joke, but Boeson's tone told it all: bad news en route.

'The tech guys contacted me,' he said. 'They're having a hard time getting into the randomiser's code.'

The phone had woken her. It was eight o'clock Monday morning. Her head was sleepy, and pounding from too much wine. Bennet was asleep beside her. Seeing him made last night's activities flood back.

'Did you hear me, Liz?'

'I heard you. Y2K not such the big panic we assumed then?' It was a little joke of her own.

'It's not that,' Boeson said. 'The guys called it code obfuscation. Muddling, basically. It's something software writers do to make their computer code hard to read, so it's tough for thieves to change or copy. Bottom line: it's going to be a while before they can break it apart. There's also more bad news.'

The technicians had found that the laptop was connected to the internet and could be accessed remotely, meaning the owner could use it without being in the bedsit. It had been remote accessed numerous times over the last few weeks, but not once physically. In other words, the user hadn't been to the bedsit in a while and there was no reason he would ever go back. The people they had watching the location were probably wasting their time.

'But the techs can trace where the laptop was accessed from?'

'Can and did. But the IP address was traced to Bonn, in Germany.'

Liz sat up. 'Sunday man is in Germany?'

'Maybe, and probably not.' Boeson explained that the Germany computer could be a proxy. Proxy servers were a common tool of online baddies. If police found the device, it could belong to an innocent user who had unknowingly bounced the signal from another location. 'Think about when you post a letter and it goes from sender to sorting office before passing on to the recipient. The sorting office is a proxy. And there could be a chain of these proxies. I can sort you out a proxy if you want to get Netflix films that aren't available in the UK.'

'No thanks. So we could be facing a bunch of sorting offices, right? So if we got the Germany computer, it would lead us to another that could be in Brazil. And from there we might follow a trail to Canada. And all these people using these computers would have nothing to do with our man. They wouldn't even know their computers had been used.'

'That's right. A proxy server would allow both perps to stay in contact and to connect their randomisers, so each can see the result of the other's spin. But Saturday man could be anywhere. There's even cloud proxies. Want to hear about that?'

'No. But there is a chance there is no proxy, right? The

Germany computer could be the one we want. Perhaps we need to find it.'

'That's not going to be easy. It means contacting the internet service provider to cough up the address of whoever has that IP. If they don't want to, we'd have to go through the German police. That's a headache all on its own. Now imagine we go through that hassle and find another computer in Peru, and Zimbabwe, and twenty other countries. If we've got three years and a million pounds spare, let's do it. I bagsy any trips to the Bahamas.'

Liz groaned. 'Tell me there's a silver lining.'

'You know I was building up to it, right? The techs found a piece of code that wasn't hidden or muddled. It was just a copyright watermark. The randomiser is owned by a company called IronClaw Digital. They make video games, and they're based in Attercliffe, right here in Sheffield. I can come pick you up right now, or do you want to head into the office for a Team Ten first?'

Bennet started to stir. She covered the microphone in case Boeson heard a male noise, especially a groan. 'Let me call you back in one minute,' she said, and hung up.

Bennet's sleepy face was overcome with sudden shock, and she knew he'd also just remembered last night. She almost laughed at his embarrassment, which immediately killed her own. 'Chess isn't this awkward afterwards,' he said, sitting up.

'One of us has to emigrate now, I guess. But not me. We have a good lead in the case and I need to jump all over it.'

'Yeah. Okay. Cool. So, what happens next? With us?'

Her memory of the lovemaking was hazy and incomplete, but she knew it had definitely happened. There was something cool about barely remembered, drunken sex, which hadn't happened since she was a teenager. He looked like he was suffering more, was barely able to look at her, and that made it easier for her.

'Don't be so embarrassed. We're adults. We chose to do what we did. Let's just have breakfast and try not to act like awkward teenagers.'

Bennet nodded and headed to the bathroom. He took his two pillows, to cover front and rear, and it made her laugh. While he was gone, she called Boeson back and told him to host the Team Ten at work, without her. She would visit IronClaw herself shortly and update him afterwards. He didn't like that, but didn't argue. She was the boss.

'And you're coming with me,' she told Bennet when he returned. 'After you cook my breakfast.'

CHAPTER FIFTY-FOUR

IronClaw Digital was at the end of Whitworth Road, which ran between Attercliffe Police Station and the English Institute of Sport, a campus of Sheffield Hallam University. It was an old three-storey red-brick building that seemed anathema to modern video games. It had once been an old factory of some ilk.

Liz was out of the car almost before turning off the engine, and Bennet had to call after her as she stomped across the car park. 'Stop. Pause. Breathe.'

She stopped. 'Oh, I remember. Time is a blessing and I should drink heartily.'

'Now let's walk there slowly. The building and the people inside are going nowhere in the next sixty seconds.'

The lobby had two receptions, one for IronClaw on the first floor and one for a martial arts studio above the second. The reception dedicated to violence was dark and empty because their trading hours were in the evenings. There was a pretty woman waiting at IronClaw's desk.

After a chat with her, they waited. Liz had expected the company to be pretty small, which showed what she knew about the video game industry. From a flyer on the wall she learned that IronClaw had forty-seven staff and two subsidiaries in France, but was itself a subsidiary and the parent company, American-based Forethought Labs, brought in revenue of $600 million last year.

'Stop pacing,' Bennet told her. Liz froze, unaware she'd been edgy.

The guy who came down the stairs was middle-aged, shorter than average and a little chubby. He had thick hair around the sides and back of his head, but none on top. 'John Hackney, general manager,' he said as he stuck out a hand towards Bennet. Liz noticed the patchy white spots of vitiligo on his hands and neck as the two men shook.

'DCI Miller,' Liz said, also extending a hand. She'd said it just to let Hackney know she wasn't some sidekick, because he'd zeroed in on his male visitor.

Hackney looked her up and down, stared at her outstretched hand, and reluctantly shook it. Then he looked at Bennet. 'Let's go upstairs.'

In the short corridor at the top of the stairs, long windows exposed the heart of IronClaw's operation. It looked like any regular office, Liz thought, which was a surprise. She'd imagined a games studio to be full of teenagers and twenty-somethings lounging around on beanbags, playing games. The staff were at computer desks and were a mix between twenty and fifty years of age.

The work floor was spacious and open-plan, modern-looking except for a dotting of pillars that were exposed bricks painted green. Against one wall was a trio of doors marked: storage, kitchen, toilets. The manager's office was a square in a corner and seemed to have been created by simply placing two walls at right angles, one of which was mostly glass and killed any privacy. Hackney led them inside, watched all the way by curious eyes.

The office was homely, apart from two file cabinets and a giant roller whiteboard against one of the corner walls. On the other and on the desk were many framed photographs. On a shelf were various mugs with pictures on them and, strangely, a saw in a glass case.

Seeing the detectives scrutinise the room, Hackney said, 'The saw was my dad's. It's a musical saw. He didn't have money for expensive instruments.'

John Hackney then pointed at a photo on the wall. Four men who strangely looked similar. 'Me and my brothers. Two sets of twins just two years apart, my poor mother. That's Paul, George–'

'And Ringo?' Bennet said. 'The Beatles?'

Liz almost laughed, thinking he was being sarcastic, until John said, 'Eric. Eric is brother four, but yes, you're right about the inspiration. That photo right there is my father with John and Paul.'

The detectives moved closer to a black-and-white picture above the musical saw. Sure enough, a man they didn't recognise was posing with a young John Lennon and Paul McCartney.

'The Cavern Club in Liverpool. Where my parents are from. My dad knew John and Paul a little before they became superstars. If only he'd been asked to join the band, eh?'

Hackney sat behind his desk and lifted another photo. It showed a boy of about twelve, grinning. 'My Lonnie. I split from his mother. She found out I was gay. Well, I say she found out – I told her. It took me till I was forty to realise. I thought I'd get that out front so there are no surprises.'

'We have no opinion on that. Now, if we could get down to business.' She sat in front of the desk while Bennet stood beside her. Hackney didn't seem to like this. Liz opened her laptop and showed Hackney the randomiser software.

'Have you seen this before?'

Hackney looked shocked. 'That's one of ours,' he said.

'We know. Can you tell us where this randomiser is from? Is it part of a game?'

'It's not a randomiser. That's the term for a game mod – modification – that changes static portions–'

'I don't know your world,' Liz cut in. 'Please, did your company make this?'

Hackney delved into his desk, rummaged around, and hauled out a drinks coaster, which he slid across to Liz. It seemed like a piece of promotional material for a game called Pirate Mutiny, with a picture of the front cover of an Xbox version. The cartoon showed a pirate walking the plank of a metal ship bellowing steam from stacks while sharks thrashed in the sea below. Behind the pirate were others, pointing massive guns at him.

'Pirate Mutiny is a steampunk game developed at our Canadian office. The treasure chests are mini-games, so basically a game found within the main game. You find these chests scattered around the game world.'

'So someone has extracted this mini-game from the larger game?'

'Yes. Cracking games is easy for hackers these days. And real big business.' Hackney leaned closer for a good look at Liz's screen. 'This one you have has been modified. In Pirate Mutiny, the player wins goodies like gold or weapons. But on yours those symbols have all been changed for words. So, ironically, this piece of software you have from our pirate game was pirated. Where did you get this? Is it part of a crime? What do *vegetable*, *kidnap* and *prostitute* mean?'

'We can't go into that. What we need to know is, can you

open up this software, since you made it? Crack it again? We want a full list of the words on the three parchment reels. What kind of time frame would we be looking at? I understand the code for this game underwent something called obfuscation.'

'Yes. We basically gave the code a code, if that makes sense. To deter hackers, or at least make them spend a lot longer than normal to steal our work. But we own the code, of course, so we have the decryption key. I can get that done for you right now, while you wait.'

Liz said that would be great. Hackney lifted his phone, dialled a three-number extension, and out on the work floor a young woman in a long skirt and long-sleeved blouse answered the call. 'I need you in here, Lucy.'

Lucy Prosser, who was about twenty-five and without make-up, hung up and crossed the work floor. A little nervous, she entered the office and eyeballed her boss's guests. She relaxed when she knew she wasn't in trouble. Hackney explained what he wanted from her, and she was happy to oblige.

She took them to her workstation, where she plugged Liz's laptop into her own computer. 'How long will it take?' Liz asked.

'Just minutes.'

And it did. She worked while they watched, until she had a screen full of code and had scrolled to the part she needed. She tapped the screen. 'Everything that's in speech marks here are the words that appear on the parchment scrolls.'

'Can you step aside, please, and don't look.'

Lucy got up, moved away, and Liz took her seat. Standing behind the monitor, so she couldn't see the screen, Lucy said, 'There's a piece of code, I think about eight lines down, that controls the random generation. It appears the randomiser, as you call it, isn't totally random, at least at first. The original code has been changed so that it is random until each reel symbol, or word, has featured once. I saw the word *scientist*. In the third parchment section. So, for example, *scientist* would appear at some point by random, but wouldn't feature again until all the other words had had a turn. Do you understand?'

Liz was too engrossed in the screen to answer. It displayed thirty words, listed alphabetically in three columns. Her eyes locked onto column one, four spots down: CAR BATTERY. Now there was no doubt: the randomiser was the tool the offenders had used to determine their crimes. Past, and future.

ACID, ARSON, CEO
BABYSEAT, BURGLE, CHEF
CAR, CRUSH, CHILD
CAR BATTERY, DEFAME, CRIMINAL
DOG, DEFRAUD, PROSTITUTE
FOOTBALL, EXPOSE, POLICE
HANDBAG, KIDNAP, SCIENTIST
TEDDYBEAR, RAPE, SPORTSMAN
TRUMPET, STALK, TEACHER
VEGETABLE, STEAL, TRAMP

CHAPTER FIFTY-FIVE

Hackney vacated his office so Bennet and Liz could take it over for a time. With pen and paper, they listed all the words in the three columns then swapped the order. They already had a starting point: TRUMPET, STALK and CHEF, which had been displayed on the randomiser when they found it. They spoke aloud as they shifted words around to make connections, fill gaps, join dots.

Bennet said, 'The Range Rover owner is a convicted criminal. So, that one, look.'

'Yes. And here, look. Defraud. Our boy lied to get the dog, remember.'

'Good. And this one. A pub owner could be a considered a CEO.'

When it was done, they had a new, much scarier list. The three columns were headed: *weapon, offence* and *victim*.

Saturday the 8th – CAR, STEAL, CRIMINAL
Sunday the 9th – TEDDYBEAR, ARSON, CHILD
Saturday the 15th – BABYSEAT, **?,** TRAMP
Sunday the 16th – HANDBAG, RAPE, TEACHER

Saturday the 22nd – FOOTBALL, **?**, CEO
Sunday the 23rd – DOG, DEFRAUD, SCIENTIST
Saturday the 29th – CAR BATTERY, **?**, POLICE
Sunday the 30th – TRUMPET, STALK, CHEF

But they had one problem. There had been two killings and one attempted, but the word *murder* or a synonym did not feature. If another entry from the *offence* reel had been employed, why had it been swapped? And why for the ultimate of crimes?

'Perhaps the murders weren't meant to be murders,' Bennet said. 'James Breakspear was already a corpse. Maybe Paul Yard, the CEO of the King Royal, was killed by accident. The word *crush* is there, so perhaps you were attributed that word. The kids who found you unconscious said the masked man was about to lift the car battery up and drop it on your head.'

Liz shook that same head. 'I don't buy it. Yard was choked to death. *Choke* or *strangle* aren't on the list. If you shove a rubber football right down someone's throat, you know you're leaving behind a corpse. Same goes for dropping thirty pounds of heavy battery onto someone's head.'

'True. And none of the words that could go where we put question marks fits with murder.'

'Also, none of this explains why Breakspear had been dead for three years and was killed by a stab wound. No, we're missing something. Something to do with the locations? Something that means the people who died were meant to. But what?'

Bennet shrugged. 'Horrible as it sounds, we may have to wait until Saturday to find the next clue. Or hope our perps get arrested for something else and give up their DNA.'

'We can get a pretty good idea of what's to come. Each word has to feature once before it can be repeated. There are ten words on each reel, and eight have been used over the last four weeks. That leaves two.'

Liz wrote them down. The remaining *weapons* were: ACID and VEGETABLE. Because *murder* had been substituted for three of the 'crimes', there were a possible five to come: CRUSH, ABUSE, EXPOSE, BURGLE, and KIDNAP. The missing *victims* were: PROSTITUTE and SPORTSPERSON. Boeson, of course, had spun the randomiser found at the bedsit and gotten VEGETABLE, KIDNAP, PROSTITUTE.

No one yet knew how this spin, or the loss of his laptop, was going to affect Sunday man next week, if they hadn't caught the bastard by then.

Bennet said, 'Two spins left gives us a small number of combinations, at least. A sportsperson could be burgled, which is plausible. But how do you crush a prostitute with a vegetable?'

'A barrel of vegetables dropped from above, for instance. There could be any way to tweak whatever combination comes up. We had a CEO killed by a football. Plus, they're open to interpretations, as we saw with the teacher handbag rape, which forced a redo.'

'Sunday man seems the more inert of the two. Teddy Burn could have been a lot worse. He could have set fire to that little girl with a flaming teddy bear. Whatever Saturday man gets, he's not going to take the easy route.'

Liz agreed. 'He's murdered or attempted to three times on the trot now. He'll surely go for a fourth. But why? Why is he killing when he doesn't have to? Simple evil streak? Or something else we're missing?'

Bennet shrugged. 'There's no way to prevent this. I'd say it's lucky we only have two crimes left to come, but it doesn't help us prevent them. We're now looking at the whole of Sheffield as a playground for these psychos, since they seem to have given up their jaunt east and moved back west. How many sportsmen and women are there in Sheffield? How many prostitutes? They can't all be protected.'

'I'm worried about what happens afterwards. When all the spins are done. Is it mission over? Or does it restart and we have a whole new round of crimes? And next time things could be a whole lot worse. We could have a raped child, murder by acid, anything. We need to catch these bastards, and before next weekend.'

'Long before, Liz. This list confirms that the handbag rape was a fudge and Sunday man had to redo it. Before his next go with the randomiser. Your attack wasn't because you were a threat.'

'I know. I see it. Police officer and car battery. Saturday man failed, and in six days he's got another crime to commit. But first he has to redo the murder of a police officer. It could be any one of thousands of us.'

'It could be you again. Your protection needs to be upped. Maybe you need to step back from this investigation.'

'You're joking, right? Run away as if scared? I'm staying front and centre. I will catch these bastards. Me. But if it worries you, I promise to keep an eye out for car batteries.'

CHAPTER FIFTY-SIX

As they were crossing the lobby of IronClaw, on their way out, Bennet said, 'I think Mr Hackney fancied me.'

'That's uncommon ego from you,' Liz said. 'Thank you.'

'For what?'

'For trying to make me feel better about Hackney trying to ignore me in there. At first I assumed it was because he thought all detectives should be men. But no. He just dislikes women in general.'

'Half the workers in there were women.'

'And every single one of them wore clothing that covered the legs and arms. No make-up.'

As they reached the exit, a shout stopped them. The young woman, Lucy Prosser, was bounding down the stairs. They met her at the bottom.

'The skin is different,' she said, a little breathless from her run.

'Skin?' Liz said.

'Your randomiser. It's the vertical slice version, but it underwent changes.'

Vertical slice was a term Liz knew. 'You mean the version of the game you showed to stakeholders? But not the finished product?'

'Yes. We improved the artwork of the assets for the vertical slice, but it underwent additional changes later in production. In your version of the randomiser, the treasure chest graphic was red wood. Look.'

Lucy showed them her phone. She had loaded the internet and googled 'Pirate Mutiny game treasure chest'. In the screenshot, the chest had rounded edges and cracks and was the normal brown of wood, not red. It wasn't the same chest from their randomiser. 'This is the gold master. The released version.'

Now Liz understood. 'You're saying the randomiser we found was not taken from a hacked version of the released game? Our version was pre-release?'

'Yes.'

'And the code wasn't hacked from your servers or made available on the internet at any point before release?'

'Oh no. We have serious hacker protection. I mean, we're all programmers, we know what we're doing. And you mean open source, right? No, open source games are free. No one would ever pay. And they're not the best graphically. We would never make parts of our game open source.'

Liz needed to sit down. If the randomiser found on the laptop had been torn from Pirate Mutiny when the game was in development and top secret, then the killer could have gotten his hands on it only one way.

As an employee. He worked here.

CHAPTER FIFTY-SEVEN

Liz and Bennet accompanied Lucy into Hackney's office. He didn't look happy at the return of his guests. Liz said, 'I would like your employee list.'

He was of course puzzled, and Lucy quickly explained. But rather than shock, Hackney expressed scorn. 'Seems like a bit of a reach. Did you know the video game industry is more lucrative than the movie and music industry combined? The big games, what we call AAA, have budgets rivalling the most expensive Hollywood movies.'

'I understand,' Liz said. 'But I'd still–'

'I'm not sure if you do, detective. Making a major game needs hundreds, sometimes thousands of programmers, designers, modellers, artists, animators, writers, translators, sound engineers, musicians, to name just a few. Production sometimes involves many development companies across the world. IronClaw itself is a subsidiary, and the parent company has offices in the USA, France, the UK and Canada.

'That's not even including advance review copies and all the playtesters. Then there's friends and family. Nobody is supposed to show off our work to their social circle, but it happens. The sheer number of people who could have had access to that mini-game code is... beyond checkable.'

'As I tried to say before you interrupted, I understand all of that. And it doesn't matter. The people we're after are committing crimes in Sheffield. One rents a bedsit in Sheffield. I believe he works for IronClaw Digital, right here in Sheffield. And that, Mr Hackney, is absolutely checkable. So. How many staff have you got and how many are on duty?'

'Fine. Who am I to argue? Forty-seven employees, twenty-one on duty and in the building right now. You want to talk to them all?'

'Yes. And I want their DNA. I have already called my people down here to test each and every one of them. It should interrupt a working day for no more than just an hour. I'd like you to inform all your staff, and let them know we don't want anyone leaving the building until it's done. We'll call them into this office, say, two or three at a time, and do the tests right here.'

Hackney considered this. 'I thought you were planning to shut us down for a few days. But what you suggest is fine. Okay. Well, Lucy and I are here. Start with us. I'll go first and show my staff it's no big deal.'

'Brilliant. Thank you.'

'No,' Bennet said. Everyone looked at him. He was staring through the window, onto the work floor. Liz stepped close and he whispered to her. 'Handsome young man at the desk by the tall plant. Looks not a million miles from the guy on the roller disco CCTV. And he hasn't stopped watching us. Sideways glances, constantly.'

Liz had watched the CCTV and agreed the young man was a fair fit, and he had serious curiosity about what was going on in the manager's office. He was tall and slim, very handsome. About twenty, which was about the age of the guy the Polish kid, Lukasz Babiarz, had described. She turned to Hackney.

'The young chap sitting at the desk near the plant. Call him in here, please.'

Hackney didn't question it. He picked up his phone and hit a single button. Liz watched the young man pick up his phone out on the floor.

'Markus, come on in here, please.'

The young man said something and put down his phone. Hackney hung up and said, 'He's just going to the toilet first.'

Markus headed for the toilet, fast, and vanished inside. Liz and Bennet left the office and approached the door Markus had gone through. Liz pushed it open to expose two more: ladies and gents. Bennet stepped past her and was about to push open the door to the gents when a dull, metallic thud sounded from somewhere beyond.

Bennet kicked open the door to the gents, barely poked his head inside, then turned and darted past Liz.

'He's gone out the window.'

She realised what the metallic thud had been, because she heard a version of it every time she went home. The clang of feet on metal steps. Markus was fleeing down a fire exit.

CHAPTER FIFTY-EIGHT

The fire exit staircase led into a small car park round back. Once through the door and on the landing, Bennet saw that Markus was already halfway across the tarmac, pelting. Bennet didn't shout – had he ever yelled for a suspect to stop and been granted that wish? Instead, he bolted down the steps.

By the time Bennet was on the ground, Markus had reached a large patch of grass behind the English Institute of Sport. He ran parallel to Coleridge Road, towards the trees and the train tracks about a hundred metres away.

Bennet had studied a map en route here and knew the River Don lay beyond the train tracks. Coleridge Road crossed the water and the tracks by bridge and there was a smaller bridge about two hundred metres from it, but Markus seemed to be aiming for a spot dead centre of the two. If he continued along that path, he'd hit the river and a dead end.

This gave Bennet confidence, but he knew he'd face a problem. Bennet was taller, but the kid had lightness, cardio, and desperation on his side. The kid would reach the cover of the trees long before Bennet got anywhere close. What would he do then?

Perhaps he knew exactly the outlay of the land and his intention was to move, hidden, alongside the river. Perhaps he figured his pursuer wouldn't follow if Markus leaped into the water.

Bennet glanced around to see if Liz was following, and he was happy she wasn't. She was at the top of the fire exit, standing amongst surprised programmers and trying to shepherd them off the landing and back indoors. For a moment he felt silly chasing a young man in broad daylight with an audience.

Markus bolted into the trees and was gone. Bennet aimed for the same spot, but his eyes scanned left and right, seeking movement beyond the branches and trunks. He saw none and figured the kid was going into the river. When Bennet entered the gloominess of the thin line of woods alongside the river, he paused to pick up a fallen branch. His head felt light and his chest was burning. This suddenly seemed like a bad idea.

He pushed forward, slow and careful, branch raised. Soon the trees ended and he was at the top of a steep, rocky bank leading to the water. Markus was nowhere. Bennet wasn't sure the kid could have swam across the Don so quickly, but he swept his eyes across the land on the other side. It belonged to a scrapyard. If Markus had somehow swum like a shark and clambered up the far bank, he now had a hundred trashed cars to hide behind.

Only now that Bennet's head and chest had stopped pounding did he realise his phone was ringing.

'Liam, what the hell are you doing?' Liz yelled down the line. 'He could have a knife. I can't see you. Move back, get away.'

Bennet didn't get away; he made his way carefully down the rocky slope, to the water's edge. 'He's gone, Liz, I lost him. Get people swarming over a scrapyard here. It looks like part of an industrial estate. Invade it. Check along Coleridge Road, too, both sides of the bridge–'

'Liam, stop, I've called it in already. Now get out of the woods before he jumps you.'

Bennet spun at a noise behind him, but relaxed as he saw a middle-aged woman up at the top of the embankment, with a dog and a clear plastic bag of elderberries. Before he could ask if she'd seen anyone running, she made a hasty retreat at the sight of a sweaty man with a wooden club.

'I'm coming back,' he told Liz, then hung up the phone. But for at least a minute he remained in place, eyes scanning for movement amongst the mounds and lines of scrap vehicles on the far side of the river.

CHAPTER FIFTY-NINE

Once the show was over, John Hackney ordered his people back to their workstations. Liz instructed him to cordon off Markus Darowska's workstation and make sure no one touched any part of it. She headed out to her car for protective equipment and on the way called Boeson to arrange for a mob of detectives and forensics scientists to attend the scene. When she opened the boot, she was startled by a voice behind her. It was Hackney.

'I can't believe this,' he said. 'I hope this doolally thing of yours isn't going to mess with our work. Do you need to do a search of the whole building and everyone else's desks and all that?'

'Possibly. I'll be taking Markus's computer away.'

'It's just a work computer.'

'I still need it. Has he got a locker?'

'We have lockers downstairs, yes. I haven't got the key for his. No clue if he's even got anything in there.'

'Don't worry about the lock.' Liz extracted vinyl gloves and put them in her pocket, and a roll of police tape. She also got her Nikon out of its case. Hackney watched. As she walked back across the car park, Hackney by her side and professing his disbelief that Markus could be a criminal, she stopped to take a picture of the building.

'Is one of these vehicles Markus's?'

'He's got a pushbike. It's by the lockers.'

'Does he have access to a motor vehicle?'

'No.'

That was puzzling. Markus, if he was their man, had been able to commit all his crimes by riding a pushbike around Sheffield? That didn't seem logical.

Inside reception, Hackney led her to a large alcove she hadn't spotted before. Here were the lockers and four pushbikes leaning against each other. 'Number eighteen locker and that red bike,' Hackney said.

Liz took a picture of the lockers and the bikes and used a length of tape to secure the whole alcove. 'I don't want anyone going inside this tape or touching the bikes or lockers.'

'What happens now?' Hackney asked.

'Now I need to do my doolally thing and question every one of your staff.'

CHAPTER SIXTY

Markus Darowska was nineteen and the address he'd registered with IronClaw was a place called The Shorn Sheep in Maesbury Marsh, Shropshire, some seventy miles south-west. However, upon searching his workstation, Liz found a key fob with the address of the bedsit in Grimesthorpe where they'd found the laptop. Bingo.

His desk drawer contained no other personal items, and upon busting open his locker detectives found the same story. Markus's workmates confirmed they'd never seen him bring anything to work other than lunch in a disposable bag and a disposable water bottle. Liz looked around the back of the building and found two cars parked near a bin store, but those belonged to staff. If Markus did have access to a vehicle, no one knew about it.

In fact there was little his colleagues could add. They knew he'd moved to Sheffield six months ago when he got the job with IronClaw, but nobody was aware of the Grimesthorpe bedsit. He'd never volunteered any information about his family or social circle, had never joined the gang on nights out. He had no Facebook, Instagram, Twitter or any other social media account.

It had taken three weeks for anyone to learn he had a little sister. Even Hackney claimed there had been little said during the interview for the job. On his CV under INTERESTS it said simply 'computers'. Hackney hadn't found out much more about the kid in the half-year since.

Because of his pretty face, at least four of the IronClaw girls had asked him on dates, but he'd refused and there was a rumour he was gay. If Markus himself had heard it, he never let on and certainly hadn't confirmed or denied it. He never eyed up the males or females, had never mentioned lovers past or present.

There just wasn't much to this quiet young man, and his work colleagues treated him like a piece of the furniture and got on with their work and their own lives. He had quite a pronounced stutter and his colleagues figured shame and frustration had made him a loner.

But he clearly knew someone beyond IronClaw's walls. This begged the question of why their crimes had been committed only at weekends. Could it be that his partner lived in another city and had to commute? There was no evidence that anyone other than Darowska had stayed at his bedsit. There wasn't even real evidence he was the man they sought. Running didn't prove guilt. The door key found proved only that he had access to the bedsit.

Two hours in, Liz didn't have much more to further the investigation. But then she got a phone call.

DNA from Markus's computer keyboard had been rushed through the lab and a profile obtained. It matched the offender profile from the valve guard found at the Grimesthorpe bedsit. Now they had confirmation that Markus not only had access to the bedsit, he'd been there. The place was his. The randomiser was his. He was definitely their guy. They'd found one.

Kind of. He was still missing. Bennet was still out helping

the search team scour the local area, but she was certain their prey was long gone. There was nothing much more she could do here, so she turned her hopes to Markus's family and his former home. There, surely, would be the evidence and the clues that would put her, Darowska and a pair of handcuffs in the same room.

She called Bennet and explained her plan. She thought he'd jump at the chance to accompany her to Shropshire, but he didn't like the idea. 'That's a long trip that might be for nothing. Dump the small stuff. Delegate more, remember?'

'If the station toilets do get blocked, I'll do just that,' she said. 'But I want to do this. Markus is nineteen and a loner, and now he knows Sheffield is a dangerous place for him. There's every chance he could have gone running home with his tail between his legs. I'm not missing this for the world. You knew damn well I'd say that, and I know damn well you want to come. So get your butt back here.'

'Yes, ma'am.'

CHAPTER SIXTY-ONE

Maesbury Marsh was a tiny hamlet and The Shorn Sheep was its biggest building, a ten-bedroomed Georgian guesthouse by the canal. The Darowska family had owned and operated it for twenty years, having moved there when Tina Darowska was pregnant with her firstborn, Markus.

As evening approached and Boeson turned into the car park, Liz caught sight of a monument sign. Atop a brick plinth, it was circular wood with the name of the guesthouse curving around the top and a cartoon aerial map of the hamlet below. There were faint black lines across the map, as if someone had done their best to rub out graffiti.

Tina Darowska had become known for her bubbly personality and eagerness to welcome strangers, which was on show when the current and former detectives exited the car. They saw a tall and handsome woman with a genuine smile, and she held her right hand in front of her as if to make sure it wasn't missed. She was minus the thumb and little finger, and perhaps wanted to make sure her guests didn't get a surprise down the line.

But upon seeing Liz, Boeson and Bennet emerge, suited and

serious, her bubbly exterior wilted. 'You're police,' she said. 'And not local. So this is about Markus, isn't it?'

'Yes,' Liz said. She introduced all three of them, but Bennet's name wasn't preceded by a police rank.

'Well, ma'am,' Tina said, correctly addressing a female officer of Liz's rank, 'if Mr Bennet here isn't a policeman, he doesn't need to be present. He can enjoy my gardens. Come inside, please.'

Liz caught a modicum of flippancy that seemed to say, come, let me hear your silliness so I can shoot it down in flames. They followed the guesthouse owner inside. In a painting-lined hallway, Tina pointed at a door at the far end and told Bennet he could use it to access the rear garden. 'We'll go into the dining room. This way, please.'

The quartet split. Bennet looked like a kid uninvited from a party, but made no complaint as he walked away. In an elegant but empty dining room, Tina faced her guests across a table with a Union flag tablecloth. 'Please explain your business here today.'

Remarkably, upon learning that her eldest child was a suspect in a series of terrible crimes, including murder, she visibly relaxed. It was as if she'd expected news of his death and anything else was good news. 'Have you got proof of this?'

'We're building a case,' Liz told her. 'Are you going to ask what crimes we're talking about?'

'No, I'm going to make tea.' And Tina quickly departed to do so.

Both detectives knew the lady needed a moment alone. But they were also suspicious, so Boeson crept close to the kitchen, just to confirm Tina was making tea and not destroying evidence. His thumbs up said all was good. And he returned to his seat.

'She's defiant,' he said. 'I've seen it a bunch. She loves him so much she's not going to believe he could ever do such a thing. She'll be screaming his innocence even as a judge hands down a life sentence.'

'I've seen that before too.' Through a long window Liz saw Bennet on the back terrace. He approached a young girl who wore jeans and a T-shirt.

When Tina returned, it was bearing tea and evidence that her make-up had been smudged by tears and reapplied. The happy eyes were sad. She no longer looked like a mother about to deflect any and all evidence that her offspring was less than a saint.

'You need to search my home, don't you? You think I could be hiding Markus?'

Liz was honest. 'If I thought there was a chance, we would have searched already. I could tell by your reaction to what we told you that you have no idea of where Markus is. But I will need to search the house at some point. It's not because I think you're hiding anything.'

'Well, although his sister, Dana, has his room now, his computer desk is set up as always and he still has a set of drawers with all his stuff. The room is how he left it apart from her few added touches. In case he comes back to stay for a while.'

'Then we'll get to that after we have a little chat.'

'I want to help my son, Ms Miller. Maybe you're wrong about him and maybe you're not. So I'll help you realise he's innocent, or I'll help you catch a murderer. Whatever it takes to get the truth out. I'll answer all your questions, show you whatever you need. But first let's start with exactly what it is you think he's done and why.'

Out on the back terrace, Bennet stopped a few feet behind a little girl of about thirteen, who was taking apart an electric patio heater that was as tall as her. He looked around, but saw no one watching.

'Hello. Can I ask what you're doing? Those things are expensive. Does your mum know you're out here?'

The girl turned to face him. She tutted, but also smiled. 'What, you think I'm wrecking it?'

'If you were twice as old and in a boiler suit, I wouldn't. But... yeah, to be honest.'

Another tut. 'It's the wiring for the reset button, okay? Won't work without a reset first. Simple.'

He would have laughed, except her line was a little advanced for a joke. And she certainly didn't look unused to the screwdriver she wielded. 'Are you serious?'

'I know what I'm doing, sir. I'm good with technology. Mum always says people don't understand me.'

She also sounded pretty mature. He had been annoyed at having to come out here and away from the action, but now he saw a chance to grab information, even if his source was still at school. 'Like your brother, you mean? Markus? You're a whizz with hardware and he's a whizz with software, right?'

A third tut. 'Not better than me, he's not. I mean on an age basis. My level at my age beats how good he was at my age. He can't do this stuff, but I know computers. I'm better than him.'

Now she sounded like a kid. 'What about video games? He programs them. Can you do that?'

'For sure. Better than he was at my age. We were always making games up. The old-fashioned games though. They're the best. We don't like these flashy new video games. I mean, shooting zombies, that's not a game, is it?'

'But Markus makes the flashy new ones. He doesn't like his job?'

'Oh, don't know about that. I'm just talking about games. Zombie shooting isn't a game. Chess is a real game. I like chess. Markus likes chess. Look.'

She pointed down the garden, where Bennet saw a giant chessboard. Bigger than his own at home. 'What about interactive games? Markus like those? You know, like where you have to do things. Forfeits or challenges. Dares. Physical things.'

Another tut. 'It's not any old chess, that. You can't get bored of this one. Me and Markus made this one special. Come on, I'll show you.'

Tina Darowska did not like questions about her son's activity since he left home, but Liz read nothing suspicious in this. Markus's move to Sheffield had been abrupt and nobody had seen it coming, and he'd admitted his new job and new bedsit only the day before he shipped out. Tina had been happy for him, but very perturbed at the suddenness of it.

But since that day he hadn't contacted his family. He had left no address and had never had a mobile phone, and although they knew his job involved computer programming, Markus had never mentioned the name IronClaw Digital. Even on the day he walked out, Tina and Markus's father hadn't pushed him for information; they had never been helicopter parents and had always tried to make their kids independent and aware that they'd have to fend for themselves one day.

They believed that Markus's rashness was because of this. In their opinion, he had secured a job and a home all on his own in order to prove to himself, and them, that he could function without help.

This was why Tina was reluctant to answer these questions. All parents experienced a day when their children flew the nest, but it was common for them to be part of the process. They would help with packing and might visit their baby's new home, and would usually be kept abreast of developments, especially in the first few weeks.

What mother wouldn't feel slighted and unwanted if a son left the family home almost out of the blue and didn't seek help and didn't make contact for a long time afterwards? Suddenly he was gone, and they didn't know where or even really why, and they had no means to get hold of him.

When Liz turned the conversation to Markus's upbringing, Tina was happier to talk. She admitted he'd always been a loner and even had a theory about why.

'His stutter and low self-esteem were what made him shun friends,' she said. 'Physical friends, that is. He preferred digital ones. There's no stutter when he's typing words or even when he speaks into a microphone. Face-to-face communication has never been his thing, even with family. From an early age he couldn't look anyone in the eye, and Dana, his sister, was his only real friend, although she's much younger and wasn't around until he was six.'

'Autism?' Liz said.

Tina shook her head. 'I wondered, but we gave him a test when he was three and he wasn't diagnosed. It wasn't shyness, either, because he had a real confidence when he wanted something. I remember one day when he was about twelve and... Anyway, I think Markus knows people, he knows how they act and react and how to get what he wants from them and...'

Tina sipped tea. She looked like she was buying time, considering the impact of what she would say next. And how it would reflect on her. 'If I'm honest, I believe Markus thinks most people are beneath him. He never had time for others, except his family. He liked his online friends. *Only* his online friends. Perhaps that's because online you can adopt a persona, can't you? Pretend you're someone else. Someone better.'

This rang true. One of Markus's work colleagues had said something similar: often he'd only talk to them when answering questions, but he never seemed reserved or shy, more annoyed. As the colleague had put it, he 'treated us like cold call salesmen at the front door. You just want to get rid of them.'

'So he lived a mostly online world?' Liz said. 'It explains his skill with a computer. Do you know any of his online friends? Did he have any in particular? Perhaps overseas or in other parts of England?'

'There was one, yes. I don't know his name. I always could tell it was the same person because although they mostly chatted by text, they'd greet each other the same way. I could always hear Markus shout it. It was a greeting in a different language each time. Just for fun, I think. So when Markus shouted a strange word, I'd know he was online with his friend.'

'And he still communicates with this friend? Might this person know where he is?'

'I couldn't say. In fact, I think they stopped chatting once Markus got his new job in Sheffield, some six months ago now. He kind of gave up his online world altogether, which I was glad about. Now he's living in the normal world. I like that.'

She didn't appear to like it. Liz said, 'I'd like to know more about this online friend. Perhaps there's information on his computer. Can we have a look at his room now?'

'I dare you to do a handstand.'

'Really?' Bennet said. 'I'm an old man, you know? But okay. Get ready to call an ambulance.'

Bennet pitched forward, up onto his hands. His keys fell out of his pocket and hit the grass a second before his knees did, hard. His ungraceful fall and grunt of annoyance made Dana laugh. He got up and slapped grass from his hands. 'So now I can make my move?'

'You did the dare,' Dana said. 'So yes. First move of the game, always a dare.'

The chessboard was made up of white, square paving slabs and green spaces of grass. Bennet lifted a wooden pawn the size of a cat and moved it two squares, onto a slab. Every slab had a question mark in chalk.

'Are you sure you want to move to a slab? Question marks are all dares. You can't move that pawn again unless you do a dare. If it's on grass, you're okay.'

Bennet moved the pawn back one space, onto grass. Dana said, 'Also, if you want to take a piece, even on grass, you have to do a dare. You have to tell me you're going to take it, and I give you a dare, and if you don't do the dare, you can't take it.'

Dana moved her first pawn onto a slab. Bennet said, 'Right, that's a dare. Okay, I dare you to jump to the moon.'

She laughed. 'No, you can't do silly stuff. Normally we write all the dares out and put them in a hat, so it's random. That way I could end up getting my own silly one. So just choose something not silly.'

'And this is the kind of game you like? Old-fashioned games with new little gimmicks added?'

'What's a gimmick?'

'A twist. A change in the rules.'

'Oh yes. We used to do dominoes and tiddlywinks and all sorts. All sorts. We both like the old ones. I wish Markus would come home so we can play more.'

'A lot of the old classics involve dice. Did you have any games with dice and gimmicks, like dares?'

Dana clapped gleefully. 'Oh, yes, I know the game you mean.'

Markus still had a computer table and chest of drawers, as his mother had said, but the items had been pushed into one corner of the bedroom to make room for his little sister's takeover. Unbidden, Boeson rifled through the drawers while Tina loaded up the computer. She didn't object. Liz noticed all the books on the shelves were about programming. She also noticed something else.

'I see a lot of male clothing,' she said.

Tina glanced at an open cupboard, where garments hung. 'Yes,' she said. 'Markus left so abruptly he didn't take anything, not even a toothbrush. He said he'd buy what he needed while in Sheffield.'

Liz and Boeson glanced at each other, thinking the same thing. Tina could claim impatience and independence had fuelled Markus's abandonment of all his artefacts, but they had another opinion. Markus had wanted a sterile presence in Sheffield. Nothing recognisable to anyone else. Nothing that could be tied to him. Nothing with his DNA on it. It suggested his murderous campaign had been planned for a long time before he left home to embark upon it.

Tina clicked on a desktop shortcut. 'Markus thinks I don't know about this website because he hid it. But Dana took over this computer and started using the same website, and she put this shortcut here. I don't know much about it. But this is where you'll find his interaction with his online friend.'

Liz and Boeson were shocked to see the website CROAK CATALOGUE appear on the screen.

Liz said, 'Mrs Darowska, I think it might be best if you left us alone to view this. There might be something you don't want to see.'

She looked doubtful – how could Markus have anything to hide from her? But she relented. 'I will wait downstairs. Please don't take anything without informing me.'

When she was gone, Boeson sat at the desk. When he clicked on the LOGIN button, the username box automatically filled with 'MKus888'. In the password box was ******. Boeson hit ENTER and they were rewarded with a profile page.

'Jackpot,' Boeson said. Liz leaned closer, intrigued.

But there wasn't much to see. It seemed to list generic I-love-life interests and nothing else, and a line said MKus888's last login was, as his mother had stated, some six months ago. Liz was disappointed. Until Boeson pointed something out.

'Friends list. Just the one friend. That was easy, if this is our Saturday man.'

MKus888's sole pal on the website was Skiffle73, and his profile loaded upon a click. Unfortunately, all it told them was that he was male from the UK, either or both of which could be false.

Boeson opened a chat box between MKus888 and Skiffle73. 'Damn. I hoped their chat history would all be right there.'

Liz spotted a little icon in a corner. 'That says it's a save-chat button. The chat logs can be saved? We need those. Where would they be saved?'

'Possibly a secret file. But I can find it.'

As she watched, Boeson typed a message to Skiffle73: !"£$%^. Once it had been sent, he clicked the save-chat button. Boeson then accessed the File Explorer program and instructed it to search for !"£$%^.

'Got it,' he said after a minute or so. 'A hidden CSV file. Don't worry, I won't talk science. It's a text file. I think we're in.'

He opened the folder containing the file. It contained dozens of such files. Boeson clicked on one. Sure enough, they were presented by text of a conversation between Skiffle73 and MKus888.

There were some formatting issues, with certain words ruined by the insertion of strange symbols, but Liz could clearly see that the conversation between the two players was eyebrow-raising stuff.

'Sign into your email and send a copy of all these files to yourself,' she told him. 'Hopefully we'll find something about our case.'

CHAPTER SIXTY-TWO

'Meet me outside,' Bennet said. 'By the sign. Quick.'

'Quick? What happened to time is a blessing and drink heart–'

'Quick!'

He hung up before Liz could respond. She left Boeson to get a few more details from Tina, if possible, and headed out. Fast. Bennet was already across the car park, by the monument sign at the entrance to the car park.

'You sound like you found something good,' she said as she reached him. His answer was to point at the sign. He had a felt-tipped pen in his hand. She was puzzled.

'Markus and his sister used to play a game,' he said. 'They drew this.'

As she watched, he started to draw on the cartoon aerial map of Maesbury Marsh on the sign. He ran his pen across the pre-existing faint lines.

First, a square that encompassed the whole map. Then lines to turn it into a grid with a hundred squares. He looked round at her at this point, seeking a response. It was a shrug.

Then he drew wavy lines and pairs of diagonal parallel lines across the grid.

With a dropped jaw, she got it. 'Snakes and ladders.'

Using an art app on Boeson's iPad, Liz created a snakes and ladders board without the snakes or ladders. Then she superimposed it over a map of Sheffield. Next, she had to work out the scale.

On Sunday the 9th of August, Markus Darowska, the Sunday man, had taken his first throw of a dice, scoring a two and landing on Mundella Place. After each throw came a spin of the randomiser, so here Markus was forced to commit the crime of burning a blind girl's teddy bear, and left behind a record of his dice score.

That meant square one was in the area of Norton Woodseats, so Liz now had her bottom-left corner of the playing board. A week later, on the 16th, he'd been tasked with raping a teacher in Hackenthorpe with her own handbag. Next, a three and the theft of a dog in Beighton.

And that made ten. Snakes and ladders boards were traditionally square grids of ten-by-ten, so now Liz had her measurements. Each side was roughly seven miles long. In the bottom left was Norton Woodseats, with Beighton occupying the bottom right. Top left: Parson Cross. Top right, Clifton, although that portion of the map cut into neighbouring Rotherham. Each side of the map was roughly seven miles long.

The killers' playing ground was roughly forty-nine square miles, about a third of the whole of one of England's biggest cities.

Markus's next throw, a four, had landed him on Arbourthorne Estate on square fourteen, but that was back over to the left, the west. So instead of zigzagging, the numbers ran left to right, like words in a book.

Next, she worked out Saturday man's throws. First a three, which saw him steal a Range Rover in Gleadless Valley, a mile east, or right, of Mundella Place. Then another three, to land on square six, home of Frecheville Community Centre. But his next throw, yet another three, took him to the King Royal in Woodhouse Mill. Square thirty. This meant he must have been sitting not at square six but square twenty-seven, which was one to the right and two rows up.

There was only one way he could have leaped from six to twenty-seven without throwing a dice.

Liz drew a ladder from square six diagonally up to twenty-seven. She said to Bennet, 'Little Dana told you that in the snakes and ladders she played with Markus, ladders represented special dares. I think we have special dares here too. You could only climb a ladder if you completed a dare. Each square landed upon represents a spin of the randomiser and a task to complete using the three criteria of weapon, crime and victim. Except for ladders.'

Bennet nodded. 'For all other squares they follow the randomiser. Weapon, crime, victim. But in order to climb a ladder, whatever crime you picked must be swapped for *murder*. That's why murder isn't on the randomiser. But what do snakes mean? And what does the winner get?'

Liz said, 'I daren't guess either one.'

'We may find out if we don't catch this bastard soon. But we need to find out where he'll strike this coming Saturday.'

Liz focused on the map again. 'Saturday man hit a ladder on square six, where he left a body at Frecheville, and climbed to twenty-seven. There, he threw a three and moved to square thirty, Woodhouse Mill. Here he killed Paul Yard outside the King Royal, so square thirty must have another ladder. This ladder must travel to thirty-three, because his next throw was a three and it put him on square thirty-six. Here, he tried to kill me.'

Bennet tapped square thirty-six in the location of Bowden Housteads Woods. 'So he's hit another ladder. But to where? If he hadn't, we'd know that he will next strike in one of six squares, since they're using a single dice. But a ladder could take him anywhere in the top half of the map. Any square except probably the final one, in Clifton.'

Liz had something else on her mind. 'Markus Darowska hasn't had to commit a single murder. Apart from his theft of a Range Rover on his first go, it's been all kills for Saturday man. How does he manage to keep landing on ladders?'

'More important,' Bennet said, 'does he consider that good or bad luck? Is he a ball of sweat and dread because he's getting a bad run? Or is it just part of the game to him?'

'Markus Darowska showed his disdain for rape by trying to find a loophole. Saturday man doesn't seem to have done that. I think murder is something he has no problem with.'

Just then Boeson came running out of the guesthouse, waving his phone. 'We just found Markus.'

'Good, maybe we can get some answers now,' Liz said.

'I'd say don't hold your breath, but that would be in bad taste...'

CHAPTER SIXTY-THREE

It appeared that Markus Darowska had leaped into the River Don, submerged himself, and swum slightly upstream underwater, his hope that his pursuer, Bennet, would go downstream in search of him. To fight the current, he had aimed for the riverbed, where surely there would be some heavy trash he could hold on to.

And there was. RUST, the Regional Underwater Search Team, had been called in to search the riverbed for dropped items, and they found Markus's shirt snagged on a twisted old roll cage someone had dumped in there. He was still wearing it.

Liz had been sorry that another human life had been lost, but her immediate concern had been that whatever information had been in Markus's head was now beyond reach. 'Have they searched him yet?' she'd asked.

Boeson had shaken his head. 'They called me as soon as they found him. In fact, it might not even be him. They did a search of his clothing while he was still snagged, but there's no ID. He had only a set of keys on him.'

Now, Boeson, Bennet and Liz sat in the car. Her phone was connected to one of the RUST team as they awaited a live update. It came half an hour later. Despite putting up a tent and plastic fences to shield the area, some of the crowd that had gathered had managed to catch a glimpse of the body as it was dragged out of the river.

'Lady from that place you were at, IronClaw,' the RUST team leader said. 'She just started screaming. I think you can take that as confirmation. It's your boy.'

Bennet got out of the car and approached the monument sign, staring at it. Liz got out and stood by his side. 'I'm just trying to get a eureka moment from the snakes and ladders board,' he said.

She knew he was doing no such thing. 'It's not your fault.'

He looked at her. She said, 'Markus was a criminal. He ran from the police. He chose to go through the river.'

Bennet said nothing.

'I know, Liam, I know. He wouldn't have jumped in the river if you hadn't been right behind him. He would have slowed down and had time to think and probably used the bridge, and he'd still be alive right now.'

His expression turned to shock. He opened his mouth to object, but she said, 'We shouldn't go after his accomplice. I mean, what if the guy is cornered and tries to climb out a high window and falls? That's on us. After all, we're told to give up high-speed car chases to avoid danger.'

She saw a little relaxing of the tension in his expression. He knew she was joking.

She fixed him with a hard glare. No more jokes. 'Markus is dead. He can take no more victims. He did that to himself. I wish we'd arrested him, but I'm focusing on the fact that no more people will get hurt.'

Bennet kissed her forehead, thanked her, and returned to the car. Liz remained by the sign for a moment, her eyes now on

The Shorn Sheep guesthouse. It was untrue that Markus could cause no more pain.

She had bid goodbye to Markus's mum with a heavy heart, knowing their next conversation might involve informing her that her firstborn had been arrested. Now she would have to tell the poor woman she'd next see him not in a cell, but a mortuary.

CHAPTER SIXTY-FOUR

Bennet couldn't remember having had so much time alone, and hadn't realised how much it would affect him. He just wasn't used to an empty house at night. The loneliness didn't set in until late because he'd been working a case. An Italian restaurant had sought his help in a fraud case. One of their managers had been off sick for five weeks with a back problem, but they'd gotten wind he wasn't as infirm as he'd claimed. Bennet's job was to watch the guy and find evidence that he was able to work.

Bennet had watched the suspect's home for two hours, but had seen the man only once, briefly, when he passed the living-room window. Around 8pm, Bennet scrolled through the man's social media and made a list of his known haunts to enquire at tomorrow, before giving up for the evening at 9pm. Once home, he made supper and watched a movie alone, which he hadn't done for months. But he felt antsy. Being alone would take some getting used to.

When the movie finished, Bennet did a round of cleaning to try to burn energy. Afterwards, still buzzing a little, he stretched out on the sofa for the night. It was summer and warm enough that he didn't need a duvet. He played some YouTube videos he wasn't interested in and hoped boredom would send him asleep quickly. But anytime his mind wandered, it would spotlight Markus Darowska.

Liz had tried to try to convince him the man's death wasn't his fault, and for a time it had worked. But it was hard not to envision things playing out differently. Now, hours later, the guilt didn't burn so brightly, but it had been joined by a feeling of failure. Criminals were supposed to face justice in a court of law. Markus's death had immunised him against prosecution. History would not record his status as a criminal.

Good for his family. Bad for his victims. If Liz could capture Markus's accomplice and close the case, that would go some way to making things... feel right.

His thoughts turned to Liz. It had been over six months since Joe's mother had died. Despite never contacting her over the years, Bennet had long entertained ideas of a renewed love affair, although he hadn't realised this until it was too late. He knew now it was why he'd barely dated in the ten years since she'd walked out. Recently he'd begun to feel it was time to move on, but he didn't want to date again simply out of grief or loneliness.

He checked the time. 11.25pm. Not too late, so he called Liz. He felt it was a long shot, but if she was up and willing, he would chat until he literally fell asleep on the call. He might even ask her on a date. Hell, he might just ask her to come and stay the night – he'd sleep on the sofa, of course.

The line was engaged. Perhaps she was on the phone to work, or her sister, or even a new lover of her own – Liz never spoke of her own love life, perhaps because she thought – knew – it would upset him. Especially after the other night. Whatever. He hung up and left it at that and closed his eyes.

Detectives don't clock off when they go home, someone had told Liz when she was a detective constable, years back. And it was true. She had left the station two hours ago, but since then had been making and taking phone calls. Even when the hour turned late and the phone calls dried up, Liz turned to the chat logs from the dark website called Croak Catalogue.

When in the zone, nothing broke through her defences, and the dingy surroundings of her bedsit faded away. She got lost in the conversations between MKus888, a known, identified offender, and Skiffle73, a possible two-time killer. The more she read, the more she became convinced she had her second man. But, of course, she had no man at all. He could serve her coffee at a café or take her next call at the bank and she'd be none the wiser.

She had already looked into the Croak Catalogue sign-up process and it required nothing except a username and password, made up on the spot and with no email verification. It was a dark website, and its visitors arrived there via untraceable stepping stones. There was no way to follow the breadcrumbs back to Skiffle73's keyboard.

Later, she pushed the sheets of paper aside, having had enough. Her mind slipped out of the zone and she became aware of the peeling walls around her, the cheap furniture, and the noises from all around outside. The people who ran the chippy below her were installing some new fryer or whatever and making a racket. Motorbikes that sounded as if they were hurt were being ridden around somewhere out back. And on the railway bridge nearby it sounded like teenagers were having a party.

God, she hated this place. She wished she had a proper

house. She wished she'd booted Dan out of theirs instead of abandoning it.

Dan. He'd made a threat against her and she'd subsequently been attacked, so he'd had to be investigated, right? Of course, but had his arrest really required his forceful removal? She had known Boeson would go in heavy-handed and she hadn't tried to stop it. How much of that was down to legit police work and how much was relaying a message to her ex? Well, the message had been understood because Dan hadn't tried to contact her since. She wondered if she should phone him and apologise. If only to kill any legal action he might be considering.

No. It might give the impression he could continue to contact her, which she didn't want. Better to suffer being dragged into court, if that was his plan.

A series of light flashes and bangs drew her to the window. The teenagers partying on the bridge had started letting off fireworks. As she watched, a firecracker started spraying sparks in the middle of the main road. Again, she cursed this place. She wished she could stay over at Bennet's house. She was always comfortable there. She envied him. Not just his house, but his job. Right now she didn't want to be a police officer.

The problem had started a few years ago after she'd mistakenly slept with a superior and soon after had been promoted to inspector. Many of her colleagues had assumed she'd climbed the ladder because of this, and it had gnawed away at her confidence.

To make things worse, her youthful looks didn't seem to gel with the public notion of a high-ranking murder detective, and people who'd normally show the role respect gave her none. It still stung when she talked to a witness or interrogated a suspect and it was the DS they focused on.

She had started to chase the big cases, eager to prove she

deserved her position by solving one. But even this had backfired as her colleagues, including department head, DCI Bates, assumed she was a glory hunter. Only Bennet had been able to dig beneath the façade to expose the truth: she just wanted people to accept her.

After helping Bennet to solve a major case, she had finally gotten some respect, and for a time she'd loved the job. Part of the reason, she now knew, was that Bates had had a laid-back attitude and effectively let her run things, but he'd still been the main face of the investigation after the super. That meant he'd take the spotlight on good days and suffer the condemnation when on the bad ones. More importantly, he'd been there to rescue her if she was headed towards a vital mistake.

But now Bates was off work and the buck stopped with her, and that was the root cause of all her stress. No more safety net. If a killer got free, it was her fault, or so she'd believe. This fear of failure was why she couldn't turn off; why she'd take on minor tasks that subordinates should deal with. Bennet knew this, and he was also right that she'd burn out if she didn't take a breath.

Ha, at least all this stress would give her a craggy, worn face, and people would cease thinking she was too neat and prim and young and pretty to be a hardcore murder detective.

Bennet. Why had they never dated? Especially after the other night. She checked the time: 11.25. Not too late to call him. She knew he was alone and hoped he'd be able to chat her stress away. She might even ask if she could sleep on his sofa, just to get away from this hellhole and snatch a few hours of peace, away from death and grief.

But the line was engaged. Whoever he was talking to this late – possibly even another woman – it had to be important. She hung up and didn't try again.

Instead, she returned to the deep web conversations between Markus Darowska and a possible faceless killer.

CHAPTER SIXTY-FIVE

Someone knocked on her door at seven on Tuesday morning, the first day of September. She glanced at an angle out of the window and saw her landlord. When she opened up, the handsome Indian man said,

'The druggies have been at our cars.'

She followed him out into the alley and felt her anger, and fear, rise. Her passenger-side back window had been smashed, and so had the BMW's. There was glass all over the back seats of both cars.

'They took my son's books. Brand new, twenty quid. What do druggies want with A-level sociology books? Anything missing from yours?'

His son was studying sociology at college, she remembered. 'They'll sell it for a pittance. I had an eight-pack box of cola on show, that's all.'

She checked the glovebox, but it contained only car-related paperwork and some rarely used make-up and knick-knacks. The boot was still locked, but she checked anyway and all was fine. Her laptop was still there, and her camera case, and everything else. Lucky, really, because the area could easily be accessed by lowering the rear backrest.

The landlord pointed at a row of houses about sixty metres away and at right angles to her own. 'CCTV over there might see this alleyway. Can you fast-track this through?'

'With the police, you mean? No. They might respond quicker, but busted windows aren't going to get the red carpet treatment. Even for me. I'll call it in though.'

She returned to her flat to get her mobile and reported the vandalism. Then she covered the busted window with a bin liner taped in place. Later, she drove to her station, where she called a window repair firm before heading inside. She also googled flats for rent. If the job didn't blow a blood vessel in her brain, that damn bedsit would.

All the staff at IronClaw Digital had been asked to attend the station for voluntary, albeit deeper interviews. John Hackney was due for his at 9am, but he called ahead. 'Make sure DCI Miller is there. She's the only one I want to talk to because she's leading this thing. I don't want some snotty DC. Make sure she's there.'

The operator told him she couldn't guarantee such a thing, but would pass his request along. Five minutes later Hackney was called back. Miller, he was told, would be happy to conduct his interview, as long as he was punctual.

He was, but then he was informed the DCI was running late – would he be okay speaking to another officer?

'Nope. Just Miller. I'll wait.'

Hackney was thanked for his patience, given tea and a Betsy Reavley paperback, and left alone in one of the cosy family rooms.

An hour later he banged on the door, which was opened so quickly the uniformed officer must have been waiting right outside. Hackney was restless. 'I'm only off work till midday and it will take me a while to get there, so I need to get going.'

'She won't be long,' the officer said. 'Please just wait.'

'You know what, it doesn't matter who I speak to. Get someone else to take my statement.'

'DCI Miller is coming in especially because you asked for her. No one else is free. It won't be long, please. Can I get you another tea?'

'Look, I–'

'Mr Hackney, thanks for waiting,' a voice called from up the corridor. It was Liz, hustling towards him with an armful of files. 'I got waylaid.' She excused the officer and stepped inside, with Boeson at her arm. Everyone took a seat and Liz again thanked Hackney for waiting.

'But let's hurry this up. I need to get back to work.'

'I know. We'll get straight to it.' She set the audio recorder running and stated the time, location, people present. 'Okay, so... You heard about Markus Darowska's death?'

'I did. Tragic. I'm very sad. We all are.'

'Okay. Tell me how you know Markus. How you met.'

'I knew he was a programmer, only eighteen at the time and a genius. I'd played a couple of his games. He'd published some indie titles on Steam. It's a gaming website. Anyway, I was impressed by his work. I wanted him working for me, so I found him on Facebook or something, called him up, gave him a job.'

'He lived about seventy miles away though. Did you help him find a bedsit? His mother told us you did.'

'Yes. Nice and close. He couldn't travel all that way twice a day.'

'Wait, no, sorry, she didn't tell us that. But now we know. Why isn't that bedsit registered as his address with IronClaw? If you remember, I looked in the personnel files and Markus's address was The Shorn Sheep, down in Maesbury Marsh.'

Hackney lifted his teacup, but found it empty. 'Markus didn't plan to stay there long. I mean, it was a bedsit. Nasty places. So we kept him registered at his former home.'

Liz ignored the bedsit dig. 'Ever been there?'

'No. I helped him buy stuff for the place, but I never went there.'

'Buy stuff? He hardly had any. It appeared the bedsit was infrequently used. Why was that?'

'I don't know about that. Maybe he got rid of stuff.'

'My feeling is he had another place to stay. Any clue where that could be? He didn't seem to have any friends and certainly no family in Sheffield.'

'That I can't help you with, I'm afraid. I really don't know much about Markus's social life. He did his job and that was all that mattered.'

A policeman knocked and entered the room, moving fast and silently. He put a cup of tea on the table and vanished. Boeson slid the cup towards Hackney.

'Markus didn't have Facebook,' Liz said.

'Okay. And?'

'You said you contacted him through Facebook. He doesn't have an account.'

'No, I said Facebook or something. Those were my words. I can't remember, but it must have been online somehow.'

Liz leaned back in her chair. 'How about the dark web? Did you meet there?'

'The dark web?' Hackney looked puzzled.

Liz said, 'Markus had a member account with a website called Croak Catalogue. Know it?'

'No, not my thing. Sounds ominous. I like video games and music.'

'You mentioned music. Ironic, because Markus's only friend on there was someone called Skiffle73. Skiffle is a kind of folk music, big over here in the 1950s. We'd like to find this person. Did Markus ever mention him?'

'No, why would he? Markus was a loner. He mentioned nothing to nobody.'

Liz shuffled some papers. 'Markus talked to this person every day on the website. Private messages. For months. But he suddenly stopped six months ago, when he moved down here from Shropshire.'

'You mean when he got the job? Well, maybe he didn't have time.'

'Or maybe there was no more need for online chat. If he was able to talk face to face.'

'Possibly. Maybe it helped him decide to take the job. Could be the reason Markus, as you say, wasn't at his bedsit often. Unfortunately, I don't know any friends he might have down here. As I told you, Markus barely spoke to us work colleagues. He could have a wife and kids and we wouldn't know it.'

Liz paused while she sorted more papers. 'What year were you born?'

'Nineteen seventy-three. Why?'

'Why did your parents call you John?'

'This was discussed. A Beatles thing.'

'Oh yes. The photo of your dad with John Lennon and Paul McCartney at the Cavern Club. But here's the thing. That photo was taken before they were known as the Beatles. They were The Quarrymen, and back then they didn't have the line-up that became the Beatles. One of the original members, from the time your father would have met them, was Eric Griffiths.'

'What of it?'

'Well, John, your brothers are Paul, George, and Eric. Your father named you all after members of The Quarrymen, not the Beatles. The Quarrymen weren't a rock band. Their genre of music was something popularised by Lonnie Donegan in the 1960s, who I believe you named your son after.'

'I don't know what this has–'

'The Quarrymen and Donegan were *skiffle* musicians. A man who loves skiffle enough to name his son after a pioneer might also adopt it as his username and add seventy-three, the year of his birth.'

Hackney leaned back in his chair. He took a long time before answering. 'I hope I'm imagining this, but it doesn't half sound like you're suggesting I am Markus's accomplice in these murders.'

'You did warn him.'

Hackney raised his eyebrows, puzzled. Liz said, 'That's why Markus ran when you called him from your office.'

'No, no, no. You were there, detective. You asked me to call Markus into the office and I did just that. That's the opposite of telling him to run, isn't it?'

'I meant before.' The eyebrows again. Liz continued: 'When you called Lucy Prosser to come to the office, you dialled her extension. Three numbers. I watched you hit them. And Lucy's extension was the last number you called before I left. Yet when you called Markus after I'd returned, you didn't dial an extension. You hit the redial button. So you must have called Markus's phone in the five minutes after I left and before I came back. You warned him that the police were sniffing around. It's why he knew to run if you called him a second time.'

'Speculation. And I've had enough of this. You didn't arrest me, so I can leave right now, is that correct?'

'It is, for about the next two seconds. Because I'm about to arrest you. For two murders, and for trying to kill me, you bastard.'

CHAPTER SIXTY-SIX

The next time John Hackney was interviewed was four hours later, and a lot had happened since. When extracted from his cell, he walked with his head high, as if to pretend the last few hours hadn't been a strain. After arrest, he'd been searched, but had only carried his car and house keys on the same fob.

Once again it was Liz and Boeson conducting the interview. 'I'd like a drink before we start,' Hackney said. 'I'll try coffee this time. Your tea is awful.'

Liz half-rose to her feet, then sat back down. 'Detective Boeson, arrange a coffee for Mr Hackney. And bring me one too.'

Boeson stuck his head out the door and lobbed Liz's order down the ranks. Liz showed Hackney a thick stack of papers. 'These are the transcripts of chats between Skiffle73 and MKus888 on a website called Croak Catalogue. I've highlighted certain portions. Shall we do this, or do you want to admit you're Skiffle73?'

'Show me what you've got.'

So she did. Nice and simple to begin with. She read aloud a

highlighted segment.

'*SKIFFLE73: I work for a video game studio, believe it or not. We make all the best video games.*

MKus888: Ooohh, giz a job.

SKIFFLE73: Okay.

MKus888: For real? You'd pay me to make games? This doesn't sound legit.

SKIFFLE73. You've seen my photo. Check the 'meet the team' section of the website for IronClaw Digital. See the manager. That's me. Now who feels silly, eh?'

Hackney made no response to this, except to slowly clap. It was as good as an admittance that he was Skiffle73.

Liz said, 'This was during your first conversation. Markus had opened the chat box because you were both on the same team on the Croak Catalogue website. This was in December of last year, so eight months ago. Two months later, Markus left home and took the job you offered him. You also helped him get a bedsit to be close to you, which you freely admitted.'

'Admitted after being tricked. And it was so he could be close to *work*, not to *me*.'

Liz showed him another highlighted piece of the transcript.

```
SKIFFLE73: The flat is only a mile from my
house, so we can get together anytime.
```

'We were friends,' Hackney responded. 'Markus didn't know anyone in Sheffield. Of course, we'd hang around now and then. My son is roughly his age, so I know how to be, shall we say, cool around teenagers.'

'And what did you plan to do when you hung around together? Markus's mother says he's homosexual, so we thought you might have had that interest together.'

Hackney laughed. 'The boy belongs on a catwalk. You think

he'd be interested in a fat old man like me?' Then a sneer appeared. 'I get it. I've come across your kind before, believe me. You think all gay men have sex with each other. Every gay man sleeps with every other gay man, correct?'

'I didn't say that. But we have two single men who work together and have a common interest.'

'Markus and I trapped on a desert island might put an ounce of worth in that obnoxious statement. But we're hardly a dying breed. There's two other homosexual men at IronClaw, by the way. And I haven't slept with either. If that's how it works, then it must be the same for heterosexual men and women. So you must have slept with dozens of your male colleagues.'

Liz ignored this nerve-piercing remark. She showed him another piece of the transcript.

```
SKIFFLE73: No, you can't ever stay the night.
My son sometimes comes over late and
unannounced.
MKus888: Doesn't he know you're gay?
SKIFFLE73: Of course he does, his hellhound of
a mother told everyone, didn't she? But
knowing it and catching me in bed with a boy
barely older than him are worlds apart. No
staying over! Although you'll be sleepy as
hell when I'm finished with you.
```

'Oh, well to hell with you, missus,' Hackney said. He crossed his legs so sharply he hit the table with a knee and made everything on top jump. 'If you've got all the answers, why even ask a question?'

Their drinks arrived at this point. Once they were on the table, Liz continued.

'Don't sound so surprised, Mr Hackney. I told you I have the transcripts. Every conversation between you and Markus. Don't make me read portions out by lying. You and Markus Darowska share a love of video games, of creating them. But, despite being at the forefront of modern gaming, it's my opinion you don't see the appeal of such games. Perhaps as one on the inside, looking out, it's akin to watching a magic trick when you already know how it's done.

'But we're getting too philosophical here. You like good, old-fashioned games, but with a twist. It's why you both joined the website Croak Catalogue, which is for people who like a bit of danger, a bit of risk. You struck up a relationship with Markus. Then you brought him closer to you, so you could play a special game of your own making. Ask me what game.'

'No.'

'Snakes and ladders.'

Hackney sipped coffee. He didn't look at the detectives. Liz gave him time, wondering which route he'd take: admit all, or lie.

Eventually, he looked at her and said, 'There's nothing in those chat logs about snakes and ladders.'

'I know, but–'

'Then you won't know that Markus invented the game. And he played it with another friend he had in Sheffield.'

'Markus had another friend here? By all accounts Markus was a loner.'

Hackney sipped again. 'Markus didn't move to Sheffield just to take a job. He took the job because he wanted to be in Sheffield. To be with his friend, someone else he met online. Tell me this, detective. You searched his bedsit. Did you find any evidence of me there? My DNA or fingerprints? Did you find a double bed? Two used cups? A high watermark in the bath from two people sharing? Was there anything in his place

259

that says I or anyone else was there? I bet you've searched my home already, haven't you?'

'Yes, but we're still searching. There was no mention of another friend in the chat logs, by the way.'

Hackney leaned forward, elbows on the table. 'Ms Miller, I've told you everything, but because of your piecemeal method of extracting information, it's jumbled up like a jigsaw. Let me fix the problem.

'I met Markus. I offered him a job because we got on. He already had a close friend here, so he came. The friend was Markus's secret from me, so he was never talked about until long after we ceased using that website. Markus's bedsit must have been half-empty and left for long periods because he was staying with his new friend. He was also a workaholic. Mostly he'd be the first into work and the last to leave. We have a kitchen there, where he'd prepare ready meals.

'I found out one day that Markus had a friend and they were both playing this sick snakes and ladders game. I was horrified. As I sit here, it sickens me to know I could have stopped it, but didn't. I couldn't. Don't be fooled by his age or that I was his boss. Markus was the one in control. He forced me to keep quiet. I hated every minute of it. But I did it because I loved him, and I didn't want to lose him. That is the reason I warned Markus when you came snooping around my work.

'Look, there is no evidence I was ever in Markus's bedsit, and I know you found no sign of Markus at my home. No DNA or fingerprints. Markus was never there. Furthermore, you found no evidence of my involvement on Markus himself, did you? You ambushed him at work, before he'd had a chance to dispose of anything. But there was nothing incriminating in his desk or his locker or his pockets. I believe he only had his keys and his phone. We never communicated by phone. You can check mine and check his, if you have the technology to get into ruined devices.

'Soon after he came to Sheffield, Markus and I drifted apart. We'd never even slept together, although I was in love. And I thought he was. But he wasn't. He had his new friend. I shouldn't have covered for him, but I did and I'm not proud of it. Now, I promise you, you will find nothing to tie me into these awful crimes and, when you do, hopefully you can stop this tunnel vision.'

He was right. Markus's bedsit and Hackney's home: both residences lacked any sign their owners had entertained guests. Liz had hoped to find a goldmine at Hackney's detached house, but not a shred had been found that discounted the story he'd just told. If Bates had been in charge, he would probably have released Hackney on police bail. Was that the right thing to do?

Liz had heard of investigations that had focused on one good suspect and story and refused to acknowledge evidence to the contrary – was she guilty of such tunnel vision? Was Hackney's story for real?

Was Markus's true accomplice, a bloodthirsty killer, still out there?

CHAPTER SIXTY-SEVEN

L iz decided to watch from the custody desk. The custody sergeant got Hackney's stuff together – just a set of keys and his shoes. A monitor showed the feed from a camera watching Hackney's cell. As he was brought out, Liz picked up the man's keys and fiddled with them.

The custody sergeant said, 'He doesn't know he's being released. Why didn't you tell him?'

Liz looked at the keys in her hand. One for his home, one for his car, one that looked like it unlocked the main doors at work, and an old door key with a piece of paper sellotaped round the barrel. Along its length it read TOILET. It looked old. 'Because I want to delay seeing a smug grin on his face. I want him to think he's being charged.'

'His clock's got eighteen more hours. Let him stew in the cell some more.'

'I'm going to have him followed.'

Hackney followed an officer down the hall, where they both stopped at the custody desk. If Liz had wanted Hackney to worry he was about to be charged, she didn't get her wish. A slight grin on the man's face said he knew he was getting released.

'Let's hurry this along,' he said. 'It's too warm in here.'

Liz dropped the keys onto the desk... but she continued to stare at them. Then she put a hand on the custody sergeant's shoulder. He got the message and said nothing. Liz told Hackney, 'I just wanted to ask you. What you want for your dinner later?'

His grin faded. 'What do you mean? I thought I was being released.'

'Oh, no, not yet. We still have you for some time yet, and we're still collecting evidence. All in good time. So. Dinner? We've had to cut down on takeaways because we were spending too much. Did you know that Yorkshire police order more takeaways than all of Scotland or Wales or London? I think we've got some frozen sausage and chips around.'

'Hospitals orders more takeaways than we do,' the custody sergeant said.

'Yeah, but they have a lot more people come in.'

'Sure, but a lot of them can't eat. Operations and sickness and nil by mouth and all that.'

'We have similar. I imagine getting charged with murder ruins your appetite. We could charge Mr Hackney now, just to see.'

Hackney gave them both a withering glare and then turned and stomped back the way he'd come.

'If he complains about that, we're in the doghouse,' the custody sergeant said. He reached for Hackney's keys, but Liz snapped them up.

'I'll keep these for a bit, if you don't mind.'

She left the custody suite, calling Boeson on the way. It went to voicemail, so her next call was to Bennet, who answered quickly.

'I just got a clue and I need a bodyguard. You busy?'

'Nope,' Bennet said. 'Stake-out. I'm sitting outside a McDonald's, watching someone eat. Sick leave fraud case. If he raises his burger to his face too fast, I've got him. My dad is bringing Joe back later tonight, but not for another few hours. You want me?'

She almost said, 'Yes, I want you, handsome'. Instead: 'My main man is busy and I need help. It might be nothing. I'm going back to IronClaw. I found a key for the toilets.'

'I went in there. There was no lock on the toilet doors.'

'Exactly.'

CHAPTER SIXTY-EIGHT

When Hackney had been booked into the police station after his arrest, he'd been asked a question by the custody sergeant: 'If anyone calls here for you, do you want us to tell them why you've been arrested?'

'My son can't know about this,' had been his answer. 'But my work will have to be told.'

He was informed there could be no picking and choosing and it had to be a yes or no to all; however, he would be allowed a phone call and could tell whoever he wanted.

He made that call to work and said to the receptionist, 'Lana, it's me. I've been arrested for a whole pile of shit you wouldn't believe. I won't be in today. Don't tell anyone about the arrest. You're going to have to call Jonas in.'

Jonas was the deputy manager and he normally worked the two days Hackney didn't on a rolling rota. When Liz and Bennet entered IronClaw's reception, the lady at the desk – Lana – called for him and down he came.

Liz introduced herself ('DCI Liz Miller, South Yorkshire Police') and Bennet ('Mr Bennet was a DCI in Barnsley, and now he's here.') – a careful sentence that was no lie yet suggested Bennet was still a policeman – and then said, 'Don't ask me about Mr Hackney. Ongoing police investigation. I'm here to search this building as part of that investigation, if you don't mind. I have no warrant but can get one if you refuse.'

Jonas was a handsome young man and he clearly liked what he saw in Liz. He did not refuse.

She showed him the key marked TOILET on Hackney's bunch. 'Oh, that's for the old room,' he said. 'Here, look at this.'

He led them behind the reception desk. On the wall behind where Lana sat was a fire system and floor plan showing the locations of the break-glass call points.

Jonas tapped the map. 'Years ago we ran both floors and the manager's office was upstairs. We downsized and the top floor was leased out by the landlord, so an office was installed in front of the old toilets and new ones put in. Those toilets haven't been used in a few years, but there's still a door.'

His finger was on Hackney's office. Or rather, a space behind it. It was split into two rooms, marked FWC and MWC.

'I want to see,' Liz told him, already heading for the stairs. In the manager's office, Jonas pulled away the roller whiteboard against a corner wall, and there it was: an old wooden door, with a lock that looked just right for her key. She sent Jonas out of the office and Bennet closed the blinds.

Once unlocked, the old door creaked open, scraping an arc through an accumulation of dust covering the floor of the vestibule beyond. It was a grim place, with peeling paint, and looked to have had no makeover since the old building was built. Better than her bedsit though. Ahead were two doors, blank except for the dried, gluey remains of long-gone lettering.

On the left door was the ghost of the word GENTS. On the right: LADIES. On the floor between the doors was a double mattress with a quilt and two pillows, but this feature was clean and new.

'The bed could explain why Hackney and Darowska always seemed to be the first at work and the last to leave,' Bennet said.

'If they left at all some nights. But why not sleep in one of the cubicles?'

'Private domains, best guess.'

'Not anymore. Take a door each?'

Bennet nodded and, habitually, stepped towards the gents as Liz aimed at the ladies. Both pushed open their doors at the same time.

And exclaimed in unison.

CHAPTER SIXTY-NINE

I n both toilets, the killers had created something akin to a police incident room. In each was a computer on a desk, whose screensaver vanished without password input to display a randomiser. On the floor was a large map of Sheffield, with a snakes and ladders board drawn on it. But Liz only glanced at these items, because the rest of the room was far more shocking.

Each back wall, above the sinks where mirrors had once been, was covered with photographs and diagrams and sticky notes bloated with scribblings. Hundreds. Liz's eyes flicked fast, trying to absorb it all at once, but they paused on items she understood: a receipt for lighter fluid, another for a trumpet. Next door, Bennet found similar for a cheap rubber football and for a car battery. They both saw photographs of the victims, their homes, and shots of them out and about, doing their thing.

There was also a sheet of paper listing three columns; the investigators had been referring to the randomiser reels as *weapon*, *crime* and *victim*, but here they were titled METHOD, MISDEED and MARK. Upon closer inspection, it was obvious they weren't just looking at memorabilia. The whole room was telling a story.

For instance, there was a photo of a school, and another showing two women walking out of the main gates: Felicity Armitage, the large woman who'd had her handbag abused; and Alice Carter, the teacher who was raped. Another photo showed them getting into the same car. Then that car was captured outside Alice's house, with Alice disembarking, waving her friend away.

Next, Felicity's house. Felicity's car at traffic lights, its occupant playing on her phone while she waited for green. Another image was a high-quality close-up of that phone, clearly displaying the dating website where Markus Darowska had found her that night.

Another photo showed Alice leaving her home out the back way, to walk the dark path where she was later attacked. Clearly, Markus had stalked the school, knowing teachers still worked during the summer holidays. He had picked Felicity over Alice because she wanted a man. Later, when he was forced into a redo, he already had the address of another female teacher, and knew of her habit of crossing the desolate land behind her home.

And another set of photos showed the dice at each crime scene. So, as Liz had guessed, the dice had probably been nothing more than proof that the crime in question was attributable to the man tasked with it.

Each toilet also had tinned food, powdered milk, a kettle and microwave, a clothing rail, on which they saw not just everyday clothing, but also one-piece plastic boiler suits with hoods and attached gloves.

Private domains, just as Bennet had said. Markus and Hackney would retire here after a shift, to work on their game. Each man's room would be off limits to the other. And when their work was done, they'd share the bed outside. It–

'Liz!'

The male toilet was the sanctuary of Saturday man, of Hackney, and of course his crimes were far more barbaric. But something in Bennet's tone told her it wasn't just shock at seeing the nth degree planning of brutal murders. Something far worse.

She thought she knew exactly what, and prayed she was wrong.

She wasn't.

———

Her bedsit, from afar. Her bedsit front door, a close-up. Dan at her door, shot from behind. Liz driving to the swimming pool; entering the building; leaving the pool after she'd gotten the call about an anonymous informant. Her car en route to Richmond Park Rise. These and dozens more photographs, some close-ups of her face. That entire Saturday was storyboarded like a movie.

Amongst the myriad sticky notes surrounding the dozens of photographs of her, one stood out because it held the only mention of her name. It said: *Miller man troubles – perhaps seduce/invite to get her to location?*

'The bastard,' she snarled.

'You've got him,' Bennet said. 'That's the thing to focus on.'

She fled the room. He followed, assuming she'd been unable to face her photographs any longer. He expected to find her numb and motionless in the vestibule, but he caught her taking the keys off the hook on the wall. She showed him one. A vehicle key that said HONDA.

'Motorbike,' Bennet said. 'But where? There's none in the car park.'

She showed him another key. It was marked BIN.

They went downstairs, out, and followed a road round the back, where they found the timber bin store they'd seen last time. Liz unlocked it and Bennet stepped inside. It was well lit because it had a wire-mesh roof. Inside were two rear-end loaders, one touching the back wall and one situated three feet away from it. Behind the latter he found a black Honda scooter.

'They must share this,' he said. 'That's why the key was in the communal area, like the bed. Now you know what to check for.'

She knew what he meant. With no idea of the vehicles used by the criminals, all had to be scrutinised. Given that hundreds of vehicles in the areas of the attacks left the scene in various directions and entered from myriad points and various times, the task of finding their owners and tracing their journeys had been and still was mammoth. Now she knew exactly how Markus and Hackney got around while researching and carrying out their crimes.

She called in the registration and wasn't surprised to find it did indeed belong to a Honda Vision scooter, although the official keeper was a female residing in Knotty Ash, Liverpool – a city Hackney might know well because he'd lived there as a kid. The bike had not been reported stolen, which she'd also expected.

In the old days criminals would steal number plates from any old vehicle, and a police officer would have to manually run the registration to learn of the deception. The Automatic Number Plate Recognition system, invented way back in 1976, had forced criminals to adapt.

Today's tactic was to clone number plates and use them on similar vehicles, so the cameras wouldn't see a problem. This bike wouldn't be flagged unless the system knew to search for it, and even if that happened, it would be the hapless owner and not the crook who'd get the door knock.

Her spirits raised. 'Is that a smile I see?' Bennet said.

'If this is the only key to that Honda, and we can place that bike at some of the crime scenes, we'll have enough to charge and sink that bastard Hackney. I need to call Merseyside Police to chat to the bike's owner though. Just in case there's some silly innocent reason why this bike is here and Hackney had nothing to do with it.'

'You should drive down there yourself and do it. Don't act like royalty just because you're an acting DCI now.'

She playfully aimed and missed a kick at his ankle. 'I can't. Hackney's custody clock is up around 11am tomorrow. I'll have to interview him first thing in the morning. But there's a mass of evidence in those toilets and it will take forensics hours to sift through. Days for some of it, probably. I'll have to edit and adjust my interview strategy as evidence comes in. I'll be at it until late. But I really don't fancy doing it in a noisy police station.'

'Or sitting in your crappy bedsit. You can admit it. And then you can ask me. I'm waiting.'

'Okay, mind reader. No, I don't want to go back to that crappy hellhole. And will you help me with the interview plans?'

'Sure. You can come to mine. We'll do a mock interview and I'll play the part of Hackney. Joe's not home until about nine.'

'Okay. I'll leave when Joe comes back.'

'No you won't,' Bennet said before he could stop himself. But he needn't have worried. She took his hand in hers.

CHAPTER SEVENTY

Bennet's father arrived with Joe at roughly nine o'clock. The kid ran into the house with a McDonald's meal, which his father found unimpressive. But he said nothing as he had something more important on his mind.

'Liz,' Joe yelled, and jumped onto the sofa next to her. She stole some of his fries.

When Ray Bennet came in, Liam was standing in the middle of the living room, a little nervous. 'Dad, this is Liz. Yes, the one who tried to hijack my investigation last year.'

Bennet had always wondered how his father actually felt about Liz. He'd never met her, but he'd had a lot of less than stellar things to say about the detective. Ray gave a smile. He was still sharp and intelligent, but he was elderly and knew this allowed him a pass if he said something untoward. Which he did now.

'Good to meet you. About time my son got himself a nice girlfriend.'

Bennet and Liz barely knew where to look, but Joe whooped with glee. 'Are you moving in?' he asked her. 'Dad says you live in a cesspool. What's a cesspool?'

Joe had the same glint in his eye as the old man. Sharp, intelligent, and aware that his age could get him a pass.

Ray was given Liam's bed and when the eldest and youngest in the house were tucked in for the night, Liam got two spare single quilt covers. 'Thin, but it's summer. I'll have the floor, you have the sofa.'

He tossed one cover over Liz's head. Leaving herself shrouded, she said, 'There's still an awkwardness between us. About what we did.'

'The chess?'

She laughed. 'Yes, the chess. We played drunk, and it's causing a bit of tension. We should play sober chess. Then it's not a drunken mistake.'

He froze. 'You want to do it again?'

She yanked the quilt cover off her head and stared at him. 'You don't?'

'I guess I'm all for unproven therapies. But what if we feel awkward again after?'

'We beat it out of us. With repetition.'

'My entire family is in the house. They could come downstairs. And you still have work to do.'

She said nothing. Held out her hand. He took it.

'Move in,' Bennet said.

She hadn't realised he was awake, since her back was to him. It was 5am. She and Bennet had worked for hours on her interview tactics and he'd drifted off at four, but the prospect of facing Hackney had kept sleep from her. She had knelt before the coffee table, where her snakes and ladders map was laid out, and yet again drilled the crimes and locations into her head.

Now, she turned to face him. But she ignored what he'd said. 'I'm just running through things one last time. Can't sleep?'

'Forget that for a moment. Do you want to move in? The negative answer will help me wake up like a slap in the face.'

'You really want me to?'

'Yes. Not because of the sex. Not *just* because of the sex. The extra person in the house will help Joe. You don't like that bedsit–'

'Cesspool, you said.'

'I did, yes. I'm sorry.'

'Don't be. It's one hundred per cent a cesspool.'

He sat up. 'Joe is worried that I can't cope without Patricia. She never refused to babysit, even at the drop of a hat if I got called into work in the dead hours. Maybe he's right. You said to me once that Joe might miss a female touch around him, and I think you're right. He likes you and you'd be beneficial around him. I think I need a woman around me too.'

'That's sweet to admit that.'

'Pots don't wash themselves.'

There was a pause. Jokes had been made, but the offer was deadly serious. Liz said, 'It would make us boyfriend and girlfriend, probably. In many people's eyes, anyway. I don't want to do it for the wrong reason.'

'I know what you mean. I feel a bit awkward being single at this age. Am I rushing into it because of that? So what? If that's one reason against, there are many reasons for.'

'But that constitutes reasonable doubt. Courts acquit for that.'

'It's a welter of circumstantial evidence, and taken as a whole it paints a convincing picture. Courts have convicted on that.'

'This could be a miscarriage of justice.'

'We're not even at trial yet. You can be on remand.'

'No need for a trial,' she said, leaning forward to kiss him. 'I plead guilty.'

When Bennet woke, at just after eight, Liz was gone. In her place, knelt before the snakes and ladders map spread on the coffee table, was Joe. He watched his son roll a dice and move a battery as a token.

'Be careful with that, Joe.'

'It's cool. Who drew it and why is it a map?'

Bennet sat up and rubbed his eyes. He checked his phone and found a message from Liz. It said she'd gone into work early to prepare. 'It's Liz's. She must have forgotten it. It's a game. You play snakes and ladders and do dares at all the places you stop on.'

'Can we play it? With the dares?'

Bennet heard coughing upstairs and knew his dad was getting up. He didn't have much time if he wanted to speak to Joe alone.

'Joe, what do you think of the idea of Liz staying here for–'

'Moving in? Yes times one thousand.'

Okay. That was easy. 'It won't be forever, just until–'

'No, she can stay forever. I like her. You like her.'

'I'm not trying to replace your mother.'

'I know. She's someone else. My mum is dead.'

Bennet got off the sofa and hugged his boy. 'We can get more done around the house, we can have more days out maybe. Things will be easier.'

'And if she becomes my stepmum, I can still scare the bad kids at school by saying my stepmum is a copper.'

'There's always that. So, you like the idea?'

'Yes. Can I help her move in?'

'Good timing there. I was going to suggest we could go to her place after school and collect her stuff. You want to do that?'

'Yes. Can't wait. I can have a proper family.'

That tugged at Bennet's heartstrings and he hugged his boy again.

'Where is she?' Joe asked. 'I want to hug her as well. For brightening my day.'

'She's had to go to work. To darken someone else's day.'

CHAPTER SEVENTY-ONE

Hackney was woken at six in the morning and offered cereal, which he refused. He was told his next interview would be at nine. Nice and early, he was informed, so he could get out in time to enjoy the sunny afternoon.

He wasn't fooled. 'My twenty-four hours is up at 11.13. You just want a last-ditch attempt to get me before you have to let me go. Well, this time I want a solicitor.'

That burned time, but not too much. Because Woodseats was the base of Major Investigation Team 2, the station had a resident duty solicitor, meaning they didn't have to call one to represent Hackney. But they did have to rouse the guy from home, since he wasn't due in until nine.

They had a tea waiting for him. He was independent of the police, but knew a lot of their kids' and spouses' names. After a quick chat about his house extension, Liz filled him in on his client and showed him into a room to meet the man. The solicitor seemed eager, knowing such a high-profile case could do wonders for his career.

Twenty minutes later, it was interview time. It was just after half nine. She had less than two hours left to charge Hackney, or he'd walk.

She started the audio and video recordings and introduced everyone. She'd brought a pretty young female DC into the room with her this time.

'You know we found nothing in your house, right?' was Liz's first question.

He answered, 'First of all, two things. The first, no comment.'

So, it was going to be like that, was it? His solicitor hadn't been given full disclosure – meaning he didn't yet know all the evidence – and the standard response to this was to advise a client to say nothing. If in doubt, say nowt.

Then Hackney surprised her. 'Unless you sort her there out.' The young DC looked shocked that Hackney had singled her out. 'I don't like women like her. Too much make-up. It's like a maggot on a fishing line. She gets rid of the face or I no comment the whole way.'

Before Liz could smash down his request, the DC said, 'It's okay. I'll do it.'

Wet wipes were brought in. As the DC proceeded to scour off the little make-up she wore, Liz contained her anger. 'You said *two* things.'

'Demand number two: for you to do something. Or to *not* do something might be more correct. But maybe I won't need it. We'll see. Ask your questions.'

Liz was happy to move on. She showed Hackney a photo of the converted toilets. Hackney tried a puzzled face at first, but then seemed to realise he was in quicksand and gave it up. He gave a slow clap, just like before.

Next, she showed him photos of the Honda Vision found in the bin store. Now they knew what vehicle to look for, CCTV specialists had been over footage through the night and had identified that bike at three locations. A bike only Hackney and Markus had access to.

'Sunday August 30th. Here we see the Honda on City Road, a short way from the restaurant where the chef who was stalked by a trumpet worked. Here we see the bike on Monday the 17th, passing a car showroom on Sheffield Road, Hackenthorpe, close to where a teacher was raped. And the final one shows the bike on August 22nd, passing a Jet petrol station on Retford Road, not far from the King Royal pub, where Paul Yard was murdered.'

'No comment.'

At this point there was a knock on the door. The young DC poked her head out and took a message, which she whispered into Liz's ear.

Next, Liz put a pair of phones in evidence bags on the table. 'Your secret phone. Markus's secret phone. Located in the disused toilets at IronClaw. The digital team have already extracted data from both.'

The solicitor asked for a pause in the interview in order to chat with his client, possibly to write a prepared statement. Hackney said no. 'Let's see it all, detective.'

She was happy to oblige. 'Then let's watch some movies. For the record, I am going to show Mr Hackney a series of recordings. These are mobile phone video calls between himself and Markus Darowska, taken in the secret bathrooms at IronClaw Digital. The first is from Mr Hackney's phone, recorded in the male bathroom at 8.19am on Saturday, August 8th...'

CHAPTER SEVENTY-TWO

The camera zooms in on the laptop. On its screen is the randomiser, whose counter reads 0.

Markus's voice, sans stutter, is on speaker: 'Okay, a momentous moment. Go number one. Let the game begin. Hit that bandit.'

Hackney's finger enters the frame and jabs the keyboard. The reels of the randomiser – or bandit, as they call it – spin with a blur. The counter jumps from 0 to 1.

The reels stop, one after the other. CAR, STEAL, CRIMINAL. Hackney turns the camera to a snakes and ladders board on the floor. He tosses a dice onto the board and scores a three. He then moves a small e-cig liquid bottle, employed as a game token, onto square three.

Markus laughs. 'You have to steal from a criminal. Ha. You've got to break into a police station. Using a car. No prison in that square. Maybe no cop shop either.'

'Numpty,' Hackney responds. 'I'll steal a criminal's car. Some drug baron or something, whatever. I only have to move it an inch to count as theft. Best of all, what police officer is going to *care about that? What criminal is going to call the police about it anyway?'*

Liz prepared another video on her laptop. 'This next recording is from the day after, early on Sunday 9th August. This time Markus is filming from his phone in the female bathroom. As we can see, there's another laptop with the randomiser and another gameboard.'

She scrutinised Hackney's face for emotion as he watched Markus roll a two and move his token onto the second square. The camera flicked to the laptop. Markus hit a key and the randomiser gave him: TEDDYBEAR, ARSON, CHILD. He immediately started to complain. He clearly didn't want to mess with kids. Hackney's response was to remind Markus that inserting a child into the game had been his idea. Deal with it or forfeit.

Hackney wore a poker face throughout the entire video.

'Let's move to the next,' Liz said. 'The following Saturday morning. Your turn again.'

Her intention here was to convince Hackney he was trapped. If she'd hoped to achieve this through overloading him with guilt or embarrassment, that tactic fell dead given his next move: he beat her to the keyboard and loaded the next video himself.

BABYSEAT, DEFAME, TRAMP.

Hackney turns the camera on himself. He is biting his lower lip as if nervous.

Markus can be heard laughing, and there are three bangs off-screen, as if someone has thumped a wall.

On speaker, Markus laughs again and says, 'If there's one type of person you can't ruin the good character of, it's a tramp. You're on crap street with this one, lover boy. Want to surrender right now? The bandit is not going to be your friend, ever.'

Back to nervously biting his lip, Hackney says, 'It's worse than that, my friend. Check this out.'

The camera turns to the gameboard. A dice sits there, displaying a three. Hackney moves his token to square six, which contains Frecheville Community Centre. And the bottom rung of the board's first ladder.

'My God,' Markus says. 'You know the rules. So now the misdeed is not defame, *it's* murder. *Jesus, J, you've got to murder a tramp. With a damn baby seat! Good luck with that. And do this one properly, won't you?'*

'What?'

'That car thing last week. I wouldn't call that stealing. You dumped it right outside the garage it was in.'

'I hot-wired it, which was a devil to learn in one day. I took it without the owner's consent. Is there some kind of minimum distance I have to drive before it counts as stealing? If the police had got me, could I have said, no, officer, I haven't stolen this because I haven't driven past that lamp post yet? Are you just jealous because it didn't get reported and I'm in the clear?'

'Even if I was, I'm certainly not jealous of this one. What if there are no tramps round there?'

Hackney shrugs. 'I'll bring one in.'

'How?'

'Well, that's for me to work out and you to be amazed at.'

'Wow. I mean, are you really going to do it? Kill a tramp?'

'That's the rules of the game. I have to.'

Liz watched Hackney's response to Markus's reaction when he was landed with HANDBAG, RAPE, TEACHER. That response was a slight grin as he watched himself banter with his comrade.

'Good old times, right?' Liz said, disgusted, when the video was over.

'Markus wanted to use a teacher that some other guy had already raped. Just because the night before I'd used a tramp who was already dead.'

'Dead by your hand, you mean?'

Hackney seemed to ignore the question. 'I told Markus. I said I smashed him up with a car seat, and he would have died from that if he'd been alive. Plus, I killed him in the first place. That counts, right? I mean, you'd agree, wouldn't you?'

Liz tried to contain her excitement at hearing a direct admission, but she was the only one. His solicitor had remained quiet throughout the videos, but now he voiced his objection to Hackney's confessing to a crime. Hackney shut him down. 'You saw the videos. They've got me for all sorts. You can leave now, you're no good to me. I'll call you for my appeal in about a year's time. Bye bye.'

The solicitor tried to argue, but Hackney wouldn't listen. The interview paused. The solicitor left, unhappy that this big case had slipped his grasp. The interview resumed. Liz delayed rearresting Hackney for Breakspear's murder in case Hackney's tune changed. He seemed ready to give her more, perhaps everything.

As if they hadn't broken stride, she started the next video. Hackney's eyes were fixed on the laptop.

'Oh yes. This next one! I mean, just watch this excuse that

Markus comes up with that Sunday night. Just watch this silliness.'

Hackney turned the laptop slightly so Liz could have the better view. She was amazed. Hackney seemed to be gloating.

'You're taking the piss,' Hackney says. The background is his kitchen.

'No, it's inside the rules,' Markus says on speaker. 'I just raped the handbag, not the woman. Check the dictionary definition. Rape is the spoiling or destroying of a thing or place.'

'No, I don't think it includes a thing. And I've already checked, because I knew you'd try this. Rape is the commission of unlawful sexual intercourse.'

Markus starts moving, and the laptop police have passes by in the background. 'Unlawful sexual intrusion counts. I intruded unlawfully.'

'Hang on, back up a sec. That laptop.'

Markus turns the camera away from himself briefly, to display the machine in question.

'Why has that computer got our bandit on it? You said you needed a machine for Croak Catalogue, that's all. Is that bandit linked to the others?'

'Well, it records my turns, yes. I just wanted one here, in case I can't get to IronClaw one day.'

'Get rid of it, you dunce.'

'No cops are going to get it. Why would they come here?'

'Because you live in a place that's probably had half of Britain's most wanted passing through. The police could kick the door in because they're chasing up some scumbag. Said scumbag could still have a key and come for a trolley dash. You want to sit *in prison and think about how right I was? What else is on it that would make the police throw a street party?'*

'Nothing. Just the bandit. I'll get rid of it. Anyway, if we can get back to business...'

'Yes,' Hackney says. 'And no. As in I'm not having it. The misdeed is rape, and the teacher needs to be the mark, not the handbag.'

'She was the mark. She was the victim of having her handbag raped. She'd count as a victim if her handbag was stolen, wouldn't she? The handbag isn't the mark. If I go on trial for this and there's a victim impact statement, the teacher will read it out in court, won't she? Her handbag won't be standing up there and telling everyone how depressed and mistrustful of men it is.'

'But the handbag was on the method reel. So even if it did count, there's no method, no weapon other than your dick, and your dick, nice as it is, wasn't on the reels, was it? So it doesn't count and you've got to try again. You only get the one fail, remember, so do it properly or I win by default.'

'This from the guy who smashed up a skeleton,' Markus snaps.

FOOTBALL, BURGLE, CEO.

While watching this video, Hackney gave a running commentary. 'With this one, Markus called me jammy. Can you believe that? Jammy because I got another ladder? The ladder meant *burgle* got swapped for *murder*. If not for that ladder, I could have just found some business owner, followed him home, see if he had kids and there was a football in the garden I could steal. But no. Now it's murder. Is that jammy? What do you say, detective?'

DOG, DEFRAUD, SCIENTIST.

'Oh yeah. Ha. This one. Markus, he starts raving about how it's impossible. I swear he thought he'd have to find a dog with a science degree and swindle money off it. I helped him out. Zara, at work, her roommate's auntie is a scientist. And she has a dog. And she takes the bloody thing to a grooming place in Beighton at weekends. That's tailor-made. And he calls me jammy!'

TRUMPET, STALK, CHEF.

The moment the video started, Hackney hit the space key on the laptop to pause it. He gave Liz a long stare, and it accompanied that slappable grin of his.

'Your chronology is all mixed up, detective. This is from the Sunday. This is Markus's go. We seem to be missing the previous Saturday. My go.'

Liz shut the laptop. She had indeed swapped the last two videos in order to play the one from Saturday August 29th last. The film evidence was supposed to chip away at Hackney's defences, with that final, most impactful – for her – recording delivering the blow that crumbled him.

But she had misjudged how this bastard would react upon knowing the game was up. Instead of wilting, he seemed to have drawn strength. He was not appalled by seeing his crimes – or at least their designs – thrown back in his face. He was actually proud, like a director at a movie premier. She would not sit here and watch him gloat over that final recording.

'I can't deny what I've just seen, detective,' Hackney said, leaning back in his seat. 'I'm bang to rights there. But you have no proof about that missing Saturday, do you? Lucky me. So, I guess the official line is going to be that whatever happened that day had nothing to do with me. It's also lucky for you. I mean, that couldn't have been easy to watch.'

He was goading her, she knew. He wanted to watch the video. He wanted to relive that Saturday, because outside of a trial he'd never get another chance. She didn't want to give him the satisfaction.

But there was a chance that folding to him would avoid a trial. He might wish to relive that day, but she absolutely didn't, and might be able to put it to bed right now.

She opened the laptop.

CAR BATTERY, EXPOSE, POLICE.

'Oh, I know what to do!' Markus virtually squeals. 'Just call in a fake crime to the cops, stand on a car battery, and whip your dick out as they drive past.'

The camera tilts to the gameboard, where the dice shows a six.

'Hang on, John, that's the second time you've already done the bandit and the dice throw before starting your video. Twice on the trot now I haven't seen you do it. You could be cheating.'

'For real? After what I had to do last time? After this?'

In close-up, Hackney moves his token six spaces from square thirty to thirty-six, where there was a portion of a housing estate, the Sheffield Parkway, and an expanse of trees marked Bowden Housteads Woods.

And the bottom of another ladder.

'Cheating, am I? Well, I'll just retake my go then.'

'No, no, no,' Markus yelps, laughing. 'I take it back. Legit go. We'll stick with killing someone instead of exposing yourself to them. And a cop of all people.'

'It didn't take you long to go from snivelling about murder to loving it. But then again you're not the one getting this bad luck.'

'Ain't that bad. Cops are all over the place. Just make a bomb out of a car battery. If you can read up how to do it and plant it and get a bobby there all by day's end.'

'Not a bobby. I'm going to use this to help us both out. There's a murder squad after us, and I don't want to do thirty years, so—'

'You're the one all over the news, John, so it's you and not me they're after. Enjoy your thirty years. Worst I did was rape.'

'Oh, sure, you'll get community service for that. We're playing the same game. Without you, this never happened. You never tried to stop me. It all falls under joint enterprise and that means if I get thirty years, you get thirty years.'

'Yeah, yeah, but that's not what I meant. None of the evidence the cops have points at me. They don't even know there's two guys. Anyway, what copper are you talking about? That bit of skirt, Miller?'

'Yeah. I don't see how a woman could be a top cop like that, but she's the one leading the bad boys after us.'

'I can't see how killing her will mean we're home free. They'll just come at us harder. Cops always care more when it's one of their own.'

'Think about it, Markus. She's their boss, the one who tells them what to do. If I cut her down, it'll be like cutting the head off the snake. They'll be disrupted.'

'No, it's more like cutting one head off a hydra. Someone else will just step up and take her place. And how will you get this woman where you need her?'

'She's hunting us. She goes where the clues are. I'll leave her a clue and she'll come to me, and step right into my trap.'

'So now you know *ninety-nine per cent* of it,' Hackney said. He shut the laptop and shoved it aside. 'Well done and case closed.'

If he'd added the ninety-nine per cent term to manipulate

her again, to make her ask more questions, he needn't have bothered. She was far from done with this smug bastard.

'And that remaining one per cent, is that because of the snakes on the gameboard? I know what ladders represent. Murder. Tell me about the snakes. There's a colossal snake on square ninety-nine, going all the way down to square thirty-two.'

'No mystery to the snakes. You go down a snake, just like in the standard game. But now you're only on ninety-nine point five per cent.'

'So there's more? Let me try again. We found various folders on your laptop. In some were copies of the, as you call it, "bandit". I assume that's from one-armed bandit. In others were videos of dice-rolls performed by you. We found this...'

Up next for Hackney's perusal was another video, three seconds long. This time it was a straight phone recording, no call or insert or audio from Hackney involved. His hand rolled the dice and scored a six. End of video.

'And this...'

She offered a photograph. It was of a computer screen showing the randomiser – ACID, CRUSH, SPORTSMAN. Its counter read five. An insert displayed a zoom shot of the date on the desktop taskbar: 5/9/20.

'But it's Wednesday the second of September, Mr Hackney. This is your *next* spin, in the future. It's fake. A fake spin, a fake dice roll. Your plan was to somehow splice these fabrications into a video phone call with Markus on the 5th of September. I'm sure a computer programmer has the skill to do that even with your basic laptop. We also found a similar video for Saturday the 12th. And for Saturday the 19th. And a final one for Saturday the 26th. You were cheating at snakes and ladders.'

Hackney clenched his jaw hard. He didn't like being ambushed. Or was he upset because he'd been called a cheat? 'I suppose Markus will never know, so it can't hurt him.'

'We worked out your planned turns and played the game.' Here she carefully considered the start of her next sentence: the last thing she wanted was to show emotion on her face or give Hackney a chance for a slashing remark. 'If you had killed a police officer, you would have climbed a ladder. Your next roll would have taken you to another ladder. And another. In fact, it's ladders all the way to square ninety-four, with just a six to roll to reach one hundred and win the game. That's some kind of luck.'

'You have been busy, haven't you? Yes, I manipulated the game in order to hit all the ladders and guarantee a win.'

'What does the winner get?'

Hackney laughed. 'You won't like it.'

'Let me judge that.'

'This game was going to take up our weekends for months. And we both work full-time. We'd need some downtime. So, when it was over, we were going to go to the cinema. Loser pays.'

'So this, all these murders, a rape, everything else, was all for about eight pounds?'

'We normally go Dutch. So I'd really only be saving about four pounds.'

Beside her, the young DC visibly stiffened. 'And you were willing to commit murder to win at snakes and ladders?' Liz asked.

'Take the scorn out of your tone, woman. You take the rough with the smooth. I did not like murdering, believe it or not. I had to do it. *My goal here was to win, win, win.*' Upon his final sentence, Hackney had virtually been shouting. Now, he calmed and softly added, 'There, I told you wouldn't like it. Now you know.'

'So I'm at one hundred per cent?'

'Ah. Not quite.'

Liz glanced at her watch. 11.01am. Hackney's clock would expire in twelve minutes. It was time to wrap this up. 'It seems we're playing our own game here. Well, okay, let me take another turn. One more video. Already filmed, of course, but faked to look as if it was shot live. It's your final dice roll. You're already on square ninety-four. Score a six and the game is yours. Let's watch your victory.'

On-screen, Hackney took his turn. But his dice scored five, not six. Instead of the winning square, his token landed on ninety-nine.

Home of what Liz had referred to as a 'colossal snake'.

'Mr Hackney, you intentionally landed on ladders, but not to win the game. Here, you deliberately hit the gameboard's longest snake to go tumbling back down. The game continues. And you get to hit all those ladders all over again, exactly as planned. You didn't cheat in order to win. Four pounds in prize money wasn't your goal here. *It was to kill, kill, kill.*'

CHAPTER SEVENTY-THREE

Hackney made no response to Liz's claim, but he didn't have time to. Two seconds after uttering the word *kill*, Liz announced that the interview would be terminated. She stopped the recording and both detectives stood.

Hackney didn't move. 'I know you need to pass the file on to the Crown Prosecution Service. You can't authorise the charge yourself. That will take time, yet my twenty-four hours is up in five minutes. I've been silly, haven't I?'

Liz gave him a slow nod. 'I called the CPS before we started this interview. That message whispered into my ear earlier? Murder charges have been green-lit. We should head out and do it now.'

'Yes, I was silly. I thought you still had to make that phone call. I thought I'd get out of here while you waited for a decision. But I imagine that if the clock expires, you'd just let me go and arrest me again in the car park.'

Liz sat down. Her DC, puzzled, copied. Liz didn't like Hackney's tone. He didn't sound like someone upset he'd misread a situation, and he didn't sound worried that he was about to be charged with murder. 'You think I'm not at one hundred per cent yet. You think there's still something I'm missing.'

Hackney leaned back in his chair. 'James Breakspear. The snakes and ladders game started last month, but he's been dead three years. You haven't asked why.'

'We'd get to that in time. Today was more about guilt and motive and evidence. Are you willing to tell me about that murder now?'

'I will. Off the clock. Authorise my release, we'll talk, and you can rearrest me afterwards. But I have a condition.'

'Oh yes. You want me to do something. Or not do something.'

'I killed Breakspear right where you found him. Where you found a bloodstain. July 22nd, 2017. He was sitting with his back against the wall in that little hidden space round the back. James bent forward to reach a shoebox by his feet, and I thrust a knife straight downwards. One stab, back of the neck. He didn't even make a noise. He just sat back and died, sitting right there. I always thought movies were full of crap when they showed people get stabbed and they just freeze and topple. But no, that's exactly what happened. Then I wrapped his body in tarpaulin, carried him to my car boot. I dumped his body that night.'

'What was in the shoebox?'

'A Tesco pizza box torn into strips.'

'Why?'

'I don't shop at Asda.'

'So how did he appear in a snakes and ladders game three years later?'

'My first ladder hit was genuine. No cheating. Suddenly I had to commit murder. I was scared, I truly was. But I was also ready. The game was Markus's idea, but I chose the location of the map, and I made sure that I included the community centre on the first line, square six, so I'd have a good chance of hitting it. When we were creating the game and took turns to pick marks, or victims, I chose the word *tramp* because James was exactly that. I chose *criminal* because he freely admitted he had to steal to survive on the streets. I chose *sportsman* because James had told me he played football for a team as a kid. I chose *CEO* because he said he'd once been a big business leader. I picked *child* because we've all been one.'

'I see. A loophole. You were giving yourself the best chance of being able to pass off a three-year-old murder as one of your turns in the game. We saw this in one of the videos. But neither that video nor your confession just now answers the question of why you killed James Breakspear in the first place.'

Here Hackney's eyes narrowed. Through clenched teeth, he said, 'And *prostitute*, I picked that word too. But although he claimed to, Breakspear never did sell his body for sex. No, no, no, I got that one completely wrong.'

'I feel these other plans have something to do with the bitterness you're displaying and how you know so much about James Breakspear.'

'Spot on, detective. Let me tell you a story...'

CHAPTER SEVENTY-FOUR

He spots one and pulls up alongside him. The young man wears a T-shirt that looks like it was cut from a potato sack and his jeans are worn and grimy, but Hackney likes the face and the sinewy arms. He rolls his window down.

The young man says, 'Call me Jamie. One hundred pounds for one hour. At your house or a hotel. I don't do cars or grimy alleys.'

They drive. On the way, the young man is determined to tell his life story. As a kid, he'd been a highly-rated footballer, but an injury put an end to dreams of superstardom. After school, he ran his own business. John doubts these claims. Pressed about how he'd ended up homeless – it was obvious – the man calling himself Jamie refuses to elaborate, and seems a little embarrassed.

John doesn't care. He cares only that tonight will be a good time.

When asked if he did this often, the man said, 'I had a couple of women.'

'No men?'

'No men. I mean, they want it. But it never happens.'

John parks a few hundred metres from his house and takes the man on a winding route to the back garden. In the living room, John steps towards Jamie. 'We can't use my bed.'

Jamie steps back. 'Because you're married, I see. With kids.'

He is looking at the family photographs around the room. John says, 'My wife will be back in a couple of hours. We have to get a move on.'

'Money first.'

John fishes notes out of his wallet. Before trawling the streets, he had investigated male prostitutes online and knows they charge anything from fifty pounds to one hundred and fifty an hour. He leaves two twenties and a ten in the wallet and holds out the remainder. 'One hundred pounds, right?'

'It was until just now,' Jamie says. 'Nice kid, nice wife, nice life. Shame to lose it all.'

John freezes. He doesn't even react when Jamie not only takes the hundred pounds, he also grabs the wallet and extracts what's inside. He tosses the wallet on the floor.

'What do you mean?' John asks, but he's got a horrible feeling he knows the answer already.

'I mean I'll do the women. Why wouldn't I? Never the men. I said that already.'

And he had, John realises. 'Are you going to rob me? That's what you do, isn't it?'

'Sort of, kind of, not really. The men who come to me are usually trying to hide the fact that they're gay. So they'll pay to make sure no one finds out they were picking up rent boys. Normally I just take what they were going to offer anyway. But I'll make a special case for you.'

'What do you mean?'

'They're not normally as well off and happily married as you seem to be. So now the price is a thousand.'

'I haven't got a thousand.'

'You will have by tomorrow night, or you won't have a loving wife and happy kids and neighbours who give you the time of day.'

CHAPTER SEVENTY-FIVE

Back in the interview room, Liz said, 'Breakspear blackmailed you. So you killed him.'

'I couldn't tell the police. I had a family and a job to worry about.'

'What happened the night you killed him?'

'He was very trusting, which surprised me. I also had a thousand pounds in my pocket when I met him, in case he had people with him. I'd found him walking a street in the city centre, and he'd been talking to other homeless people. But for the handover he sent me to the community centre, and he was there alone. It was obvious it was where he lived. He was just sitting against the wall, like he was meeting an old friend and didn't have a single worry. I put the box by his outstretched legs, so he'd have to lean forward.'

'And then you stabbed him. Once, back of the neck. He sat back, bled all down the wall, and died. And you saved yourself a thousand pounds.'

Hackney scoffed at that. 'Not a thousand. It would have been a priceless deal, detective. There would have been another thousand, and then another. If I hadn't killed him, I wouldn't be here right now. I'd be down the bank, begging for another loan to pay him.'

'You say you had the money to pay him with you, but a shoebox full of cardboard says otherwise. You knew he'd be alone, and you took no money.'

'I just can't get anything past you, can I? Anyway, I saved many thousands of pounds. And he helped me win another four pounds.'

Hackney seemed to like his own joke, which angered Liz further. 'But you didn't win the game. The fine people of the emergency services put an end to that.'

'No, we made provisions for police interference. Like in boxing, in the event of unforeseen stoppage, we go to the scorecards. I was ahead when Markus died, so I win.'

'No, Mr Hackney, not the police. I mean the fine boys and girls of the medical services. They saved my life. You failed to kill me.'

'You think I lost by default? You know nothing.'

'But I do. I know ninety-nine point nine. All that's left is to find where you concealed Breakspear's body for three years and, hopefully, the murder weapon.'

'Very good. The knife is in the shoebox I tricked him with. The shoebox is at the location where I dumped the body. I hoped not to need this demand, but it seems you have me over a barrel. It's very simple. I said I don't like that girl next to you, and I don't like you, Miller. You're my nemesis. All I ask is that when I'm taken to the desk and charged with these crimes, it's not by you. I don't want you getting that glory. Give me that, I'll give you one hundred per cent.'

'This is a word I planned never to use in this case, but here it is. Deal.'

CHAPTER SEVENTY-SIX

The location was just over three miles north-east of Woodseats Police Station. Unwilling to wait for forensics and a search team, Liz told Boeson to arrange the backup and then grabbed her car keys.

'We should wait,' he said. 'If that place is a crime scene, it's been one for three years and nothing is going to change in the next half hour.'

'I want to make sure we don't send fifty people to a red herring,' Liz countered. 'It's somebody's garden and it's better if the owners know the score before everyone invades the place.'

Fair arguments and not without sincerity. But Liz also itched to get out there. Knowing he couldn't stop her, Boeson got on the phone as he watched her leave.

But she wasn't so impatient that she couldn't detour to watch a certain event. Liz lurked in the custody area and watched as an officer escorted John Hackney to the desk. The killer didn't see her, but she clearly saw his face as he was charged with two murders and one attempted. By the pretty young DC he'd insulted back in the interview room. The lady had been honoured to accept the task, and had reapplied her make-up before the grand show.

Strangely, though, Hackney didn't seem that upset about it. In fact, he had a slight grin.

CHAPTER SEVENTY-SEVEN

Intrigued by the idea of gimmicky additional rules in a game of snakes and ladders, Joe invented some of his own. He would roll first. If his dad hit a snake, he'd pay Joe five pounds. If Joe hit a ladder, his dad would have to drive to the real-life location of that square, find a shop, and buy him a toy.

'What's in it for me?' Bennet asked.

'Every time you pass me, I'll do half an hour of chores.'

'And for the winner?'

Housework. Lots of it for a month if his dad won. 'None for a month if I win.'

Deal. Once Joe was washed and dressed for his afternoon school start, they had half an hour spare and began the game. Joe's grandfather, Ray, was pulling weeds in the backyard. Joe's first roll was a six, which immediately took him to the ladder in the square containing Frecheville Community Centre. Giggling, he said, 'Ha ha, toy shop time.'

Bennet couldn't avoid thinking of Hackney and Markus, playing their own modified game. Bennet was supposed to go to the location of that square and buy a toy for his son. Hackney had gone there for a much darker reason. He imagined Markus laughing at Hackney: *ha ha, murder time.*

Bennet was about to roll the dice when his phone rang. It was Liz. He walked to the living-room window, his back to Joe.

'You left your map,' he told her. 'I'm playing it with Joe. Seems very bizarre after what we know.'

'I'll leave it with you then. But don't do anything that will set me on your tail. I just called to say it's done. Hackney's admitted it all.'

'How good are you?'

'Teamwork, remember. That's the Sheffield way. Did you Barnsley lot always want the credit for yourselves?'

'Very funny. Was the Range Rover on Overend Drive his first? Or have these guys been at this for months?'

'His first in the game, apparently. He also came clean about what happened to James Breakspear.' Liz ran through Hackney's story of his lethal clash with the homeless man.

With Joe within earshot, Bennet had to be careful about word choices. 'Do you buy that he did something like that and then nothing further for three years?'

'I don't know. Maybe more will come to light one day. But it's almost over. We should go out to celebrate.'

Joe suddenly squealed. 'Here! Square three.' Bennet turned. Joe had his finger on the map. 'Overend Drive.'

Bennet gave a thumbs up and turned back to the window. 'Think you could stomach the King Royal again?'

'For sure. But you didn't pick up on the fact that I said this thing is *almost* over.'

'I just didn't want to talk shop. Go on, tell me.'

'Hackney told me where he hid the body of Breakspear for three years. An empty house in Danewood Grove in Castlebeck. Although it's no longer empty. I'm heading to my car now. Listen, my phone is about to die, so I'll have to chat to you later.'

'Nice one. Okay, you go have fun. Oh, how many of your own drinks have you had to make today?'

'None, for your information, smart-arse,' she said, then blew a raspberry and hung up.

Joe said, 'King Royal! Here.' He jabbed another place on the map. 'Square–'

'Thirty,' Bennet said at the same time, and he laughed at Joe's face of awe.

Ten minutes into the game, Bennet owed his son five pounds and a toy, because the former had hit a snake and the latter had hit a ladder. But a handful of low-numbered rolls by Joe had allowed his dad to catch up. Now, he scored a six and leaped past Joe, onto square thirty-three. Bennet laughed and Joe moaned. Owed: half an hour of homework.

Joe peered closely at the square. 'Granvill*ee* Road. The Sheffield College.'

'Granville. Don't emphasise the *e*. But well done.'

Bennet checked his watch. They'd have to set off for school soon. Joe rolled, scored five, and started bouncing his token. When he passed his father's, he said, 'I took over you again, so this should cancel out homework.'

'Nope. Rules are rules.'

Joe thumped his token onto square thirty-six. Seeing the green of Bowden Housteads Woods, Bennet was reminded of Liz's attempted murder. He suddenly didn't want to play the game any longer, at least on a map of Sheffield.

Joe peered closely at the square. 'Castlebeck.'

Joe yelped in shock as his father snatched the map right off the coffee table, sending the dice and tokens flying. The portion of the woods where Liz had been attacked was in the top half of the square, but poking into the bottom-left corner was a northern segment of Castlebeck. And there he saw it. Danewood Grove, where Hackney claimed he'd buried Breakspear's body.

Immediately he thought of Markus, who'd been tasked with HANDBAG, RAPE, TEACHER in Hackenthorpe. 'I have to go, Joe. I'm sorry. Your granddad will take you to school.' As he ran out of the house, he called Liz, but her phone was dead. He swore, got in the car, and burned rubber.

Markus had fudged his mission, but had been given another shot at it. Rules were rules: same crime, same weapon, same victim-type.

Same location.

Hackney had failed to kill Liz in square thirty-six, but he was allowed a redo. And he'd just sent her right back there.

CHAPTER SEVENTY-EIGHT

Castlebeck was bordered on two sides by woods and fields. She made a few turns in the housing estate and found Danewood Grove. The street was neat and quiet, with only a handful of residents visible. As she drove slowly, checking house numbers, she spotted the little piece of scrubland Hackney had described.

She parked at the kerb and got out. The area was surrounded by a waist-high wall and about ten feet wide and twice as long. An old, green telephone junction box sat in the centre, while thick, tall weeds claimed every other inch. It appeared to be a surplus piece of land where Danewood Grove and a neighbouring street intersected.

Given its condition and the box, Liz doubted the area belonged to either of the properties alongside. She could search the Land Registry for an owner, but why waste time when she could hop the wall and search? Nobody was going to confront her.

Something didn't seem right. The wasteground was so overgrown that a body could, with effort, be obscured, but could it remain undetected for three years? Surely whichever firm owned the junction box would have sent an engineer in that time. Kids would have played in there. If Breakspear's corpse had been buried, this would have disturbed the weeds and left a visible clear spot. If his interment had occurred before the area was overgrown, the grave would have been equally obvious.

And why would Hackney have picked such a place instead of a remote area, like the nearby woods? Digging a hole and burying a body was a lengthy chore. He didn't live here and would have drawn attention, especially at night.

If she was suspicious of Hackney's honesty now, she became downright convinced he'd lied to her when she approached the wall and looked down. The ground was laid with paving bricks, which the thick weeds had sprouted between. Nothing could have been buried here without massive, improbable work.

She kicked the wall in frustration, and was about to turn and leave. Then she saw it.

Near the junction box, barely visible because it was low in the weeds. Something brown. To confirm, she had to get closer, so she sat on the wall and swung her legs over. She made two steps, kicking aside weeds that scratched her calf, and a little more of the item was displayed, including a company logo. Now she knew what she was looking at.

A shoebox. Just as Hackney had said.

CHAPTER SEVENTY-NINE

B ennet arrived at Castlebeck Avenue, and could go no
further. The entrance to Danewood Grove had been
cordoned off by two police cars nose to nose. A crowd of
onlookers had gathered around it. Beyond the cordon he saw
more vehicles, at least ten, and perhaps two of them were
civilian-owned. A uniform tried to get him to drive past, keep
going, nothing to see here, but he spotted Liz's car and got out.

Hearing him shout her name, Liz approached, told the
officer Bennet was good for entry, and he was allowed past the
police tape. Bennet saw another cordon ten metres away, and
again perhaps a hundred metres distant, blocking access from
the other end of Danewood.

In the middle of this double-secured forbidden zone, by a
walled area full of weeds, he saw men in the unmistakable
heavy-duty gear of the Bomb Squad. No forensics or police
vehicles were going into the inner cordon until the all-clear had
been given. He realised that most of the gawkers were residents
ejected from their homes. He thought he knew why.

'You found a bomb?' he asked, and grabbed Liz in a hug.

Watched by colleagues, she pushed him away, although she apologised.

'Possibly. There was a strange shoebox.'

'Hackney sent you back to square thirty-six. To kill you.'

'Boeson told me you called en route here and said that.'

'I called him when your phone was dead. He said you'd already called a team in. Did you already suspect Hackney was planning to kill you?'

'Not at first, stupidly. I was too eager to finish this thing.'

She explained that she'd become suspicious after finding a shoebox sitting all alone, and had remembered one of the videos they'd found in the secret toilets. In it, Markus had mentioned making a bomb out of a car battery. Only then had she realised she was close to Bowden Housteads Woods – right in the area Hackney needed her if he hoped to redo his murder attempt.

'I stayed away from the shoebox and called it in. But we still need to search that area and possibly the gardens around it. He might not be lying. Once we know the bomb is diffused, or not a bomb at all.'

'Does Hackney know his plan failed?'

'Not yet, and I've arranged that no word gets to him. I want to walk into his cell and see his shock that I'm not d–'

Boeson yelled her name and she turned. 'All clear,' he said as he approached. 'No explosives in the shoebox. But it's full of useless bits of wires and metal, so we were probably supposed to think that Bonfire Night was coming early.'

'It could be full of evidence then. So this could be genuine. There could still be a grave.'

Soon after, the inner sanctuary was opened up, and the mass of vehicles clogging the outer started moving. It was like a drag race: they burst away at speed, then just as quickly stopped because they'd only had to cover fifty metres. Liz and Bennet got in her car, which she parked right outside the crime scene.

Forensic officers and detectives started pulling on protective gear.

As Liz suited up, with Bennet watching, she said, 'Keep your distance, nosey civilian.'

'Fancy delegating bomb disposal. How lazy is that? I think this DCI role has gone to your head.'

'Do you feel sick? Oh, no, you're just green with jealousy.'

He had no comeback. She was right.

Ready, Liz joined others in the wasteground. He leaned against her car to watch. Down at the entrance to the street, residents eager to return to their houses were getting restless at the delay. He was glad he hadn't been forced to remain way back there. For a moment, he wondered if he should try to get his job back. He could–

'Liam!' He saw Liz in the wasteground, watching him. 'I forgot my camera. I delegate you to bring it to me.'

Bennet saluted. He opened her boot and then flipped the lid on her camera case. Inside, he should have seen foam padding for the device and its accessories. Instead, he saw an empty space with wiring and metal parts and–

Bomb, he thought, half a second before it exploded.

EPILOGUE
TWO DAYS LATER

The video showed the perpetrator smash the passenger side window. And then use the hole to climb into the back seat of the car.

As she'd suspected.

Because of the distance, the darkness and the quality of the video, Liz couldn't see what the man was doing inside her vehicle. But she knew. He was folding down the back seat, to access the boot. To get at her camera case.

A glass tube about three inches long had been connected to the lid of her case at a forty-five degree angle, pointing towards the back of the vehicle. At the top end of the tube were two electrical contacts; at the bottom, held there by gravity, was a small amount of mercury. It was vital the two forms of metal remained apart. The steep angle of the tube would guarantee this, even if the car hit a bump or travelled downhill.

But if the lid of the case was opened, the liquid metal would flow down, smother the contacts and close the circuit. It was known as a mercury switch. Apparently the old vending machine at her station employed this simple system in order to trigger a tilt alarm. Most people, however, knew the term because of its use in another type of device. Home-made bombs.

The shrapnel bomb Hackney had installed in her camera case had been loaded with metal and sharp plastic parts from a busted-up car battery. Exactly as advertised.

After learning of his guilt through the chat logs, Liz had put a surveillance team on him, in case he neglected to turn up for his voluntary interview. Interviewed after the explosion, he had claimed to have known about the watchers: he had planted the bomb and got home mere minutes before the stake-out cars arrived. Knowing he was under suspicion had pleased him, he'd said. After failing to kill Liz, he had immediately set up plan B, but it required his capture and confession.

The bomb was in place; the bogus body-dump site was ready. If he was arrested at his interview, all he had to do was offer Breakspear's body in order to get control of Liz's movement and send her to her doom.

Make sure DCI Miller is there. She's the only one I want to talk to because she's leading this thing. I don't want some snotty DC.

Hackney's words when he'd called the station before his first interview now sounded so haunting. He had wanted her at his interview in order to guarantee she wouldn't be off investigating another crime that morning. God forbid she should die somewhere outside square thirty-six and ruin the game.

He had been smart, she had to give him that. He knew a bomb at the location would be found and diffused long before Liz got near. But once the area was considered safe, everyone would pile in to analyse and search and photograph. Hackney had already seen Liz's camera bag when she was parked at IronClaw; he'd watched her retrieve it to photograph Markus's desk. Of course she'd do the same at a possible body dump site.

Liz had wanted to show Hackney his failure in the most

direct way possible: by waltzing into his cell, very much alive and well. That hadn't been possible because she'd had to go to hospital for a few bruises and lacerations, after which she'd been due to face questions from an internal enquiry team. Besides, she wouldn't have trusted herself not to fly at the man and beat him senseless.

However, Hackney had requested to speak to her and she'd agreed. Her boss hadn't liked the idea of a chat outside of formal interview, but Liz had insisted and a phone was delivered to Hackney's cell.

It didn't match a face-to-face encounter and he'd had time to process his defeat, but she got to hear the dejection in his voice. 'You win,' he said. 'It was all about the game, so now I wish you a speedy recovery. I'm glad no one got hurt in that bomb. I'm very sorry for all of this, you know.'

He thought his bomb had hurt nobody? He hadn't been informed about Liam Bennet? The story was all over the news. Even if Hackney didn't hear that way, he'd soon know about his final victim when the explosion was added to his charges. But she wouldn't be the one to tell him. She also knew his sorrow was solely because the game was over. 'If you're sorry, make amends.'

'I will. I miss Markus now. Before, I didn't. Maybe that was because the game was still on. Or I had too much worry about getting caught. Or... I don't know. But I do miss him now. He was my... we... I should talk to Markus's mother. Can you arrange that?'

Was that the real reason for his call? She could have said no. She could have told him that Markus's mother wouldn't care for an explanation or an apology. Instead, she became a gamemaster herself and played him.

'We'll see. But nobody's going to do you any favours if you continue to lie or withhold information. You need to be truthful and helpful in order to show that you are remorseful. The first step down that path is to give us Breakspear's burial site. Not another bomb.'

He had agreed and directed police to a patch of woodland in Shirecliffe. Investigators had found proof that Breakspear's body had lain here and this had been of some comfort to Clara, his sister, and other members of his scattered family. Another action by Hackney had failed to please Clara though.

'I want to help his sister,' he'd told Liz during that same phone call. 'I want to donate money to her. To help with his funeral.'

Liz would later relay this offer to Clara, but it would field only anger. Hackney would never know this, though, because Liz's response to his offer was:

'I'm not going to waste her time. She won't want anything from you.'

'Pride, is that? Dirty money and all that? Maybe Markus's mother will take it. When I talk to her.'

'Save it for a defence lawyer,' Liz had snapped, then hung up.

On the subject of Clara, she had taken no satisfaction from knowing her brother's killer was now locked up and planning to plead guilty to all charges. Learning the truth about James's fate had injected her with a new resolve to turn her life around. She had gotten a part-time job and was back at Liz's bedsit, which Liz would continue paying for a few months to help her out.

Liz no longer lived there. She had a new home.

The lavish funeral of Paul Yard, Hackney's second murder victim, had lit a fire under Clara and made her intensely more unwilling to condemn her brother to a pauper's burial. Luckily, the council had delayed proceedings while they tried to find her. She had been able to step in and take over. Family had helped her give James a decent send-off. Liz had heard that Barry the crime nerd planned to include the snakes and ladders crimes in his book and would dedicate it to the dead victims.

Liz got up and handed Boeson back his iPad, which he had brought round to show her the newly discovered CCTV from outside her bedsit. She walked to the kitchen window and stared out. Boeson said, 'Will you be okay?'

She nodded.

Long after he'd gone, she continued to stare out the kitchen window, watching Bennet's son and dad pretend to fish in the backyard.

Would she be okay? Would *any* of them? Only the blessing that was time would tell.

THE END

AFTERWORD

Fiction writers often tweak reality to fit a story. If you're a police officer, don't be offended if I have your comrades bending procedure a little. If I've erased your house to plant a bogus road, it's nothing personal. If it seems I've nicked your uncle John for a character, that's just coincidence. If you fit all three, though, send me an email, because that's worth a chat.

Various people helped bring the Yorkshire Murder Thrillers from my head to your hands. The main trio of suspects are Betsy Reavley, Ian Skewis and Tara Lyons. I don't need to thank them here because I've done so already — to see proof of this, please buy the first two books in the series, Dead Cold and Cold Blood.

A NOTE FROM THE PUBLISHER

Thank you for reading this book. If you enjoyed it please do consider leaving a review on Amazon to help others find it too.

We hate typos. All of our books have been rigorously edited and proofread, but sometimes mistakes do slip through. If you have spotted a typo, please do let us know and we can get it amended within hours.

info@bloodhoundbooks.com

Lightning Source UK Ltd.
Milton Keynes UK
UKHW011434210822
407591UK00002B/459